W9-AKX-826

Tyra ran her tongue over the ice cream, closed her eyes and savored the rich, creamy delight

"This is fan—" She stopped in the middle of the sentence, and when she opened her eyes, she was staring into the pools of naked desire in Byron's eyes. She lowered the ice cream cone from her mouth.

"Byron…"

"It's all right. You caught me off-guard. Aren't you going to finish your ice cream?"

She nodded, and as soon as the ice cream touched her tongue, her discomfort disappeared. She reached across the table and stroked the back of his hand, not thinking what her touch might precipitate. He turned his hand over and caressed her palm with his own.

"Byron, tell me why you called me tonight. I…I have to know."

"I'm a loner, Tyra. I have always enjoyed being alone. I like people and enjoy being with those I find interesting. But I've always liked the peace and quiet of being alone. I always did my best thinking walking by myself in the park. Tonight, I suddenly felt as if the bottom had dropped out. I sat in my den trying to work, and suddenly I felt so lonely that I couldn't stand it. And you were the only person on this earth that I wanted to see."

Books by Gwynne Forster

Kimani Romance

Her Secret Life
One Night with You
Forbidden Temptation
Drive Me Wild
Private Lives
Finding Mr. Right

GWYNNE FORSTER

is a national bestselling author of more than twenty romance novels and novellas, as well as general fiction. She has worked as a journalist, a university professor and as a senior officer for the United Nations. She holds a bachelor's and a master's degree in sociology, and a master's degree in economics/demography.

Gwynne sings in her church choir, loves to entertain at dinner parties, is a gourmet cook and an avid gardener. She enjoys jazz, opera, classical music and the blues. She also likes to visit museums and art galleries. She lives in New York with her husband.

FINDING
Mr.
RIGHT

ESSENCE BESTSELLING AUTHOR
GWYNNE FORSTER

KIMANI™
ROMANCE

If you purchased this book without a cover you should be aware
that this book is stolen property. It was reported as "unsold and
destroyed" to the publisher, and neither the author nor the
publisher has received any payment for this "stripped book."

To all of my fellow volunteers in the Obama Campaign
for President of the United States—you helped make the
impossible dream come true. And to President Barack
Obama, who is the man for our time.

 KIMANI PRESS™

Recycling programs
for this product may
not exist in your area.

ISBN-13: 978-0-373-86124-8

FINDING MR. RIGHT

Copyright © 2009 by Gwendolyn Johnson-Acsadi

All rights reserved. The reproduction, transmission or utilization
of this work in whole or in part in any form by any electronic, mechanical
or other means, now known or hereafter invented, including xerography,
photocopying and recording, or in any information storage or retrieval
system, is forbidden without written permission. For permission please
contact Kimani Press, Editorial Office, 233 Broadway, New York, NY
10279 U.S.A.

This is a work of fiction. Names, characters, places and incidents are
either the product of the author's imagination or are used fictitiously,
and any resemblance to actual persons, living or dead, business establishments,
events or locales is entirely coincidental.

® and TM are trademarks. Trademarks indicated with ® are registered in
the United States Patent and Trademark Office, the Canadian Trade Marks
Office and/or other countries.

www.kimanipress.com

Printed in U.S.A.

Dear Reader,

Thank you for making *Private Lives,* my previous Kimani Romance title, such a success. I deeply appreciate the loyalty of my readers, which I have been so fortunate to enjoy since the publication of my first novel in 1995. Many of you still write to me regularly, and I look forward to hearing from you.

My heroines are usually independent, educated and capable of making their life's journey a successful one. In *Finding Mr. Right,* Tyra Cunningham is not an exception. But because her siblings think she needs a man and needs help in finding one, Tyra does a few foolish things, including looking past "Mr. Right," in order to show her brother and sister that she is capable of finding one. There is a lesson in there, and I hope you catch it. My grandfather used to call it cutting off your nose to spite your face.

Byron is a tribute to those of you African-American men who are great fathers and who put a premium on loving your women and nurturing your children. And he is precisely what Tyra needs.

During 2009, Kimani Arabesque will release reprints of three of my popular Arabesque books, *Swept Away, Fools Rush In* and *Scarlet Woman.* All three of these books won national awards. They've been out of print for a while, so I hope you will have a chance to read the reissues.

I enjoy receiving mail, so please write me at P.O. Box 45, New York, New York 10044, and send a self-addressed, stamped envelope if you want a reply. My e-mail address is GwynneF@aol.com. Please visit my Web site at www.gwynneforster.com. For business purposes, reach me through my agent, Pattie Steel-Perkins, Steele-Perkins Literary Agency, 26 Island Lane, Canandaigua, New York 14424.

Sincerely yours,

Gwynne Forster

Chapter 1

Tyra Cunningham stood at her bedroom window watching her younger sister, Darlene, drive off for her first day of work as an attorney. The early June breeze was blowing through her hair and drying the tears she hadn't realized were welling up in her eyes. She'd done it. Nobody would have thought it was possible. With the responsibility she'd taken on for her fifteen-year-old brother and thirteen-year-old sister not to mention herself, she'd produced remarkable results. Her brother, Clark, was a civil engineer working in Baltimore, and her sister had just been hired by one of Frederick, Maryland's most distinguished law firms. In the meantime, she had managed to educate herself. Of course, she'd had Maggie's support, but she'd made the important decisions and taken responsibility for the family.

She raced down the stairs and into the breakfast room. Maggie, who had been her parents' housekeeper before they had died in an accident, indeed, before Tyra's tenth birthday, sat eating her breakfast. "I feel like celebrating, Maggie. I don't have to worry about either of them any more. Mom and Dad would have been real proud, and that's all I ever wanted. I hope you know that I couldn't have done it without you, though."

"The Lord always provides. Now, I wish He'd provide you with a man. It's not a good idea you strolling around here with three decades under your belt and never even looking at a man."

"I look all the time. I just don't see any brothers who make me want to go to the trouble."

"There's a difference between browsing and looking. When I was your age, I would have been considered too old for marriage, that is, if I'd still been single. When you gon' have children...after menopause? You young people act like youth is eternal."

"Oh, Maggie. For the first time in memory, I feel footloose and fancy-free."

"I know, chile. You've had to be a grownup since you were seventeen, and now you feel like you're seventeen. But take my word for it, that's not for you." She refilled her coffee cup. "Tyra, I'm serious. If men want a family, they look for a younger woman. If they fall for you before they think about family, you're lucky."

"You know more about this than I do. My one foray into dating wasn't very good, but I'm still hopeful."

As she headed up the broad, winding stairs of the house, she was proud that she had not only preserved what her parents, both physicians, left to her and her siblings, but had doubled its value. Their big, white-brick Georgian mansion stood out even among the elegant homes surrounding it. She put on a straw hat and sneakers, got a pair of shears and went out in the back garden to trim the hedges and cut away the dead blooms from daffodils and jonquils before the hot Maryland sun made it unbearable.

Boredom set in almost at once. What was she going to do with the rest of her life? She had a degree in psychology and was qualified to be a psychoanalyst, but she hadn't pursued a career because she'd been so focused on raising Clark and Darlene.

She went back inside and sat on a kitchen stool and waited for Maggie to come up from the laundry room in the basement. "What am I going to do with myself, Maggie? I plan to get a job. But a job isn't the answer for what I'm feeling. It's as if they went off and left me. I'm used to Clark being away, but Darlene's the baby, and she's on her own now."

"You're lonely, and you're gonna find out that it's not loneliness for Clark and Darlene. Being a woman means more than wearing a dress and putting on lipstick."

"All right. All right. I get the message. I've sent out job applications, but with no response so far. I only started last Thursday, so I guess it's too soon."

"You've got the empty nest syndrome that parents get when their children leave home. You'll get over it. Excuse me." She went to answer the telephone in the kitchen. "She's here, Clark. Just a minute."

"Hi, Sis. I'm bringing home a friend for dinner and overnight, so you and Maggie fix something real nice. Be there at about six."

"All right. At least this will give me something to do. With Darlene at work, this place is awfully quiet."

"I can imagine. For years, you've been busier than you had a right to be. See you around six." Tyra hung up the phone.

"He's bringing a friend home for dinner, Maggie, and she's spending the night. He wants us to serve something special, I guess. Wonder who she is and where they met. I'll put some flowers in the guest room. At least, this gives me something to think about."

"I was going to serve roast pork. Oh, well. I'll just dress it up," Maggie said. "Let's see. Cold mint-pea soup; roast pork with mushrooms, roast potatoes and asparagus. A salad, and let's see…crème caramel. Coffee if anybody's got room left. That's not so much, since everything's light except the pork and potatoes. I need some more lemons, mushrooms and some cognac for the dessert."

"Good. I'll phone the grocer and the liquor store."

Tyra finished setting the dining room table, put a bowl of hyacinths and sweet peas from her garden in the center of the table and sat down to watch the local news. A while later, she heard the doorbell ring, glanced at her watch and saw that it was already ten minutes to six.

"I'll get it, Maggie."

She opened the door and gasped. Standing beside Clark was a strikingly handsome man, who stood a good two inches taller than Clark's six foot three. He was a good-looking man who wore success the way peacocks wear plumes. And the way he fixed his gaze on her unnerved her. Annoyed with herself, she looked down at her long, blue denim skirt and flat sandals. Her T-shirt flattered her ample bosom, but that was all it did.

She gathered her wits. "Come in. Clark, the time got away from me, and I haven't even dressed for dinner. I'll be right back." She ran upstairs before Clark could introduce her to his friend. Why had she assumed that his guest would be a woman? Well, at least they hadn't made chicken-à-la-king. Men preferred food that stuck to the ribs. She took a sponge bath and changed into a long, red-silk dress and heels. The shoes raised her height from five feet eight and a half inches to almost six feet. She liked being tall.

"Byron Whitley, this is my sister, Tyra," Clark said when she returned to them. "My kid sister, Darlene, should be here in about half an hour. And this is Maggie Jenkins," he said, as Maggie served hot hors d'oeuvres. "Maggie is our house-keeper and surrogate mother. Maggie, this is Byron Whitley."

"Welcome, Mr. Whitley," Maggie said. "I hope you'll visit us often." She cast a sideward glance at Tyra and smiled as if triumphant.

Tyra had never learned to drink, mostly because she felt that she had to set a good example for her siblings, especially her sister. Nonetheless, she leaned back in her chair, crossed her legs and, after deciding that she could use something to steady her nerves, she asked her brother to make her a vodka tonic.

Clark stared at her. "You sure? In that case, you'd better eat some of those little canapés Maggie served."

Tyra looked at Byron. "This morning, my responsibility for my brother and my sister ended. Clark has been on his own for the past five years, and today our sister, Darlene, began her first day at work. She's an attorney. I think I deserve a drink."

"You do, and I'll join you," Byron said, looking intently at her as if there were no one else other than the two of them. When he raised his glass to her, she shifted in her seat, uncomfortable with the sexual tension between them.

She heard the front door open and was about to go to greet her sister when she realized that Darlene had gone directly up to her room.

"Darlene's here," she said to Byron. "We'll eat in a few minutes."

Byron focused his attention on Tyra. "What do you do, Tyra?"

"I'm a psychoanalyst, but I think I'd make a good counselor."

He rubbed his chin with his thumb and forefinger. "Yes. I expect you will be. Counseling can be very rewarding."

So Clark wasn't matchmaking, thought Byron. He hadn't told his sister anything about his coming to dinner. Indeed, she hadn't expected her brother's guest to be a man, given her attire when she first greeted them. He smiled inwardly. When she saw him, she dressed in a hurry. He liked that, and he liked her. A woman who looked as if she might be in her late teens came into the room, her face all smiles. He noted that she had the Cunningham looks, but she certainly didn't have the bearing of a lawyer.

"Hi, all," she said.

Clark walked over to her, put an arm around her and said, "Byron Whitley, this is Darlene, my baby sister. She did a decent day's work today for the first time in her life. Darlene, this is Byron Whitley."

"I'm glad to meet you, Darlene."

"Thanks. I'm glad to meet you, Byron." She turned immediately to her older sister. "Hi, sis. Did I keep you guys waiting?"

Not much escaped him, and if he didn't know better, he'd swear he'd just been given the brush off by someone who was anxious to portray herself as something that she wasn't.

"No, you didn't," Tyra said to her sister. "Let me check with Maggie."

Tyra strode to the kitchen, her suspicions rising. "What's going on here, Maggie? Did you get a look at Darlene? From head to foot, she looks the way she did ten years ago with her hair in a pony tail, no makeup, jeans that are too tight and sneakers. She didn't leave here this morning looking like that."

Maggie didn't seem concerned. She handed Tyra two bowls of cold mint-pea soup. "Here. Put those in Clark's and Mr. Whitley's plates. I'll bring in yours, Darlene's and mine."

She knew that Maggie's nonchalance was her way of avoiding things. "Okay, but don't you think Clark and Darlene are up to something?"

Maggie's withering look was not unusual. For years, she'd used it as a way to express her disapproval without saying a word. "What on earth could they be up to? You ever know Darlene to keep a secret? Clark's too smart to be in cahoots with Darlene about anything that's supposed to be a secret. After you take those bowls in, would you come back and cover that platter while I light the candles?"

"Why don't you cover the platter and I'll light the candles? I don't want to rearrange your handiwork," Tyra said.

She put the soup at each place setting and looked in the top drawer of the china cabinet for the lighter. When she couldn't find it, she searched for a match. She lit two matches, both of which quickly burned out.

"Let me do that for you."

She looked up at Byron Whitley, towering over her in a way that few men did. When he smiled and extended his hand for the matches, her left hand went to her chest as if to lower her heartbeat. He took the matches from her hand, lit the candles and asked her, "Would you go to dinner with me Sunday evening?"

She wanted to say no. Indeed, she thought she was going to decline. Not because she didn't like him, but because she did. And that was the problem. She didn't know whether he liked her or knew that she was attracted to him and planned to take advantage of that fact.

"Will you?" he urged.

"I'd love to. Thank you." Embarrassed because she'd agreed so readily. He raised an eyebrow, but she pretended that she didn't see it.

After Maggie said grace, Clark asked Darlene about her first day at work. "I think they were all being nice to me. I liked the orientation that Mr. Harris gave me."

"It was probably very thorough," Byron said. "That firm knows its business. You've landed a good position. What area are you in?"

"I'm in contracts."

"Good," Byron said.

With Tyra's help, Maggie served dinner. She believed that

serving one course after another made a meal more enjoyable. For dessert, they each got three heaping scoops of crème caramel.

Byron tasted it, closed his eyes. "I'm never leaving this place. After a meal like this, I could sit here until it's time for the next meal."

"Oh," Tyra said, "I'm not sure I'd like to see roots growing from you."

Darlene giggled. "I doubt he'd grow the kind of roots you have in mind, Sis."

Her comment had a suggestive overtone. "What kind of roots do you think I have in mind?"

"Let's just say you're not thinking of carrots." Then, as if to dispel any misunderstanding, Darlene turned to Byron. "I'm out of line, but this is kind of funny."

Byron's laugh shook his body. "She's got your number, Tyra."

"Yeah," Clark said. "She's used to getting away with it. If Tyra sent her to her room, she'd stay there five minutes, come out, say she was sorry, hug Tyra and that would be the end of it."

"I'm not a pushover." Tyra felt uncomfortable under Byron's intense stare. "Let's go into the living room and play some music," she suggested, to break the tension.

She and Darlene helped Maggie clear the table and clean the kitchen. "What are you up to, Darlene?" Tyra asked her.

"Nothing. Just relaxing after a hard day's work."

"Don't make jokes, Darlene. I know you. And nothing's going to convince me that you worked hard on your first day on the job. Nothing! Go in the living room and pick out some music, anything but hip hop."

"I don't do hip hop any more, Sis. You're way behind. I'm going upstairs for a minute."

Maggie put away the dish towel, removed her apron and

looked at Tyra. "You didn't have to come in here to help me clean up. Why you trying to avoid that man? I saw how he looked at you, and you saw it, too. He's not wearing a ring, so what's your problem?"

"If you're trying to shove me into his lap, you can forget it. I'm not about to throw myself at him."

"You're not fooling me, Tyra. He's gotten to you. You're thirty-one years old, and men your age are getting married. So quit fooling yourself. Leave that tray here. I'll take the coffee in. Find another excuse to avoid Mr. Whitley. If a man like him looked at me the way he was looking at you, I'd be in there where he could see me. I'm gonna have to sit you down and talk to you."

"All right."

Byron Whitley met her in the hallway. "Are you avoiding me? If you're not interested, say so. I won't be offended."

Well, you couldn't get more direct than that. She forced herself to meet his gaze. "I always help Maggie in the kitchen. She's the housekeeper, but she's been part of our family since we lost our parents in an automobile accident."

"And you became mother to Clark and Darlene, I presume."

"I did with a lot of help from Maggie, who's been with our family since I was nine. She's a widow now, and this is her home. What time do you want to have dinner Sunday?"

"I'd like to pick you up at six-thirty. There's a wonderful little restaurant I know in Buckeytown. It's mainly Italian, but they serve great Maryland-style crab cakes."

"I...look forward to Sunday."

"Me, too," he said without a trace of a smile. "Since you're not avoiding me, let's have some of that coffee I smell."

"It's in the living room." When did Maggie pass them with the espresso? Surely she hadn't let the man fluster her to the point that she didn't see what was going on around her. She got through the evening by focusing on the music, changing the CDs and finding music by performers that Byron and her family preferred. At the end of the evening she announced that breakfast would be served from seven to seven-thirty, said good-night and went to her room. She had some choice words for Clark and Darlene, but saying them would have to wait.

The following morning, Clark and Byron said goodbye to Tyra. She promised Clark that she would give him a call. Once she had assured herself that both her brother and sister were settled in at work, Tyra placed a three-way call to them.

"What do you two mean by setting me up with Byron Whitley? Take care of your business and stay out of mine."

"Now look, Sis," Clark began, "that wasn't really my intention. If I'd thought about it…"

Darlene interrupted. "So what's the big deal? If you looked for a year, you wouldn't find a better prospect than Byron. He's tall, handsome, and he's got a brilliant legal mind. You should be thanking Clark. And Byron liked you. Anybody could see that."

"Yeah," Clark said. "And he's the right age—forty. Don't tell me you didn't like him. I could see that the minute you opened the door and looked at him."

"I'm warning both of you. I can find a man on my own. I don't need help from either of you."

If Clark was trying to be a matchmaker, she'd no doubt frustrated him. Although he may not have planned it, Clark had already warmed up to the idea. "Byron says he has a dinner date with you this coming Sunday. I hope you're not going to disappoint him."

"If you hadn't meddled in my personal life, Clark, you wouldn't have to worry about that."

"He's a great guy."

"Remove your halo, Clark. Let me know if you'll be home this weekend."

"Since you're not interested in Byron, Sis, can I go to dinner with the two of you Sunday?" Darlene said. Tyra threw up her hands. "Oh, stop acting so innocent. I'll show you both a thing or two. See you tonight."

Byron sat at his desk trying to focus on a case. He seemed unable to think about his legal strategy. He'd spent the previous night at the Cunningham home, hoping to be distracted from the case. But he hadn't counted on that much of a distraction. He wanted to see Tyra Cunningham again, and he knew himself well enough to know that if he enjoyed her company at dinner, he'd want to see more of her—much more. She'd made a strong impression on him: not even the delicious crème caramel dessert had gotten his attention.

His intercom light blinked, and he pushed the button. "Mr. Whitley, your dad's on two," his secretary said.

He waited until the paralegal left his office and then picked up his second line. "Hi, Dad. How're you doing?"

"I'm fine. I was thinking how nice it would be if I took Andy fishing with me this weekend. Do you mind if he stays over with me Saturday night?"

"That much is fine, Dad, but I have something to do Sunday evening, and I have to check with Aunt Jonie to see what her plans are."

"If he's home by five Sunday, that should do it," Lewis Whitley told his son. "I know you'll have a fit if a day passes and you don't see him. But he could spend Sunday night with me, and he'd love it."

"Don't tell him until Friday, otherwise, he'll pester me about it the entire week. I'll be in touch."

Andy was his life, just as he and his sister had been the center of his father's life. He tried to be both mother and father to the boy. Andy had never known his mother since she'd died a few days after his birth. He looked at the picture of the child that he kept on his desk and smiled. The boy looked as much like him as Byron looked like his father. What would his life have been like if Lois had survived.

He flexed his left shoulder in a quick shrug, his way of reminding himself that he couldn't undo the past and that he had to get on with life. He had already realized that he wouldn't be over Lois completely until another woman claimed his heart. But four years was a long time to wait.

He always played it straight, and he couldn't commit to a woman unless he thought she would be a good mother for his son. So far, he hadn't come close to finding a woman like that. A rueful smile flashed across his face. *Wonder how long I'll be able to say that.*

The following Friday night, Tyra sat on the deck in back of her house, waiting for the hamburgers and hotdogs to grill. She almost always cooked dinner on the grill in the summer when Maggie took the night off. The housekeeper didn't have regular days off. She took a day off whenever she needed to, provided her absence didn't conflict with Tyra's plans. She never worked on Sundays. Tyra hadn't expected Clark, and when he arrived, she put more hotdogs and hamburgers on the grill along with two more ears of corn.

"This is a surprise," she told him. "Darlene and I thought we'd be eating without you."

"I wanted to talk to you and saying anything important to you over the phone is never a good idea." He straddled a chair and rolled up the sleeves of his hoodie. "Byron Whitley is an exceptional man, and I don't want you to treat him as if he's an also-ran, an ordinary Joe. He's not. There are seven lawyers in his firm, and he hasn't lost a case in the fourteen years he's been practicing."

"Okay. He's a great guy. But I won't have my brother choosing a man for me. I can do that myself."

"Yeah?" Darlene said. "Not according to Maggie. She said you wouldn't have the slightest idea what to look for in a man."

Tyra rolled her eyes skyward. "I know Maggie's smart, but her words are not gospel. From now on, leave it to me to get my own man. So lay off, please. I know you mean well, but it is humiliating."

"Are you keeping your date with Byron?" Clark asked.

"I told you I was, but if you ask me one more time, I'm going to phone him and cancel it. I know you both love me, but I want you to let me take care of this part of my life myself."

"Okay. Okay. I'll lay off, but if you need me…" Unwilling to risk aggravating her more, he let it hang.

Ordinarily, Tyra would have asked Darlene's opinion about which of two dresses she should wear to dinner with Byron. But since she had asked her siblings to back off, that meant not consulting them about anything to do with Byron or any other man. She chose a pale yellow sleeveless silk-chiffon dress that flared below the hips, black patent-leather shoes with three inch heels and a small black purse. She selected a black wrap in case the air conditioning in the restaurant was too much.

The doorbell rang precisely at six-thirty, and Darlene rushed to open it. Tyra took her time walking down the stairs and, at about halfway, she heard Byron say to Darlene, "What happened to your pony tail? I hardly recognize you."

"That was then. This is now," Darlene said. "Next time you see me, I may have a completely different look."

"I doubt it," he said.

"Hi, Byron. I meant to answer the door, but Darlene beat me to it." She took the bouquet of pink, red and white peonies that he handed her and smiled. "How did you know that I love peonies."

"Just luck, I guess. I'm fond of them, and those were so beautiful. I was wavering between the peonies and roses."

Tyra looked over her shoulder at Darlene. "I'm thirty, Darlene, so I think I can go on a date without a chaperone."

"Oh, sorry. I just thought you might want coffee or something."

"Thanks, but we have to leave now," Byron said. "Maybe next time. Goodbye."

He helped Tyra into the front passenger's seat of his Cadillac. Once she had fastened her seat belt, he closed the door, walked around the car and got in. *Not bad,* Tyra thought.

"I like the way you look. You're…well…very special. You're beautiful and elegant."

A grin formed around her lips, and for some inexplicable reason, she felt like teasing him. "I wouldn't call you beautiful, Byron. There are other words that describe you. But you're elegant, and thank God, you're tall. Oh, and I like the way you look."

Laughter rolled out of him. "I noticed that you Cunninghams like to pull a guy's leg. Clark's good at it, and Darlene's a prankster. I hope you're more sober-minded."

"You don't like jokesters?"

"I didn't say that. And I warn you I can give as good as I get."

She settled back in the comfort of the Cadillac's soft leather seat and crossed her legs. "I'm no slouch, either."

They arrived at the restaurant, a rustic setting that she thought would probably be cozy and even more romantic in the winter when the stone fireplace sparkled with a roaring fire. White lace curtains with red tiebacks graced the windows, and offered relief to the red-brick walls. White linen tablecloths and napkins, white candles and long-stem goblets adorned the round tables that were designed to seat two or four. A bowl of white and pink lisianthus sat in the center of each table.

"Byron, this is so…beautiful. Thank you for choosing this restaurant. I imagine it's even more idyllic in winter when it's cold."

He sat across from her and smiled as if trying to put her at ease. But, his smile had the opposite effect. It rattled her composure. He spoke softly. "What a lovely picture you painted. You wouldn't happen to be an artist, would you?"

Her gaze drifted from his remarkable eyes to his wrist and hands. His fingers were long and appeared strong. How would they feel on her body?

"Do you paint?" he asked again.

Get a hold of yourself, girl. "Yes, I suppose I do. I make stained-glass art. I would love to make stained-glass windows for a modern-design church. I have all kinds of ideas, but I'm not good enough yet to carry them out."

"I paint with watercolors. I've used oils, but I prefer water colors, because I think they're best for the landscapes and seascapes that I do. I also play the piano. I'm pretty good at that."

She sat forward. "You are? Gosh, I envy you. I'd give anything to play the piano. I'd settle for any instrument. I just want to play music. I love music. You're…why are you looking at me that way?"

"I'm sorry if I've made you uncomfortable. I'd never want to do that. So many things were flying around in my mind just then. It's amazing that we have so many interests in common."

"Would you care for drinks, sir?" the waiter said, interrupting the conversation.

Byron looked at her. "What would you like?"

"Something light…and safe."

"I'm glad to know that you trust me." He turned to the waiter. "Please bring her a Chardonnay spritzer, and bring me the wine list."

They ordered their meals. Tyra was sure that she enjoyed the dinner but she hardly remembered tasting it.

"I take it you don't eat much?"

"I do, I'm just a little overwhelmed. If I took a doggie bag, it would be gone in fifteen minutes."

"I'm not sure I should ask what overwhelms you, but I'd certainly like to know."

"The ambiance got me when we walked in. And of course, there's you."

He swallowed heavily, and his face darkened in a frown. "I guess it wouldn't be nice of me to ask what you meant by that last part."

"Thanks, because I'm not sure I could explain it. The food was wonderful. I'm glad you brought me here."

"It's a beautiful evening," he said. "The sun sets late in mid-June. Would you like to drive through Sugarloaf?"

Tyra would say yes to most anything that would prolong her time with him. The man exuded charm. But in her experience, anything presented on a silver platter should be carefully examined. She'd do that. But in the meantime, she'd find a man without anyone's assistance or intervention.

Chapter 2

The next morning, Tyra arose at sunup. She went into her flower garden and sat on the little stone bench beneath the rose trellis. Her parents had put the trellis and bench there a few weeks after they bought the house, and some of her fondest memories were of them sitting there on a summer evening, laughing, holding hands and sipping ice tea. Over the years, Tyra had gone there to find solace and direction. But as time passed, she needed the comfort she found in that little spot less and less. Tyra wondered why she'd gone there at this particular time.

"What are you doing out there so early?" Maggie called from her bedroom window. "You all right?"

"I'm fine, Maggie. Just musing."

"I'll start the coffee, and we can muse together. I'll be down in a minute.

"So what's up?" Maggie asked Tyra a few minutes later when they sat together drinking coffee.

"I need to get a job. I haven't had a response to any of the jobs I applied for, so I think I'll do better if I try something else."

"I expect you're right. If it's money that's bothering you, I can live on less than you pay me. All I need is a home."

"This is your home, Maggie. I'm happy to say that we don't have a financial problem. I've invested what my parents left us. I've paid off the mortgage, and we don't have any debts." Indeed, the value of the trust funds had nearly doubled in the twelve years since the family had received their inheritance. Nevertheless, Tyra remained vigilant and had become as good a money manager as the man she hired to keep a check on their resources. "I'll get busy with my job search as soon as I've eaten."

True to her word, Tyra sat at her computer investigating online job listings. She thought she saw a good job prospect and telephoned the number on the screen.

"You're definitely overqualified for this job, ma'am. Anybody who's finished sixth grade can do what we want." Tyra opened her mouth to say, "You should have put that in the ad," but thought better of it, thanked the woman and continued her search. She doubted that she would have enjoyed a job that didn't challenge her mentally. After applying for more jobs online, someone from the Legal Aid Center that she had spoken to earlier called her back.

"Miss Cunningham, this is Barbara Johnson. We have a position for a counselor that I overlooked when we spoke before. Would you come in tomorrow at nine for an interview?"

"Yes, I'll be glad to. Thank you."

The next morning at nine, Tyra stepped into the Legal Aid Center wearing a white linen suit and tank top, white sandals and bag.

The sisters liked to pull rank, but regardless of status, they appreciated class when they saw it.

Two hours later, she'd been interviewed by a supervisor, examined by a medical doctor and fingerprinted. She had also filled out a questionnaire that contained at least two dozen questions, and she was ready to say, "No more."

"This will be your office," Barbara Johnson said, "and your secretary sits next door. After two weeks, you'll be asked whether you want to keep her or hire one whose skills and personality better suit you. We'd like you to begin tomorrow, but if you prefer you can wait until Monday."

Nothing needed her urgent attention. Indeed, if she didn't start work the next day, she'd spend the rest of the week waiting for Monday. "I can begin tomorrow, Ms. Johnson. Would you tell me who I report directly to?"

"Mr. Riddick is in charge of counseling. He'll introduce you to your associates when you come tomorrow."

"Thanks, Ms. Johnson. You've been so helpful."

As Tyra left the center, she encountered a young good-looking brother. "Things are definitely looking up around here," he said as he held the door for her. "I'm Christopher Fuller, and I hope you're going to be working here."

"I'm Tyra Cunningham. Glad to meet you." She extended her hand, smiled and kept walking. She liked his looks, but she suspected that he could be full of himself. He didn't seem to doubt his attractiveness, and that type had always bored her.

There I go prejudging men. I'm supposed to be looking for a guy, not necessarily to marry, but to get Clark and Darlene off my back. She thought for a second. *Maggie, too. If they saw me with that guy, they'd mind their own business. He's a looker. But something tells me he won't measure up to Byron. Still...*

Tyra plotted to find a man, who might make her reaction to Byron Whitley seem like a child's delight with a new toy.

Meanwhile Byron was arriving at the conclusion that Tyra could be important to him and that he wanted to see more of her. He rarely made a mistake when it came to women, and he didn't think he'd made one with her. He'd gotten a wallop when he first met her. He knew he could lose interest in Tyra simply by staying away from her and by seeing other women. But to his astonishment, he didn't want to do that. She intrigued him, and he wanted *her.*

"I'm wasting time," he said to himself, recognizing something that was out of character for him, and lifted the telephone receiver.

"Ms. Cunningham's not home, Mr. Whitley," Maggie said when he asked for Tyra. "She ought to be back anytime now. I'll tell her you called. You want her to call you?"

"Thanks, but I'll try reaching her again later. Goodbye."

He tapped the fingers of his right hand on his desk. "Now what?"

He phoned his aunt, his mother's sister, who lived with him and took care of four-year-old Andy when he wasn't at home. "My dad and Andy caught some striped bass this past weekend. Dad cleaned them, and I put them in the freezer. Would you mind cooking them for dinner? Andy is proud of them, and the sooner we eat them, the happier he'll be."

"I'll be glad to cook them. You know I love fish. Why don't you call your dad and ask him to have dinner with us tonight?" Jonie said.

"Good idea. Would you mind calling him? I'll be busy for the next few hours."

"I'll call him. If you bring home some vanilla or strawberry ice cream for desert."

"Will do. Andy will be ecstatic."

He hung up and buzzed his secretary. "Ask Mrs. Foxx to come in, please." For nearly a month, he'd been trying to figure out why the woman wanted him to be her lawyer. Rich

as she was, she could have any lawyer she chose. He decided
to stop guessing her reasons and ask her.

"Before we go further with this case, Mrs. Foxx, would
you tell me why you want me to take your case? I'm a crim-
inal lawyer. Yours is a civil suit and you're not asking for
money. Why?"

"I want an apology in *The New York Times,* and you can
get that for me." That wasn't reason enough for her insistence
that he take her case. She had met him at a reception in the
mayor's office and asked for his card. He remembered her.
Any man would remember a woman who looked like her. But
blond hair and blue eyes didn't turn him on. The opportunity
arose earlier than he'd expected.

"I shouldn't take up so much of your time, Mr. Whitley.
Why don't we discuss this over dinner and drinks. We'd both
be…more relaxed, and we'd get more done."

He forced a half smile. "I don't discuss business after my
working hours, Mrs. Foxx. No, thanks. In fact, I advise you
to get another lawyer. This case is not for me."

He stood and extended his hand. "Thanks for considering
me."

She took his hand and held it. "It would have been nice.
Very nice." Head held high and shoulders back, she walked
out of his office as if her brazen suggestion had not been
thwarted. He buzzed his assistant. "Get me some information
on Mrs. Foxx's husband, please."

"I have a file on them, sir. I'll bring it right in."

He flipped through the file. *Hmm.* Just as he'd thought.
She'd married a rich man many years her senior and she was
paying the price. He put the file in his out-box and buzzed his
secretary. "Whenever Mrs. Foxx calls, I'm unavailable."

A glance at his watch told him that if he wanted to speak
with Tyra, he'd better call right then. He dialed her number.

"Hello, Tyra, this is Byron. How are you?"

"I feel as if I could jump across the Potomac. I just got a job, and I think it's perfect for me, that is, if I get some interesting clients."

"Congratulations. That's good news, indeed. What will you be doing?"

"I'll be counseling at the Legal Aid Center, and they want me to start tomorrow."

"This is wonderful. I marvel at how much you and I have in common. When you get down to it, a lawyer is a counselor."

"I hadn't thought of the similarity, and I definitely wouldn't compare what I'll be doing with what you do."

"Yes, but if you're successful, a lot of people won't need me. I called because I want to see you. We could go to the Kennedy Center or hear Kiri Te Kanawa at Wolf Trap. If that doesn't suit you, I could pack us a picnic basket and we could go to Meridian Hill or the Tidal Basin and just be together. The sun doesn't set before nine-thirty."

Her silence told him that he had either surprised her or that she didn't care for his plans. Well, he had patience. Finally she said, "I love the picnic idea, but I haven't heard Kiri Te Kanawa sing in a long time, so—"

"There's no reason why we can't do both, and I'd be much happier. The concert is Saturday evening. We could have our picnic Friday evening in Meridian Hill and at the same time listen to a baroque ensemble. Would you like that?"

"Byron, you've discovered my weaknesses. I think it's a great idea."

"Then I'll be at your house Friday afternoon at five-thirty so we can pick a good spot."

"I'll be looking forward to seeing you."

He hung up. She'd hesitated, and he wondered why. She was attracted to him, and they both knew it, so what held her back? If she was in a dilemma about him, he'd make up her mind for her the first chance he got. And if an opportunity didn't come along naturally, he'd make one.

Byron Whitley was rushing her, and although she wanted to see him, she also wanted the experience of finding the kind of man she liked for herself. She didn't need a matchmaker to fix up her life. She closed her eyes and imagined him kissing her. Her annoyance at Clark and Darlene had all but disappeared, but she still intended to show them that she was capable of managing her own love life. She was attracted to Byron…at least so far, but they didn't have to know it.

"You going in for a swim?" Barbara asked her the next day at lunch. "The pool's right behind us. It belongs to the Parks Department, but it's never crowded. A lunchtime swim can relax you for the rest of the day."

"I didn't bring a swimsuit, but I'll have a look at the swimming pool." She took the elevator to the ground floor and followed the signs. At a door marked POOL, she read a plaque: "Gift from Morris Hilliard to the Legal Aid Center workers with gratitude." Very interesting, she thought, wondering what the center had done for Morris Hilliard. Streams of water cascaded from a single, fifty-foot wall, in a waterfall of rainbow colors. Blue and white tiles paved the entrance to the pool and the area surrounding it.

She glanced at the man sprawled out in a red chaise longue. She couldn't see his face, but his swim trunks advertised his seemingly more than ample equipment. She walked in the opposite direction in hopes of seeing his face without him noticing. The dark glasses did little to camouflage him, because they hardly covered his eyes. Christopher Fuller. She should have known.

Pool or no pool, it doesn't seem appropriate for the office. But oh, the tantalizing picture he made lying in that chaise.

She shrugged, and admitted to herself that she had no right to judge Christopher Fuller.

In the staff cafeteria, she bought a quiche, a bottle of lemonade and an apple, went back to the pool, and took a table in a shaded area to eat her lunch. Several people went for a swim, but she focused on her meal.

"I was wondering when I'd see you again," the male voice drawled.

She looked up into the face of a man she didn't know. Seeing that he was tall and easy on the eyes, she let herself smile. "I don't think we've met," she said after dabbing at the corners of her mouth with her napkin.

"And what a pity that is," he replied. "I'm Matt Cowan. Are you going to tell me who you are?"

"I'm Tyra Cunningham."

He pulled up a chair and sat down. "Don't let me interfere with your lunch. What do you do here?"

Very direct she thought. "I'm a counselor. Some people would call me a psychoanalyst, but they'd be wrong." He crossed his legs and appeared to get comfortable, so she continued eating.

"What is your field?"

She stopped eating and stared at him. Curiosity was one thing, but rudeness was something she wouldn't tolerate. "Psychology," she said. "And that's the last question I'll answer."

He stood and wiped the front of his left trouser leg with his handkerchief. "Sorry if I annoyed you. I tend to do that to people."

"You didn't annoy me, Mr. Cowan. I stopped you before you got that far."

He smiled. "I'd like to know you better. But right now, I have to meet a client. We'll pick this up again later."

"Mr. Cowan, I had a cat who ignored me until he wanted something. He didn't let me pet him or even touch him. One day I decided to let him know who held the power."

Matt walked back and stared down at her. "What happened to him?"

"He loved milk and liver. When he didn't get either for three days, he began following me around the house, rubbing against my leg and looking up at me and meowing. He got plenty to eat, but not what he craved. After a week, I relented, and he no longer treated me as if I were his servant. He was at my heels all the time."

"And the moral of this story?"

"I don't appreciate arrogance."

"Okay. I stand corrected. Why don't we have lunch tomorrow?"

"I'll let you know."

He looked at her for a minute. "I'm about to be late. See you."

She didn't think she could get along with him. He was an alpha male type, and he probably went to the gym every morning before getting to work.

She saw Barbara Johnson as she left the pool area and went back inside the building. She wasn't sure of Barbara's title or of her precise responsibilities, but she was certain that Barbara knew everything about everybody who worked for LAC, as the employees called the center.

"Barbara, are all of these lawyers full-time employees?"

"Good heavens, no. Fuller, Parker and Jenkins are full-time. All the others are either salaried part-time employees or volunteers."

She knew she was taking a chance, since Barbara could have been involved with someone at the center, but she asked any way. "What about Cowan? He struck me as being a lawyer."

"He is, and he makes certain that everybody knows it."

"Hmm. No love lost there."

"At first glance," Barbara went on, "it seems like the pickings here are good. But scratch the surface, and you'll find that this place is about as devoid of real men as a baseball stadium in January."

Barbara couldn't have been more correct or more discouraging. No telling what was behind that. She forced a smile. "What a pity. They're such a good looking bunch, too."

"Yeah, but you can't judge a man by his appearance."

"Nor a woman." Realizing that her last comment might have been misinterpreted, Tyra tried to make up for it. "I know you're very busy, but perhaps we could have lunch."

"Sure," said Barbara.

"See you later." Tyra went back to her office, wondering about her decision. She could be a counselor somewhere else, but the real appeal of the job was its available bachelors. So far, the two clients she was assigned—a teenage runaway and a woman who wasn't sure she wanted to leave her abusive husband—were depressing cases to work on. She welcomed Byron's call that evening with enthusiasm.

With Andy in bed and his Aunt Jonie sitting outside on the deck as she did most summer evenings, Byron had a sudden sense of loneliness. He knew it was natural to feel that way after Lois's death, but her loss was buried deep inside of him in a place that no once could touch. Without thinking, he picked up his cell phone and dialed Tyra's number.

"Hi. This is Byron. Did I call too late?"

"No. It's only nine. How are you?"

The word *fine* came to mind, but he didn't feel fine. He'd spent the day smiling and pretending. "I'm not sure how I am, Tyra. I think I'd feel better if you were here." He knew he'd shocked her, but it was no use pretending.

"You've surprised me, Byron. If something's wrong, I'm sorry. I'd fix it if I could."

"I'm not certain you can't. Ever since I met you, I've been

a little off kilter." And he had. Things that usually satisfied him just didn't anymore.

"Are you unhappy?" she asked. He heard in her voice the softness and compassion that he'd missed for four long years.

"I wouldn't go that far, but I'm obviously not myself, either. And I shouldn't be dumping this on you."

"That's what friends are for. Look, come by and let's go some place and get an ice cream cone."

"That's a wonderful idea. In fact, I think it's just what I need. Can you make it in twenty minutes?"

"Twenty minutes it is." She brushed her teeth, dabbed a bit of perfume behind her ears and went in the family room where she knew Maggie was watching television. "I'm going out for a few minutes."

"If it's who I hope it is, make good use of the time," Maggie said as she threw a handful of popcorn into her mouth.

"No comment."

Tyra grabbed her pocketbook from the back of the dining room chair, took her hair out of a ponytail and closed the front door behind her. As the Cadillac drove up, she started down the walk. Byron got out of the car and met her.

"Hi." He slipped an arm around her waist, bent over and kissed her cheek. "I'm not moody, but—"

"Oh, you don't have to explain," she said, taking his hand. "We all need a lift some time. You'd do the same for me."

He opened the passenger's door for her and helped her in. "You're right. I would, and I won't forget it."

Without thinking Tyra reached over and patted his hand. "Were you really feeling depressed?"

"Yeah. If things aren't going right, I usually fix them. Right now, I'm feeling better."

She thought it best not to comment, but still, the idea that she could make a man like Byron Whitley forget about whatever was bothering him was good for her self-confidence. She wanted to hug him.

She knew she'd better be on her guard with this man. She slid down in the comfortable leather seat. *What the hell,* she said to herself. *I'm thirty-one, and it's time I did some living.*

She'd thought he would take them to a place nearby, but since she lived on the outskirts, he began driving in a different direction

"I'm surprised you didn't ask where we were headed."

"I knew you were taking us to a place that sold ice cream. What else did I need to know?"

He parked and turned to her. "You're growing on me. So you'd better be careful."

"Thank you for warning me."

She wasn't prepared for the cozy, romantic atmosphere inside the massive ice-cream cone-shaped shop. Under hanging lanterns, white pillar-candles were nestled in arrangements of yellow, red and blue nasturtiums atop wrought-iron marble-top tables. Soft music filled the air. With his hand pressed against her back, Byron guided her to a table with a view of the moonlit sky.

They seated themselves, and he picked up a menu. "Whatever flavor you can imagine is here. What would you like?"

"As much as I love ice cream, I feel as if I can't eat anything. I mean, Byron, it's so…perfect."

"I'm glad you're pleased, but I'll be disappointed if you don't have some."

"I know, but not to worry. The chance of my leaving here and not tasting any ice cream is close to nil. I'll bet they don't have pomegranate ice cream."

A grin flashed across his face. "Let's see. Last time I was here, it was on the menu, and it was delicious."

"I'll have a double cone."

"Good. That's what I'll start with." He called the waitress.

"Two double scoops in a cone of pomegranate, please. I'll get an apricot cone for dessert."

If she wasn't careful, she'd fall for him. The waitress brought their ice cream and some napkins. Tyra ran her tongue over the ice cream, closed her eyes and savored the rich creamy dessert.

"This is fan—" She stopped in the middle of the word. When she opened her eyes, she was staring into pools of naked desire. She put the cone on the plate that the waitress had placed in front of her.

"Byron—"

"It's all right. You caught me off guard. Aren't you going to finish your ice cream?"

She nodded, and as soon as the ice cream touched her lips, her discomfort disappeared. She reached across the table and stroked the back of his hand. He turned his hand over and caressed hers. It was too much.

"Byron, tell me why you called me tonight."

"I've always been a loner, Tyra. I have always been that way. I enjoy being with people who are interesting to me in some way. But I liked the peace and quiet of being alone. I always did my best thinking walking in the park or in the woods by myself. Tonight, I suddenly felt lonely. I sat in my den trying to work, and suddenly I felt so alone that I couldn't stand it. And you were the only person that I wanted to see. You can't imagine how happy I was when you suggested we get together."

"I see."

"I won't ask what you are thinking." He leaned forward. "Can we spend some time together? I mean a lot of time. Is there a man in your life?"

"The answer is no."

"Do I stand a chance with you?"

"Well, I haven't left my house at night on the spur of the moment to go any place with a man other than you."

He sat back in his chair and gazed into her eyes as if to make certain that he had heard her correctly. "Not only do you and I have a lot in common, but there's something else important going on here. At first I thought it was just physical attraction. But you've quickly proved me wrong. And it isn't one-sided, either. Are you willing to explore it?"

"What can I say? The same feeling that hit you hit me. But let's go slowly."

"You're telling me not to rush you?" She nodded. "All right, I won't," he said, grinning from ear to ear, "but I certainly won't take things so slow that you'll think I'm dragging my feet."

"Would you mind spelling that out?" As soon as she said it, his expression brightened, and she wished she hadn't asked him to explain.

He leaned forward, his eyes twinkled, and a smile—just short of salacious—framed his lips. "I mean, when I kiss you, I won't pour it on. I'll make it sweet and tender, and when I touch you and stroke you, I won't be too possessive. I'll be careful."

For a full minute, he had her spellbound. She thought of him sinking into her body. Her fingernails scored the palms of her hands, and the pain brought her back to her senses.

She stood. "It's getting late. We should go."

"Of course," he said. He paid the bill, took her hand and walked with her to his car. On the drive back to her house, they didn't talk. He put a CD into the player, and the sound of Chet Atkins's guitar enveloped them. Byron parked in front of Tyra's house and walked her to the door.

"Give me your key, please." She did, and he opened the door, walked in with her and closed it. "You made me feel special tonight," he said. "You were there for me." His left hand stroked the side of her face, and his right hand held her arms, eased across her back and gathered her to him.

She knew he meant to kiss her, and she wanted it so badly that she could hardly wait. Her heart beat so wildly that she feared she would faint. His eyes darkened. When he lowered his head, she rose on tiptoe to meet him. He ran the tip of his tongue across the seam of her lips, testing them. She opened her mouth and sucked him in. His groan stunned her. A prickly sensation shot through her, making her tremble uncontrollably. He gathered her into his arms and held her there.

"I'd better go while I still have my sanity," he whispered after some minutes. "I'll call you when I get home."

She kissed his lips. "Drive carefully. You're carrying precious cargo."

"I promised not to rush you, but if you say things like that to me, keeping my word won't be easy. I won't be like a long distance runner but more like a sprinter."

She floated up the stairs in a world of her own. *If he could make me feel like that with just a kiss...I could be wrong, but how do I know he's the one? But before I get involved with him, shouldn't I see what else is out there?*

Chapter 3

Byron drove three blocks, stopped and put the car in park. Overwhelmed, he hadn't reached his car before he wanted to turn around and go back to her. What the devil was wrong with him? He was his own man—always had been. But this sudden need for a woman he'd seen three or four times boggled his mind. He wasn't upset. He just couldn't understand it. He'd never felt about any woman the way he felt about her. It was if some vital part of him was missing the moment he left her. He shook his head, put the car in gear and continued home. It was probably a fluke. But she made him feel so good. God, please let it be real.

He hadn't told Tyra about Andy. She didn't know he had a son and, until that moment, he hadn't thought it important. But it was. For if his feelings for her persisted, his having a child could become an issue. He'd have to do something about that, and soon.

He drove into his garage and entered his house through the

passageway that connected the garage and the kitchen side door. Vowing not to allow anything to spoil his good mood, he took a bottle of ginger ale from the refrigerator, sat down in the family room, kicked off his shoes and flicked on the television. He switched between late-night talk shows, but didn't see or hear much of either. Tyra had seemed to want him as much as he wanted her. Lord, she was so sweet. And she had an air of innocence that didn't seem to fit with what he knew about her.

He remembered that he'd promised to call her and looked at his watch. A quarter to twelve, twenty minutes since he left her house, but too late to phone. But if he didn't call, she'd probably think he wasn't a man of his word. He dialed her number and prayed that the phone wouldn't ring in anyone's room but hers.

When she answered the phone by saying "Hi," he knew he'd done the right thing.

"I almost didn't call, because I was afraid I might awaken you or your family. But I didn't want you to think of me as unreliable. I've been thinking about you, and about us, and I can hardly believe that I had you in my arms. If it doesn't happen again and soon, I'll think I imagined it."

"Not to worry, Byron, if I thought you forgot it, I'd remind you." Her laughter, warm and hearty, floated to him through the wire.

That comment surprised him. He hadn't known many straightforward women. He was used to women who liked to play games with a guy. "It's really refreshing. I hope the time soon comes when you'll feel free to kiss me whenever you want to."

"You promised to go slowly."

"It seems to me that I'm crawling at a snail's pace."

"Really? A roller coaster is more like it. I enjoyed being with you tonight, Byron, but I'd better get to sleep. I have to get up at six-thirty."

"Stay sweet. At least I'll see you Friday at five. Good night." He'd wanted to add *sweetheart,* but he knew she'd say he was moving too fast.

"Good night, dear."

She hung up. He sat there staring at the receiver. She'd said, *good-night, dear.* Was he dear to her? He'd give anything if he understood women, any woman. He took a shower, dried off, slipped into bed and let the cool sheets tantalize his naked body. What he wouldn't give if she were there to wrap her arms and legs around him! He couldn't help laughing at himself. Every man had at some point knelt before a woman. Who was he to complain about the order of things? He had to wait, and he'd be glad to cool his heels while he waited for Tyra Cunningham.

Tyra strode into the Legal Aid Center office building the next morning feeling like a lottery winner, until Christopher Fuller blocked her way.

"Feeling frisky this morning, are we?" he said with a rakish grin. "I thought I saw you in the pool area yesterday at noon fully dressed. A beautiful woman like you should take a dip so we can appreciate you fully."

She caught herself before she did something she'd later regret. "Not all of us are exhibitionists, Mr. Fuller."

His eyebrow shot up. "When you've got it, flaunt it."

She moved around him, and as she passed, she said, "When what you're flaunting isn't so special, you're wasting your time." His shoulders seemed to sag, so she knew she'd hit him where it hurt. He'd hoped she had seen him sprawled out in the lounge chair. She admitted to herself that he appeared well endowed, but he could bet she'd never know for sure.

But of all the men here, he's the one who's after me. He's the only one that I don't want near me, she said to herself. As far as she was concerned, all he had going for him was below his waist, and she didn't need that from him.

    She found a note on her desk from Lyle Riddick, the man Barbara Johnson said was her supervisor and whom she hadn't yet met. *"Ms. Cunningham, could we meet in my office at ten this morning. Thank you, L. Riddick."* She reread the note. At least he said thank you. Since he didn't say what they would discuss, she couldn't prepare, so she began drafting a questionnaire designed to obtain essential information from her clients—questions that would help her determine the best way in which to help them. Tyra walked into Lyle Riddick's office at exactly ten and stopped short. Was she in a bird sanctuary?

    "Come in. Come in, Ms. Cunningham. I surround myself with my favorite things…to the extent that I can. And birds and squirrels are among my delights. My yard is full of squirrels, by the way." He stood and shook hands with her. "I've been away at a conference. Delighted to meet you."

    "Thank you, Mr. Riddick. I hope the conference was worthwhile."

    "Indeed it was. Are you satisfied with your assignment so far?"

    She leaned back in the chair, assessing the man as best she could.

    "Thank you for asking," she said. "I haven't had anything to do really. I'm sorry for being so blunt, but you asked, and I always try to tell the truth."

    "Honesty is a good thing. I have a case for you. The boy's name is Jonathan Hathaway. He's a great kid, but he's got some family problems. If you have extra time after dealing with this problem, I'd like you to counsel Erica Saunders. After twenty-five years of marriage during which she never held a job and lived off her husband's earnings, she got bored, had an extra-marital affair. She feels she's being mistreated because her husband is divorcing her and refuses to pay alimony. She's depressed, almost suicidal and thinks the whole world is against her. I thought you might be able to help her."

She stared at him. "I hope you don't think I'd sympathize with her."

"I think we'll work well together, Tyra," he said with a hearty laugh. "And please call me Lyle. We have a couple of young turks here, but I see that you're able to keep them in line."

"Yes. I've met both of them, and I don't anticipate a problem."

"Good, Ron Parker took a turn with the Saunders case, but I decided he wasn't the person to deal with it. Stop by his office and get the file. If you have any problems, I'm right here."

She thanked him and left. A knock on Parker's office door brought a response that was more akin to a growl than a greeting. He stood when she walked in.

"Well. Well. Things are looking up around here. I hope you're the secretary I ordered. Hmm."

Another one of those. "Mr. Parker, I'm Tyra Cunningham, and I've been assigned Erica Saunders's case. Lyle said you have her file. May I have it?"

"Walked right into that one. No hard feelings, I hope. I didn't know we were hiring women." He searched through a stack of folders on his desk and handed her one of them.

"Thanks. I'm sure that's not all you don't know." She couldn't get away from him fast enough. Another lesson learned. If she'd met him at a party and he'd asked her for a date, she would probably have gone out with him, though she doubted she'd have done it a second time. She wouldn't say that Ron Parker was a problem. Nor did she expect him to be one, but he was obviously accustomed to getting what he wanted, and he seemed to want what didn't come easily. Or so it seemed. On the way back to her office, she stopped to get coffee.

"Can we have lunch today?" Matt Cowan asked her when she bumped into him in the coffee room.

"I have to prepare for a new client this afternoon, so it's probably not a good time."

He dropped three packets of sugar into his coffee and stirred, all the while gazing intently at her. "You have to eat, don't you? Why not have dinner with me."

She smiled, because she didn't want him for an enemy. But she couldn't imagine why anyone would care about a having lunch with someone who didn't matter. "All right, but I'm planning to read while I eat."

He put the coffee cup down and put both hands in his pants pockets so that his suit jacket hung at his sides and back. To her mind, exasperation was the only word that could describe him.

"Are you brushing me off?"

She didn't try to control the smirk that formed around her lips. "Would anybody dare to do that?"

Matt ran his fingers through his silky curls, a testament to his Native American heritage.

She looked at her watch. "It's eleven o'clock. Meet you in the lunch room at twelve thirty."

"I'd almost given up hope."

"Well, you're nicer than I thought you'd be," said Tyra.

"Are you trying to get a rise out of me?"

"No, but your brusque manner doesn't impress me. Fuller and Parker impress me to the extent that I don't like their company."

"But I'm just another guy, eh?"

"I didn't say that, and don't put words in my mouth. See you at twelve-thirty. I have to work."

"I'll look forward to it."

She went back to her office and closed the door. What would Byron think about that? It was just lunch, but it was still a date. She told herself to tread carefully, and not risk ruining her relationship with Byron just to prove that she could find her own man.

She headed to the cafeteria to meet Matt for lunch and, to

her surprise, he was already there waiting for her. She had assumed that he would be late. Once they had gotten their food, she decided to initiate the conversation. "How old are you?" she asked him.

"Thirty-five."

"Are you married?"

He didn't seem a bit taken aback, considering her question. "I am. But I'm at a different state in my life. I want stability and a family. Right now, I don't have either."

"Is it you or her?"

"It's a combination of things, and it's too bad. What about you?"

"I'm sorry. As for me, I've never married or even come close to it. But I met someone recently who seems interesting."

"He's a lucky guy."

She was surprised that he was so open about such personal matters. But she realized that he was vulnerable and seemingly very unhappy.

"Are you separated now, Matt?"

He nodded. "Yeah, but it suits me. The longer it lasts, the more I learn about myself and the happier I am."

She sipped sweetened ice tea as she waited for Matt to finish his apple pie. She didn't look at him. She couldn't, because she knew he would see the pity in her eyes.

As they left the lunch room, she asked him, "Do you think you and your wife could make a go of it if she worked harder to understand your needs?"

"Maybe, maybe not. Neither is what the other needs."

"Thanks for your company, Matt."

"I thank you. Just talking about it has strengthened my resolve to put my life in order. You're a good listener, and I'll bet you're a good counselor."

"See you later."

She sat down at her desk, leaned back and exhaled. She

understood the wisdom of letting Byron know her feelings, and that meant letting him know her dreams and aspirations. She cared for him, and she wanted him.

At two-thirty, a tall, handsome and well-dressed teenager walked into Tyra's office and extended his hand. She liked him at once. "Ms. Cunningham, I'm Jonathan Hathaway, and I hope you can help me," he said. She asked him to have a seat.

"Thanks. My seventeen-year-old girlfriend is pregnant, and her dad won't let us marry."

"Did you date her without his permission?"

"No. I went to her house practically every evening, took her out or stayed there and did my homework with her. Sometimes he was at home, and sometime he wasn't."

"I don't think the courts can give you permission to marry this girl so long as she's under eighteen, but you do have some rights, and we'll see that those rights are honored."

"Thank you, ma'am. I sure hope so."

She talked with him for half an hour and realized that they might be forced to go to court. "Where does your family stand in this, Jonathan?"

"They're angry. She could stay with us and my folks would help me pay for everything, but her dad won't allow it."

"What is he demanding? He must want *something*."

"Oh, he does. He's asking for money."

Tyra bit back her anger. "I'll see what we have here and collect the resources that we need, Jonathan. Meanwhile, try not to worry. She'll be eighteen in about six months, and her father will have no legal jurisdiction. Of course, we want marriage for the two of you before the child is born, if possible. You're my number one priority."

"Thank you, ma'am. I know you'll do what you can."

She said goodbye to Jonathan. She'd lost track of time and realized that it was past time to go home. She quickly packed up her things.

"How about a drink?" She looked up and saw Christopher Fuller holding the lobby door for her.

"No thanks. I'm in a hurry to get home."

"If you're in a hurry, why'd you stay so late? What were you doing? Making out with Cowan?"

"What I was doing is none of your business. I don't have a damn thing to do when I get home. I just can't stand you." She whirled around and bumped into Matt. "Matt, this idiot says I've been making out with you. I'd appreciate it if you'd straighten him out."

As she rushed off, she heard Matt say, "Come off it, Fuller. You wouldn't know a lady from the pigs you lie around with. You've had one warning. If you don't want a second one, you'd better change your tone."

When she got home, she went to her bedroom, closed the door and kicked off her shoes. She'd decided it would be foolish to jeopardize her relationship with Byron merely to put her siblings in their place.

Byron was a block from his house when he remembered his promise to buy Andy a bicycle. A four-and-a-half year-old could handle one he reasoned. He turned the Cadillac onto Genstar Drive and headed for the Francis Scott Key Mall. Once inside the mall, Byron passed a bookstore window and saw a children's book about Frederick, Maryland heroes. He went in and bought it. Andy loved stories that he could retell in his day school and was fast earning the title of class storyteller. Byron made a note to read the book first so that he could answer his son's questions, and he knew there would be plenty of them.

Byron found the bicycle that he wanted, remembered to get a helmet and headed home. He pulled into his garage, left the bicycle and helmet in the car and entered the house through the kitchen. In his haste to greet Byron, Andy nearly fell out of the chair.

"I need a new story, Daddy. Kisha told one today, but nobody clapped."

Byron lifted the boy into his arms and hugged him. "Why didn't you clap?"

"I didn't want her to be as good as me."

"As good as I. You should have clapped. You're good at it, and you can afford to be gracious to other children who try to tell stories.'

"Yes. But she wasn't as good as I am."

"Fine. Next time, I want you to lead the applause for her. Got it?"

"Yes, I will. But I don't like the idea."

Byron put Andy back in the chair and went up to his room. A search of the yellow pages in the telephone book gave him a choice of several gourmet restaurants, and he chose one. After ordering, he showered and dressed in black jeans, a T-shirt and black sneakers and went downstairs.

He handed his son the book he'd bought earlier. "Let's read, Andy."

"What's the story about?"

"Important people who lived in Frederick long ago."

"Good. I'm going to read slow, so I'll remember it and I can tell it at school tomorrow." The boy read the picture story in about fifteen minutes. "I love the story, Dad."

Andy loved reading. Indeed, the boy had a sizeable library of books. It was becoming difficult to find new ones that challenged his skills. *I'm going to have to start writing stories for preschool children,* Byron said to himself. "If I get Andy's imagination to working, it should be fun."

At five-thirty, he rang Tyra's doorbell, and, to his disappointment, Darlene opened the door. "Hello, Darlene. Are you the Cunninghams' official doorman?"

"Hi, Byron. I think I detected a bit of sarcasm. Who do you want to see? Tyra or Clark? Clark's in Baltimore."

"Darlene, give me a little credit. I wouldn't be here if I didn't have a reason. Do you mind if I come in and wait for Tyra?"

"Sure. Something tells me that I get on the wrong side of you without trying."

"Darlene, I told you I was expecting Byron at five-thirty." Tyra walked in. "Hi. I'm sorry, Byron."

He leaned over, kissed Tyra's cheek. "It's all right. We'll make up for it." Tyra cast a glance in Darlene's direction, took Byron's arm and ushered him out of the house.

"Do you realize I've never been to Gambrill Park?" she asked him as he opened the front passenger door for her. "And I've lived here all my life."

"Something tells me that, when you were a teenager, you didn't do much dating."

"You're right. I didn't. I was seventeen when we lost our parents, and responsibility for my siblings and our home fell to me. I was scared to death of setting a bad example."

He got in the car, eased his arm across her shoulder and turned to her. "I've waited all day for the greeting that Darlene deprived me of."

She turned to him, snuggled closer and parted her lips. Heat plowed through him as she sucked his tongue into her mouth. He knew he should stop, but when he attempted to pull away, she clung to him. He braced his hands on her shoulders and eased her away from him. Her face bore a dazed expression.

He held her as close as he dared. "It's still daylight, sweetheart. We could draw quite a crowd." He'd meant it to be funny, but she didn't smile. "What is it, Tyra? What's wrong?"

"Nothing, I guess. I suppose I'm only now learning who I am. I surprise myself sometimes when I'm with you."

Her words brought an inward smile and gave him a feeling she would never understand. If he was the man to teach her who she was, nothing would please him more. He knew she wasn't an innocent. A woman without any sexual experience wouldn't relate to a man as she did. But she'd missed something, and he couldn't wait to fill the void.

"Don't think you haven't shown me a different side of myself. The good thing is that I like who I am with you," he said, as he headed out Yellow Springs Road to Gambrill Park. "I've already picked out a space for us. It's close enough to the bandstand, but far enough to protect the eardrums."

After parking the car and locking it, he took a wicker picnic basket and a shopping bag from the trunk, walked with her to a big boulder and put the basket on it. "This boulder will not only make a great table, it's a good back rest."

"What's in that?" she asked, pointing to the shopping bag.

"A blanket to sit on, and two longs-sleeved shirts, one to protect your arms from the mosquitoes and the other to protect mine. I also brought along some repellant. Mosquitoes hate that."

He spread the blanket and sat down beside her. "Would you put your head on my shoulder for a few minutes?" he asked her. "I'm not rushing you, but I'd like you to be a little closer." He was still hot from her kiss in the front seat of his car.

She did as he asked and put one arm around his back and the other across his chest. "I could go to sleep right here," she said, her voice low and inviting.

"Tyra, you don't want me to rush, so don't feed my imagination with statements like that."

"It was an innocent remark. What time does the music start?"

"It started when you appeared at your foyer."

When the sound of musicians tuning their instruments reached their ears, Byron handed Tyra a copy of the evening program and opened his own. "You read it to me," she said. "I'm too comfortable to move, and I'd have to let go of your waist."

He read it to her and added, "We're in luck, or at least I am. I love Italian baroque chamber music."

"Me, too. The problem is that it puts me right to sleep."

"We'll have our picnic in a few minutes. I don't suppose you can eat and sleep at the same time."

She kissed his neck, and he wished she'd warned him. "I guess not. I don't remember ever dreaming about food. And that's weird, because I love to eat."

He covered the boulder with a blue tablecloth, set the table with the matching plates and utensils the caterer supplied and placed their food on it.

"This is wonderful, Byron. A feast beneath the stars in a fairy-tale environment, listening to beautiful music in the company of a man who is literally a heartthrob. If I act a little giddy, who could blame me?"

He leaned over and kissed her cheek. "Don't expect me to behave when you talk like this." He held a glass of white wine to her lips. "I've been drunk on you since the minute I first saw you. If you keep talking like that, I'll start staggering." It was all right to joke and tease, but he was serious. "Tyra, I asked you if there was a man in your life, and you said that there wasn't. Will you give me a chance to be the man in your life?"

She seemed taken aback. "Isn't that what you're doing now?"

"No, not yet."

"If I know up front what your motive is I might cooperate."

"Fair enough." He swatted the side of his neck to discourage an offending mosquito. Then he opened the shopping bag and took out the shirts he'd brought.

"Thanks. You're a very thoughtful man."

"If you give me a chance, Tyra, I'll always take good care of you. Always."

Chapter 4

On the way home from the concert, Tyra mulled over Byron's words, and especially her memories of his gentleness throughout the evening. He'd done everything but feed her by hand. Now, he wanted her to confine her male companions to him.

Tyra didn't want any man but Byron. Yet, she wasn't sure that not seeing other men made sense. She could count on one hand the men she'd dated and still have fingers left.

"You're very quiet," Byron said. "Is there a something bothering you?"

"I'm not sure. There isn't another man in my life, but I'm not certain that I want to promise you that there won't be. There are times when my attraction to you frightens me. I love being with you. and I'm happy when I'm with you But suppose I'm making a mistake? Don't you ever doubt your feelings, Byron?"

"I appreciate what you're saying, even though I don't like it. I especially appreciate your honesty. I'm forty years old, and I know who I am. I don't doubt my feelings for you one bit. Are you telling me that you don't trust a relationship with me?"

"I didn't say that. I'm wondering if I've had enough experience to know…I mean to judge what I'm feeling. It happened so suddenly, and it…seems like we're moving too fast."

"No relationship stands still, Tyra. It either grows, or it begins to die. Are you afraid?"

"Believe me, it's definitely not dying."

"If you want to stop seeing me, tell me right now."

When she turned to look at him, she saw that the firm set of his jaw did not match the softness with which he spoke. Maybe she shouldn't have been so candid. "No, I don't want to stop seeing you. I love being with you."

"But you don't trust the relationship."

"That's too harsh. I trust you, and I… Oh, why did I start this."

He parked in front of her house, cut the motor and turned to her. "Will you or won't you stop seeing other men and give us a chance?" He looked into her eyes, unsmiling, and she knew what would come next if she said no. If the truth were known, he had no cause for concern. *Don't make the biggest mistake of your life, girl. He's asking for the truth.*

"I will, Byron," she said at last and breathed deeply in relief, "but you promised not to rush me."

He slid an arm around her. "I know I did, but I had to know, because we need to talk. Instead of going to the concert tomorrow night, will you have dinner with me?"

She hid her surprise at his change of plans. "What time?"

"I'll be here at six-thirty. Okay?"

"That's fine," she said and stroked the back of his hand almost absentmindedly. "It'll be a long day."

"Does that mean you'll be eager to see me?"

"That's what it means." His eyes seemed to devour her. Then a half smile played around his lips.

"If we weren't right under this streetlight. I'd kiss you

silly." He got out, went around and opened her door and headed up the walk to her house.

Unwilling to let him leave so soon, she said, "Why did Clark invite you to spend the night here? I don't get the sense that you two are really close friends."

"Our offices are in the same building and, occasionally, we eat lunch together. At the time, he was an expert witness on a case I had here in Frederick. The judge wanted the trial at nine o'clock, and that didn't suit me, but it suited Clark, so he suggested that I spend the night here. As an added incentive, he raved about Maggie's cooking, because he knew how much I love good food. He didn't mention you, and it's a good thing that he didn't, because I don't like being set up."

"He told me he was bringing a houseguest, but he certainly didn't describe you. I thought he was bringing a girlfriend."

Byron stepped closer. "It happened when you opened the door. Why don't you stop fighting it?" He brought her into his arms. "Kiss me. I'm starved for you."

She reached up to kiss him playfully on the cheek, but he moved to capture her lips. She tasted his hunger and his driving need. She pulled his tongue deeper into her, answering him with her own rising passion. He grabbed her buttocks and fastened her body to his. She could feel him then, and heat began to simmer in her loins as she pressed herself to him until, nearly frantic with the need to explode, she undulated wildly.

Out of her mind with desire she grabbed his hand and rubbed her left breast with it until he began to pinch and squeeze it. "Do something," she moaned. "I'm aching."

She thought she would die from the feeling of his long fingers on her skin as he released her breast from her scooped-neck dress. Lifting her, he sucked her left nipple into his mouth while he teased and pinched the other one. She'd never felt anything in her life like the throbbing between her legs. And still he suckled her.

"Oh, my lord. I can't stand this," she moaned, shaking from the onslaught of his passion.

He released her breast and wrapped her in his arms. "We're going to have to do something about this, sweetheart. Do you feel anything for me other than passion? I know you feel that. Do you? Do you care for me?"

"Yes. Oh, yes, I do. What…what happened a minute ago?" When he stepped back in order to see her face, she wondered if she'd said the wrong thing, if he'd think her immature.

"If we had privacy, we probably would be making love this minute. At least, that's what we both need right now. Have you ever had a truly satisfying sexual experience?" She shook her head. "It's something for us both to look forward to."

She wanted to ask him why the thought brought a smile to his face, but she figured she'd revealed enough for one evening. "I don't think we'd better consider that right now."

"I agree. I'll see you tomorrow at six-thirty. Kiss me, and this time, please don't turn up the heat."

"I didn't turn it up. You turned it up."

"Did not."

"Did so, and I can prove it." When he raised an eyebrow, she reached up and touched his lips with hers until, frustrated, he brushed the tip of his tongue over the seam of her lips until she opened to him. He plunged into her demanding, asking, begging for what he needed until she capitulated and loved him as sweetly and as tenderly as she could, stroking his face, nibbling on his tongue and moaning softly.

"You're…you're precious to me," he said when he could get his breath. "Don't forget that."

Long after Byron left her, Tyra stood in the darkened foyer coming to terms with her feelings for Byron. There was no point in fooling herself. Byron Whitley was the man for her, no matter how he happened to come into her life. When she was in her teens and twenties, she didn't have an opportunity to play the field. Now, she was thirty-one and too old for it. She wanted a family of her own.

She turned on the hall light and started up the stairs, rubbing her hands along the banister that she'd slid down so many times in happier days before her parents died. *I've been so busy trying to relive the youth I missed, that I almost missed out on the prime of my life. I'm through with that. Byron asked for a chance, and I'm going to give him one.*

Byron's problem at the moment did not involve questions about his feelings for Tyra. He knew he loved her. The questions that gnawed at him were how she would react when he told her about Andy, and how would she and his son get along. Maybe having had to nurture her siblings when she herself still needed nurturing had turned her against children. Maybe she'd find it difficult to love another woman's child.

I should have told her before it got this far, before we began to need each other. But what the heck! The die was cast when we met, and I didn't have a reason to tell her anything personal. Besides, it happened so fast.

He tiptoed into Andy's room and stood beside the child's bed marveling at his son as Andy stretched, hugged his teddy bear and sank into a deeper sleep. He knew that, in spite of his feelings for Tyra, he'd close his heart and his mind to her and get on with his life if she couldn't accept his child as her own. He leaned down, kissed the boy's forehead, turned out the light and closed the door. Life could play cruel tricks, but if he were fortunate this time, he'd have a real home and family. But he wasn't going to rush it. He'd introduce her to Andy when the time was right and not before.

With his mind at ease, he turned his thoughts to one of his clients. He didn't like the man, because of his alcoholism. The man swore that he could stop drinking, if he wanted to and probably believed it. He agreed to take the man's case because his teenage daughter needed help. Yet, he had a nagging feeling that his client was basically selfish, that he didn't really have his daughter's interest at heart. After reading two similar cases, he shrugged. What would be would be. A peaceful sleep awaited him the minute he put his head on the pillow.

"You mean you won't be home for dinner tonight, Sis?" Clark said to Tyra.

"Right. I'm going out to dinner." She almost never left the house when Clark was at home because they had so little time together. "If I'd known you'd be here, I wouldn't have made plans, but—"

He raised his hand to assure her that she didn't have to explain. "I should have let you know. But I'm so used to your being here all the time that I didn't think to do it."

"That's my life in a nutshell," she said to herself. "I probably won't be out late," she said aloud.

"A guy or a girl?"

She gave him a withering look. "If I had a date with a girl, Clark, I'd cancel."

She dashed up the stairs to dress, and he called after her, "You mean you aren't going to tell me his name?"

She ignored the question. "I have to get dressed. Answer the door before Darlene gets to it, will you?"

As she hurried to the bathroom, she heard Clark say, "What? If Darlene's been flirting, I'll have a talk with her." She closed the bathroom door and stepped into the shower. She and Clark had spent hours lecturing to Darlene about her flirtatiousness. Wasted hours. Flirting was Darlene's way of communicating with the opposite sex.

Deciding to dress conservatively, Tyra put on a silk-chiffon, flared lavender dress that had a criss-cross waist-defining middle and fell below the knee, a string of cultured pearls and pearl earrings. Looking in the mirror, she was pleased with herself for choosing a dress that wasn't an advertisement for sex. Not a bit of cleavage was showing. But suppose he wanted to… *Cut it out, girl. You don't want a duplication of last night.*

When the doorbell rang, she could feel her blood race. Her fingers shook when she tried without success to zip up her pocketbook. She walked on wobbly legs to the head of the stairs and looked down.

"Well, I'll be damned! How's it going, man? My sister didn't tell me that she was expecting you. Come in. She'll be down in a minute."

She started down the stairs and stopped. Both men stood at the bottom of the stairs looking up at her. She grabbed the banister and continued down the stairs. Suddenly, Byron's face lit up in a wide grin, as he moved to meet her.

"You seem a little shaky," he said. He put an arm around her waist and kissed her. He turned and started down the stairs using his arm to support her. Clark stood at the bottom of the stairs, an expression of shock plastered across his face.

When they reached the bottom of the staircase, Byron patted Clark on the shoulder. "Get used to it, man." What she would have given to record the expression on Clark's wide-eyed face.

"Well, hell! Have fun." He walked away, turned and gave his sister a stern look. "Curfew's at eleven o'clock."

"Is he serious?" Byron said to Tyra.

"He'd better not be. But if he is, I'll advise him not to bring a woman here unless he wants a dose of his own medicine." She took Byron's hand and yelled to Clark who she knew was in the family room sitting in front of the television. "I'll be back home tonight, but don't count on my doing that all the time. Good night."

"You think you should have said that to Clark?" Byron asked as they settled into the car.

"He knows I said it to put him in his place. He could

have been teasing, but how do I know? Let's forget about him for now."

"You never ask me where I'm taking you. How do you know I'm not driving you to some secret lair?"

She settled into the soft leather seat and turned on the radio to a classical music station. "Being spirited away to your secret lair? I'd be so excited I'd probably pass out. Just thinking about almost takes my breath away."

"Are you saying you like to live dangerously? I wouldn't have thought so."

She didn't look at him. She couldn't. A delicious feeling coursed through her body as her mind recalled the previous evening and imagined his hands and mouth doing all kinds of things to her in preparation for the pleasure to come.

"Where's the danger in going off to a cave or some other isolated spot with you? I bet I'd have the time of my life."

The car skidded to a stop. "You'd better not talk like that if you don't mean it."

"Why are you so sure I don't mean it? If you took me off some place, wouldn't I have a great time?"

He started the engine, looked over his left shoulder and drove away from the curb. "To answer your question, I'd do my best to make it an occasion you would remember for the rest of your life."

"I can't wait."

He brought the car to a stop in front of a building that looked like a private home in a block of row houses. "Here we are," he said.

"Huh? I thought you said we were going to a restaurant."

"I said dinner." Her stare brought a torrent of laughter from him.

"What's so funny?" she asked. "Please let me in on the joke."

When he began laughing again, she tried to shake his

shoulder. At last, controlled and evidently sober, he said, "This is a restaurant, and you've just proved that you're all bark and no bite. After bragging about the excitement of being intimate with me, you were scared to death that I was taking you to a room and you'd have to pay up. Be glad I didn't take you at your words."

She pretended to pout. "It's not nice to laugh at me. You're not as sweet as I thought you were."

He wiped the grin off his face and grasped both of her shoulders. "Do you think I'm sweet? Do you?"

She'd never seen him as open and vulnerable as he appeared at that moment, and she told herself to be careful. His eyes and the huskiness of his voice revealed a need for… yes, for affection and understanding.

She stroked the side of his face. "Yes, I think you're sweet, and if we were somewhere else, I'd hug you real tight."

He closed his eyes and brought her close to his body. "I want to kiss you, but I don't dare. Let's go inside."

What he needed from her went far beyond a kiss. He needed *her* in the fullest sense of the word. He'd chosen the Sonata Restaurant because its rounded, boothlike banquettes gave diners a good measure of privacy.

"Right this way, Mr. Whitley," the maitre d' said. "Your table is ready."

"Do you have any more secrets?" Tyra asked him. "I love this one. Thanks for choosing it."

"You make doing things to please you a delight. What would you like to eat? I confess I'm not very hungry."

She put her menu on the table, placed her hands in her lap and seemed to study him. "You said you wanted us to talk. Is what you have to say going to make me unhappy?"

"I don't know. It shouldn't."

"I see." She picked up the menu, glanced over it and said,

"I'll have cold cucumber soup, broiled lamb chops with wild rice and asparagus tips and raspberry sorbet for dessert."

"I'll have the same plus a good burgundy wine," he told the waiter.

"What will madam drink?" the waiter asked.

"The same," she said, ignoring Byron's raised eyebrow.

When she had eaten half of the raspberry sorbet, she pushed the remainder aside. "This is killing me, Byron. You haven't told me anything that you couldn't have said over the phone."

He knew that, but he hadn't wanted to upset her while she ate. And if he were honest with himself, he'd admit to procrastinating. "Tell me exactly how you felt about having to raise Clark and Darlene?" Her deep frown didn't surprise him. They had touched on that before.

She leaned back and looked straight at him. "I loved them so much, and the responsibility for taking care of them was merely an extension of what I'd been doing when our parents weren't at home. If you're asking if I resented it, no I didn't. And Maggie helped me."

"I've observed your relationship with Maggie. She isn't motherly toward you. She treats you as if you're head of the house. Do you want to have a family of your own, or have you had your fill of raising children?"

"I long to have children, Byron. That is if I get the chance at all, but I still want to try. What about you? Do you want to have a family?"

She seemed to be holding her breath in anticipation of his answer. When he reached across the table and took her hand, he realized how desperately he needed her to understand. "Tyra, I probably should have told you this earlier, but our relationship didn't warrant it."

"You're not married!" she gasped.

"No. My wife died two weeks after she gave birth to our son, Andy. He's four and a half."

Her face clouded up in a frown that he couldn't decipher. After a few seconds, she said, "Oh, lord, Byron. I'm so sorry. Who takes care of him while you work?"

"I didn't want him to be raised by a succession of nannies and babysitters. My aunt had recently been widowed and lived alone, and I invited her to live with me. She's been a godsend, but I'm the one who's responsible for Andy's up-bringing. I bathe him, put him to bed at night, read to him—or did before he learned to read—and hear his prayers. I'm his father."

"Are you going to let me meet him?"

"Eventually. Yes. What I want to know is whether my having a child changes your attitude toward me."

She seemed taken aback. "Why should it? If I discovered that you didn't take care of your son, that you didn't love him and do everything for him that you could or that you ne-glected him in any way, my attitude and my feelings for you would definitely change. But I don't believe you're guilty of any of that." She leaned forward. "Tell me about him. What is he like?"

"I am certainly biased, but I think he's a wonderful kid. He's very smart, reads well for his age, counts and is trying to learn arithmetic, although that's his idea, not mine. He's becoming a good storyteller, and his day school teacher often gives him that role at school. Andy's affectionate, but he's very impatient and definitely exacting. He can tell time, and if I tell him I'll be home at six, he wants to see me there at six, traffic notwithstanding. I don't complain about that, because I've taught him that he can depend on me. He loves music, and he'll sit quietly without saying a word for half an hour while I play the piano, no matter what I'm playing. He and I have a wonderful relationship."

"Is he obedient?"

"Yes he is. I let him argue his case for a few minutes, and then I tell him what's final. He accepts it."

"Does he look like you?"

"If you put his picture and mine at that age side by side, a stranger would think it's the same child. Yes. He looks as much like me as I look like my father. Oh, he's just begun learning to play the piano, and he loves it."

She massaged her forehead with the tips of her fingers, and watching her do it, her face creased in a worried frown. He couldn't help being anxious. She hadn't even hinted at answering his question whether knowing about Andy made a difference in her attitude toward him.

"You know my family. Tell me about your parents and siblings. Are you close to them?"

She had a right to ask that. If you didn't know a person's family, you were missing vital information about that person. "After my parents divorced, my father raised my sister and me. My mother married someone else and moved with him to Eugene, Oregon. I was seven, and from that time on, she wasn't a part of my life. Not my choice or my father's choice, but she didn't make it possible for my sister and me to visit her and she didn't visit us.

"My sister, Nannette, lives in Florence, Italy, with her Italian husband, who's a surgeon. My father's a doctor, so we grew up well off. He's seventy-two, but still busy with a full practice. I'm close to my father and to my sister, and I talk with her at least once a week. I've been thinking that my dad would love you, because you and he share similar outlooks on a lot of things. I'm proud that my father raised my sister and me alone, though I now realize that I must have missed something not having a mother."

Now that he'd told her, he couldn't bear not knowing what she thought or how she felt. If she had to think about it, or if her acceptance was contingent upon anything, he didn't want to know. She could forget it. He had a strange, dull feeling.

"Tyra, I asked you a while ago whether knowing that I have

a son changes your attitude toward me. Your answer was 'Why should it?'"

She seemed flustered, as if she didn't understand him. "Honey, I told you that I'd walk away only if you weren't a good father. Don't you remember?" Her right eye arrowed slightly, as she looked at him in an intense gaze. "If you're asking whether I'll love your child, of course I will if he'll give me a chance," she said.

He inhaled deeply. It was what he needed to hear, not some sugar-coated answer about loving Andy because he was his child, but an honest and sensible response. He knew Andy would learn to love her. But as long as he hadn't committed to Tyra, he couldn't bring up that subject.

"I've never introduced Andy to anyone I was seeing, because I don't want him to get attached to someone who proves to be a temporary relationship. Oh, you know what I mean. But there's nothing temporary about my feelings for you, and I want you to know everything about me. I want you to care for the man I am, not what I appear to be." He had to know one more thing. He was in too deep, and he wanted to be sure where he stood with her. "Do you resent my not telling you about Andy on our first date?"

"No, I don't. But after what we shared last night, I needed to know where you and I are headed. With your telling me about your son and your family, I'm satisfied that you're sincere." She paused for a moment. "The funny thing is that I never doubted your sincerity. But I feel that I know you better now."

Maybe if he did it casually rather than taking her home with him to meet Andy, it would work out better. "Do you like to fish?" he asked her.

"I did when I was little. I used to fish with my dad in the Monacacy River. Why?"

"My dad loves to fish. Perhaps you can join us sometime."

"I'd love that, Byron, even if I don't get a single bite."

"Then, I'll arrange it."

Tyra wanted to ask Byron if Andy would join them when they went fishing. But she had already decided that if he seemed inclined, she would encourage him to let her meet his son, but she wouldn't push it. She knew the implications, and she didn't doubt that she would meet his father before she met Andy.

"Would you like something else?" he asked her.

She shook her head. "Thanks. It was a delightful meal. If you're not in a hurry, could we walk a little?"

"Of course. But if walking is a way to prolong the evening, I have some other suggestions. We could go to the carriage company, hire a hansom and take a ride, or we could go to the Frederick Hotel's supper club, have coffee, a liqueur and dance. In either case, I could have you in my arms. What would you like?"

"If I choose the hansom ride, will you take me dancing another time?"

"Of course I will. Ready to go? I need to hold you, and I don't want to do it standing in your foyer."

"What's wrong with my foyer?" she asked in an attempt to bring a little levity into their conversation. The seriousness of their after-dinner conversation had nearly exhausted her. The subject had obviously weighed heavily on him, and she didn't understand why. Surely he should have understood that she would find a way to show love to a four-year-old, motherless child, no matter who his father was. But she wasn't going to worry about it. Andy was extremely dear to him, and he'd just served notice that any woman who couldn't love and care for his child would have no part in his life. On that score, she agreed with him.

"Nothing's wrong with your foyer except that every minute I'm standing there with you, I'm distracted. I feel as if I should look over my shoulder for Darlene or Maggie."

"Distracted? I wonder what you'd be like if I had your undivided attention?"

"I'm going to do my best to make sure you find out."

"Do you have any pictures of Andy?"

She knew at once that she'd said the right thing, for his face beamed with pride. "You bet." He opened his wallet, removed two pictures and handed them to her.

She studied them. "Byron, he's a beautiful child. And you're right, he looks just like you." She handed the pictures to him. "You're blessed to have a healthy, happy and intelligent son."

"I know, and I'm grateful for it. I could have been left with no one."

She reached up and stroked his face. "Are you over your wife's death? I know it's hard."

"Yes, I'm over it."

As they left the restaurant holding hands, she asked him, "How far is it to the hansom carriage? I thought it was right around the corner."

"It's right around the next corner. Would you like to walk, or shall we drive there?"

"It's a balmy night, let's walk."

She looked up at the full July moon, at the sky as clear as crystal and squeezed his fingers. "What is it?" he asked.

"The moon. The sky. The night. It's so idyllic. I wish it could last forever." A brisk wind brushed the hair away from her face, as tiny bit of debris whirled around her feet. Lights twinkled in every building that they passed. It seemed to Tyra that neither residents nor merchants were willing to sacrifice the beautiful night.

"I also noticed how perfect the night was. I'm so busy all

the time, that I rarely notice things—such as this night—that give me so much pleasure. When I'm with you, though, my senses work overtime."

"Where do you want to ride, mister?" the driver of the hansom asked Byron. "For twenty-five extra, we can take a drive through Gambrill."

"Want to?" he asked her.

"He's a romantic, so maybe he knows something. I'd like it if you have time."

He helped her into the carriage and tucked her close to him. "The night is young, and you're so beautiful," he sang. To the driver, he said, "Gambrill sounds fine."

With his arms around her and her head on his shoulder, she was as one with him. "For tonight, at least, I have you," he said. She wanted to know what he meant and asked him. "I know what I want and what I need," he said. "But I know that not even the next piece of bread is guaranteed. So I'm treating this evening as the precious experience that it is."

She pondered that, but didn't respond. Byron could relax. She was not going to let him down.

Chapter 5

When Tyra walked into her office the following Monday morning, she was more besotted with Byron Whitley than ever and in no mood to tolerate advances from any other man. So when Christopher Fuller walked up behind her as she opened the door of her office and patted her on her bottom, she swung around and, without thinking, let him have the weight of her briefcase across his face.

"What the hell is wrong with you, woman?" he growled. "Who do you think you are?" He stood inches away from her.

She didn't back away. "If you ever put your hands on me again, this briefcase isn't all I'll hit you with. I should sue you for sexual harassment."

"Who'd believe you?"

"Everybody. You'd be surprised what your colleagues think of you. If you're charged with sexual harassment, what do you think it will do to your career. Now please let me get into my office."

"You haven't heard the last from me," he said.

"You'd better hope you've heard the last from me," Tyra replied and stormed off to her office.

She sat down at her desk, made a note of the incident, dated it and filed it under the heading, C. Fuller. If she left her job, he'd probably be the reason.

The incident didn't occupy her thoughts for long. Memories of the previous evening with Byron crowded her mind. She had never seen a brighter, clearer moon or felt a softer breeze than when she sat snug in his arms in a red-bordered hansom carriage. The only sounds were the rustling of the trees and the clickety-clack of the horse's hooves.

She could still hear his voice. "I need to kiss you." And she had raised her head from his shoulder and parted her lips for the thrust of his kiss. She hadn't known that a man could find so many ways to cherish a woman, yet he'd promised her much more than he gave. And she knew he was a man who delivered what he promised. The telephone rang interrupting her thoughts.

"Tyra Cunningham speaking. What's the problem, Jonathan? Your girlfriend's father has forbidden you to come to see his daughter?"

"He says he'll have me thrown into juvenile detention. If he does that, I won't be able to finish high school with my class, and I'll have a record. All I'm asking is for an opportunity to look after her. I've been giving her a part of my allowance. Now, I don't know how I'll get that to her."

"Has she been to social services?"

"He wouldn't let her to do that, and she's scared of him."

"You wouldn't expect him to approve of his sixteen-year-old daughter having sex, would you?"

"No, ma'am. But if we hadn't had to sneak around to see each other, we'd probably have been more careful."

"You're not going to juvenile detention, so don't worry

about it. Get a post office box, and give her one of the keys to it. That way, you two can communicate, and you can contact her through the mail. I would advise you not to go against his wishes."

"Thank you, ma'am. I'll ask my dad to do it today. He's fed up with Mr. Tate."

She hung up and looked through her messages, hoping there was one from Byron, although she knew that he normally didn't call her at the office. She saw one from Lyle, her supervisor, and called him.

"Can you see Ms. Saunders today, preferably this morning?" he asked her. "She'll fall apart if she doesn't get to see a counselor."

"Okay, but I'd rather it be my last appointment."

"Fine. She'll be satisfied as long as she gets to see someone today."

Tyra prepped herself for what she expected would be a trying experience with Erica Saunders. A few minutes before her appointment, she went to the coffee room for a bagel and a fortifying cup of coffee and encountered Matt Cowan there.

Matt poured a cup of coffee for her. "How's it going, Tyra? Any more problems with Fuller?"

"He hasn't learned to keep his hands to himself, but I corrected him. If he needs further instructions as to where his hands belong, I'll let the legal system educate him."

"Something's wrong with that guy. He's the last person who should be working in a place like this. I imagine he's been fired from more than one job. He's capable of nastiness, so be careful, Tyra, and watch your back."

"Thanks, Matt. I'll try to. See you later. I have a three forty-five appointment."

Minutes after she sat down, Erica Saunders walked into her office. "You Miss Cunningham?"

Tyra stood. "Yes. Have a seat. How may I help you?"

Erica Saunders gazed around, taking in everything before she sat on the edge of the chair. "I never heard of anybody black being named Cunningham. Where you from?"

"We have half an hour, Ms. Saunders. Why do you need to see a counselor so urgently?"

"If you gon' be my counselor, you gon' have to be patient, 'cause nobody rushes me, and nobody bullies me. You got a file on me big as from here to New York, so you know what my problem is."

"Ms. Saunders, I was given your case because no one else is prepared to take it. You have a reputation for being uncooperative. If I can help you right now, tell me what the problem is. Otherwise, don't come here and waste my time." She looked at her watch. "You're the one with the problem. Not me."

"That's why I always like men for counselors," Erica said under her breath. "My husband closed his checking accounts, so I can't get any money, and I'm broke."

"Then the best thing for you to do is agree to reasonable divorce terms. You'll have some money then. Why don't you find a job?"

"You're supposed to be helping me, not him."

Tyra leaned back in her chair and glared at the woman. "In the twenty years of your marriage, you didn't work one day. You had an elegant home and a housekeeper. You and your husband have no children. According to these files—" she tapped the thick manila folder with her finger "—you have access to your husband's checkbook. Am I right?"

"I did have, but I just told you he closed the checking account, and I'm flat broke."

"I'm giving you a voucher to take to this agency—" Tyra handed her a card "—where you can get food and shelter. This is all I can do for you."

The woman stared at her. "You sending me to beg for food and a place to stay? My husband's rich."

"And so were you until you got caught sleeping with other men. You made your choice, Ms. Saunders. I'm closing your file. Good day." She hadn't expected Erica Saunders to give in so easily, but after two years and five months it was time to drop her case.

After Erica Saunders left, Tyra phoned Lyle. "Lyle, this is Tyra. I've closed the Saunders file."

"Good! I've thought that for some time, but I just couldn't make myself do it."

"I'm leaving now. See you tomorrow."

Matt Cowan walked out of the building along with Tyra. As they stepped through the door, he removed his jacket. "This heat's not for me. Say, Tyra, did I see you in Gambrill at the concert with Byron Whitley last Friday night?"

She couldn't have been more surprised by his question. But why should she have been? They were both lawyers. "Yes. You know him?"

"Only professionally, but I gather he's a helluva lawyer. Way to go," he said, giving her the thumbs-up sign. "See you Wednesday." She hailed a taxi, sank into its air-conditioned comfort and headed home. She would have been happier if Byron had been waiting for her.

Byron was speaking by cell phone with his father. "...then arrange something. Invite me to dinner or something."

"You don't need a special invitation to have dinner at my house. You can come any time you please."

"Come on, Dad. I know that, but I want you to ask Jewel to prepare one of her special dinners, and I want to bring a friend."

"Humph. Why didn't you say so? Who is she? That's strange. Andy hasn't mentioned anyone to me."

"Andy hasn't met her. I don't introduce my women friends to Andy, because I don't want him to get the wrong impression. If I settle on one for sure, he'll meet her."

"There's some logic to that, but his reaction to her should help you make up your mind about her. Kids are very perceptive."

"So they say, Dad. But not yet. I've met her family, and she should meet you, since I can't take her to Florence, Italy, to meet Nannette. What do you say?"

"If you took her to Italy I imagine your sister would greet her with open loving arms. What's your girl's name?"

"Tyra. Tyra Cunningham. I like her a lot, Dad."

"I'm sure you do. Lois was the last woman you brought home. Are you over her yet?"

"Yeah, I am. I don't dream of her any more, and I don't have that feeling of guilt that if she hadn't gotten pregnant, she'd still be alive."

"And you wouldn't have Andy. Don't think such thoughts. You can't alter the divine plan. Come over Friday night and bring her with you. I'll see if I can find a date."

"Thanks, Dad. I'm in your debt."

"No such thing. You're my son, and it's to my advantage to check out a prospective daughter-in-law."

"Hey, wait a minute. I haven't gotten that far."

"I stand my by statement. See you Friday at seven."

"Yes, sir."

Byron hung up and leaned back in his desk chair thinking about what he'd just done. It hadn't been an impulsive act. He did nothing on impulse. He trusted his own judgment, so any uncertainty about Tyra wasn't the reason he wanted his father to meet her. He packed his briefcase, locked his desk and took the elevator to the basement of the building that housed the Whitley, Chambers and Jones lawfirm. He shed his jacket, laid it on the back seat, got in his car and headed home.

When he stopped for a red light, he was soon in another world. He imagined he held Tyra in his arms. She was always so soft and sweet, so giving. How could a woman be all the things that she was, feminine, sweet, sexy, smart, competent, knowledgeable and fun? He hated being away from her. His dad would like her. He was sure of that. She was… The sound of other motorist's horns brought him thoughts back to his surroundings as he saw that the light had turned green. He realized that he'd wanted to show her off to his dad and that the dinner at his father's home was a ruse enabling him to do that without making a grand gesture. He expected that he'd have a hard time waiting for Friday.

At home, he listened while Andy read a story. Pride suffused him when the child finished reading the book, looked up at him and said, "Daddy, do I make you proud? My teacher said I must make you proud."

"Yes, I'm proud of you." He battled the lump in his throat and held his son tightly in his arms. His love for the boy overwhelmed him and his eyes filled with tears. Thank God, he no longer counted the cost.

"Something in your eyes, Dad? Want me to get you a tissue?"

"Thanks, but my handkerchief will do the trick. What do you want me to play?"

Andy clapped his hand. "Oh, goody. I thought you forgot. Play 'Barcarolle'. No. Play 'Take Five.'"

He frowned. "You didn't give it much thought. They are as different as two pieces of music can be."

"I know, but I heard 'Take Five' on the radio this afternoon, and I want to hear it again. You can play 'Barcarolle' tomorrow."

He sat down at the Steinway grand, gave his fingers a practice run over the keys and launched into "Take Five," Paul Desmond's great jazz composition. He could hardly believe that the child tapped his knee in perfect timing with one of the most difficult jazz pieces. He wanted to teach his son to play the piano, but he hadn't found a teacher he trusted.

It was 8:45 p.m. when he finally phoned Tyra. "Hi, sweetheart. I hope you had a good day."

"I made some progress with my cases, and that was good. What about you?"

"Not particularly eventful. We're wrapping up a suit that's been dragging along for months. Today, I said, 'Enough! We're going to trial.' Neither side wants that, so we'll have a settlement sometime this week. That's a relief.

"Tyra, my dad has invited us to his home for dinner Friday. Can you make it?"

"Your…your father? Well, sure. Of course I can make it. What time?"

"I'll pick you up at six-fifteen? Is that all right?"

"Uh…sure. Look, Byron. This is such a surprise. Are your father and I going to get along? I mean, is he going to like me?"

He couldn't help laughing. "Sweetheart, how's he not going to like you?"

"I don't know, Byron, Besides, what'll I wear? What does your father do away from his job? I mean what does he do when he's not in his office or in the hospital?"

"He's in surgery three mornings a week and has office hours from eleven to five Monday through Friday. At other times, he fishes and plays the piano. He's seventy-two and still good looking."

"I'll bet he is if you look just like him."

"What did you say?"

"I said I'm sure he is."

"Chicken! You didn't have the guts to repeat it."

"Lack of guts has on occasion stood me in good stead."

"For instance?"

"Like when I was mad enough with one of my coworkers to take his ears off, but didn't have the guts to do it."

"That's not lack of guts. That's using common sense. He probably wasn't worth it. I'd go to the wall for you, sweetheart, but I stop at going to jail."

"Thanks for letting me know that your affection has its limits."

"Doesn't yours?"

She didn't want that kind of teasing to evolve into a serious conversation, so she said, "I'm still having conversations with myself about that."

"You mean about *me,* don't you?"

"Talking to myself about you would be a waste of time, Byron."

"I don't know how to take that. Look, I just heard a thump. Andy may have rolled out of bed. I'll call you tomorrow."

"Call me back if he's hurt. Kisses."

"Kisses."

Tyra went into the family room where she knew she'd find Maggie watching television and sat beside her on the sofa. Maggie turned off the television and looked at Tyra.

"What's the matter, hon? Anything wrong?"

Tyra remembered the times when she'd gone to Maggie with her problems, and the woman, always welcoming and kind, would ask, "What's the matter, hon?" She put an arm around Maggie's shoulder. "I wonder what I'd do without you?"

"You'd do just fine. Is it Byron?"

She nodded. "He wants me to go to his father's home with him Friday night for dinner. I can't believe he wants me to meet his father. We haven't…I mean we just met two months ago. What if his father doesn't like me?"

"Don't make jokes. Whether he likes you is up to you. Every father wants his son to have a beautiful woman in his life. If she is a good match for his son in other ways, like intelligence and education, so much the better. But he'll look at you for the kind of woman who'll make his son want to stay home and curl up with her in front of a fire on a cold winter evening."

"Byron said his dad would like me. I have no idea what to wear. If I was going to a restaurant, there'd be no problem.

But to dinner in a private home when I don't know the people, that's presents a problem."

"Wear something that Byron likes, something soft, feminine and dressy. Doesn't he like that melon-colored silk chiffon?"

"Oh, that's a good idea. It's figure flattering, but it doesn't show too much cleavage."

"That's what you want. Let the old man see that his boy is getting something nice."

"Maggie! Shame on you!"

"No point in sugarcoating it. That's what it's all about. Byron wants his dad to meet you 'cause he's getting in deep, if he ain't already there. And he wouldn't mind knowing what his dad thinks of you."

"He has a four-year-old son from his marriage—you know he's a widower, don't you—and I haven't met his son yet. He's more important to our relationship than Byron's father."

"Nobody asks a four-year-old to pass judgment on an adult, although some of them are pretty good at it. When you meet his son, you'll know that he is committed to you. Now quit worrying about it. By the way, what about Byron's mother?"

"She's not in the picture. When Byron was seven, his father divorced her because she had an affair with another man. She lives with him now, or at least did, and has made no effort to contact Byron or his sister, who lives in Italy."

"He got a stepmother?"

"No. His father raised the two children on his own, and it's something that I gather Byron is very proud of."

"And well he should be. If I were you, I'd wear my hair down Friday. Men like that." She got up, braced her back with both hands and straightened up fully. "Don't worry about Byron's father. Just be yourself, and he'll love you. I'm going to bed. Good night."

"Good night, and thanks for listening." She turned the

lights out in the rooms downstairs, left a light in the foyer, and climbed the stairs. What did she mean to him?

"You said you didn't hurt yourself and that you don't have any pain anywhere. So why are you crying, Andy?" He'd asked the question at least ten times, but the boy's response invariably was to sob even louder. He decided to try a different tactic. "I'm going to bed. If you don't tell me before I leave this room, you get no cherry-vanilla ice cream for one month, and you won't be able to con Aunt Jonie into giving you some, because there won't be any in this house. Now, what will it be?"

Andy sniffled several times and wouldn't hold up his head. "I…uh didn't want you to know I rolled off the bed."

"Why, for goodness' sake. I'm your father, and it's my duty to take care of you."

"But I'm four years old, and I'm not supposed to fall out of bed. I don't want to have to sleep in a crib. That's for babies."

He didn't want to laugh, because Andy's distress was real. "I hope you're joking, Andy. I wouldn't make you sleep in a crib. You're too big for that. And I certainly wouldn't punish you for falling out of bed. Why would you think that?"

"In the story I read this afternoon, Bubble fell out of bed, and his nanny was ashamed of him and sent him to sleep in his crib."

"That was Bubble's nanny in a story. I'm your father. How did you fall out?" Andy's arms tightened around Byron's neck. "I was playing soccer. I mean I dreamed I was playing soccer, and when I kicked at the ball, I think that's when I fell out."

"All right. Give me a kiss, and go back to sleep."

"Can I have cherry-vanilla ice cream tomorrow?"

"Yes, you may." He tucked the covers around the child, adjusted the air conditioner and kissed Andy's forehead. "Good night, son."

"Good night, Daddy."

He went to his room and sat in the dark for a minute and then got up and opened the blinds. The moonlight reminded him of the carriage ride with Tyra. He'd soaked up her sweetness like a sponge, and he doubted that he would ever get enough of her. Whenever he was with her, the world seemed so right. Whether she hugged him, kissed him or argued with him made no difference. She was there with him, a boundless joy.

It wouldn't surprise him if Andy acted out with Tyra. The boy was not accustomed to sharing his father with anyone. Aunt Jonie kept a little distance between herself and Andy, for she didn't want to assume a mother role with her nephew. He'd handle it when he got to it, and he knew he could count on Tyra to use good judgment in dealing with a child. She wouldn't love him at first but, if Andy gave her a chance, she would learn to. Now, if he could get that suit settled and if things worked out Friday night, his world would once again be standing on its legs and not on its head.

He got home from work Friday evening, showered, shaved, went over Andy's reading and arithmetic with him and fell across his bed, exhausted. They had settled the damage suit and although he knew his client would be satisfied, he'd given up more than he wanted to. He turned over on his back and put the lawsuit behind him.

"Daddy. Daddy. Wake up. Tyra wants to talk to you, Daddy. She wants to know if you're all right. Here's the phone, Daddy."

He rolled over and sat up. "What time is it, Andy?"

"Wait a minute. Your watch says six twenty-seven. Here's the phone."

"Hello." He barely recognized his gravelly voice. "Tyra? This is awful, sweetheart. I came home exhausted, checked Andy's homework, showered and laid across the bed. I didn't intend to go to sleep. No, I don't want you to meet me at my dad's place. I'll call him, and I'll be at your place in half an hour. I'm sorry about this."

He hung up, called his father and explained. "I was arguing a case for four solid hours today. See you at about seventwenty." He put on a gray pinstriped suit, a white shirt and a pink and gray paisley tie.

"Where're you going, Daddy?"

"I'm going to your grandfather's house, and I'm late."

"Is Tyra going, too?"

"Yes, she is."

"Tyra has a pretty voice. Where does she live, Daddy?"

"About fifteen miles from here, and I'd better hurry. I'll answer the rest of your questions tomorrow."

"Okay."

Fortunately, Tyra didn't live in Frederick, but in its suburbs just off Route 70. If there was no traffic, he'd make it by seven. His father lived closer to Frederick than to Baltimore, so he didn't expect to get there too late.

Tyra opened the door and stared up at Byron. "You shouldn't haven driven so fast. Please don't speed like that."

He picked her up, swung her around, set her on her feet and hugged her. "I don't as a rule, but there was no traffic. You look beautiful. Absolutely beautiful. You always look great, but this dress is…something else."

"I'm glad you like it. I didn't want to wear anything too revealing."

Both of his eyebrows shot up and then slowly returned to their normal positions. "I see what you mean. Where's Maggie?"

"She and Darlene went to see a movie. I'm ready when you are."

He glanced down at her feet. "Hmm. You're taller tonight. Where's your handbag?"

She handed him her key. "I don't need one."

"Thanks for your confidence, and thanks for calling and waking me up."

"I was upset, because I didn't know what happened to you. You're never late. Andy is an exceptional four-year-old. He asked my name, and when I told him, he asked me how I spelled it. He already knows the alphabet?"

"Andy reads at second grade level, and he can manage some third grade books. He's working on arithmetic. That's his idea. I encourage, but I don't push him. He loves to read, and he loves to learn."

"That means you've spent a lot of quality time with him. I'm happy to hear it. Whatever constructive time you invest in a child pays rich dividends."

"True." He headed to Route 40 and a shortcut to his dad's house. "Andy had questions about you, and he'll have some more tomorrow. By the way, he thinks you have a 'pretty voice.'"

"How sweet of him. I would expect your child to be smart. But if he didn't have the voice of a small child, I could have mistaken him for a much older child. He said, 'Dad's asleep. You want to talk to him?' I told him I did and he said, 'Just a minute, please.'"

The closer they got to their destination, the more nervous she became. Finally, Byron said, "Look, baby, you have to stop twisting your hands. This is not going to be torture. My dad is a great guy."

"I believe you, but my nerves don't."

"That's the craziest thing I ever heard." He turned into a narrow lane over which hung a trellis of brides' bushes in full white bloom, and she gasped at the beauty of it as the dying sun rays peeped through.

"This is idyllic, Byron. How long has he lived here?"

"Since before I was born. He wouldn't leave here for

anything. He has a large garden, a terrace and a swimming pool in the back of the house. It's all well protected, and he's happy here." The big white brick house loomed in front of them.

"He lives in this huge house by himself?"

"Yes, but his housekeeper-cook comes every day except Sunday. He has a lot of friends, too." The sensor in his car opened the gate, and he drove through and parked in front of the house.

"I'm surprised he has a locked fence."

"I told him to install it when he put the swimming pool in, and he's glad he did. Most of the properties out here are fenced." He got out, opened her door and took her hand. "Dad may have invited a friend to join us. I'd better warn you women like him a lot."

"Why are you telling me that?"

"So you'd stop being nervous. The devil made me do it." He hugged her with one arm as he rang the bell.

The door opened and she looked into the face of a tall, svelte man in an off-white linen suit, white shirt and red tie. His face transformed itself into a warm grin that seemed to glow. Her nervousness gone, she stepped into the house and hugged Lewis Whitley.

"Now I know why he wanted me to meet you. He wanted to show off. Welcome, Tyra. I'm pleased that you agreed to come to dinner with Byron so that you and I could get to know each other." She saw him look over her shoulder and give the thumbs-up sign to his son. "Come on in, son. She's a lovely lady." When they embraced, she could see that it was genuine and that they did it often.

As if he wouldn't be outdone, Byron put an arm securely around her waist and said, "Dad, this is Tyra Cunningham. Tyra, I don't have to tell you that this is my father, Lewis Whitley."

"No," she said, happier and more self-confident than she'd been in a week. "You're the spitting image of him."

"Come in, you two. Meet my neighbor. We're friends. She's not man-hunting." Tyra stifled a gasp, looked up at Lewis and relaxed when she saw the twinkle in his eyes. He had a mischievous streak. But that shouldn't have surprised her; so did Byron. They walked into the living room, and her gaze landed on the huge stone fireplace at one end and the enormous Persian carpet that covered the other half of the room near the fireplace where comfortable seating had been arranged. Good taste everywhere and evidence of the money with which to indulge it. At the other end of the room sat a Steinway grand, and a music stand facing a floor to ceiling picture window.

"Nora Smith, this is my son, Byron, and his friend, Tyra Cunningham." They finished the introductions, and Lewis served drinks and snacks, sat down and made himself comfortable. "Tyra, this is the house in which Byron grew up. I hope you'll spend a lot of time here."

"Thank you, sir. Do you play the piano?"

"Yes, I do, and the violin, too. Next to my work, I get the most pleasure out of music." He sat forward, his face bright and animated, already immersed in the subject. "I can play for hours and not realize the passing of time."

"Does Byron play the piano with you when you're playing the violin?"

"When he was a teenager, we did that all the time. I have more music for piano and violin than any other kind. We still play together occasionally. Do you play a musical instrument?"

"No, sir. When I was growing up, I didn't have the opportunity to learn, but I'd give anything if I could play the piano."

"Buy a piano, give me an hour—preferably two—of your time every week, and in one year, you'll be playing, that is if you practice. How badly do you want to learn?"

She wanted to look at Byron for advice, but forced herself not to. "I want it badly enough to buy a piano, come here for two hours every week and practice." She turned to Byron. "What do you think of that plan, Byron?"

"He's a wonderful teacher. Could you teach her on Monday evenings, Dad?"

Lewis leaned back in his chair and looked at his son. "I'm not sure your presence would be a help, but let's try it that way. Let Byron know when you're ready to start."

"Thanks. I will. You can't imagine what this means to me. Byron told me I should study, and I hadn't made a move toward getting started." Tyra looked at the other guest. "Do you play an instrument, Mrs. Smith?"

"Good heavens, no. I gave that up when I was ten. When it comes to music, my only talent is for listening."

"Dinner's ready, Mr. Whitley," announced Mrs. Owens, the housekeeper.

Lewis introduced his housekeeper to his guest, said the grace, tasted the wild mushroom soup, looked at his house-keeper and gave her the thumbs-up. "Up to your usual high standard, Mrs. Owens."

At the end of the elegant meal, Lewis told his housekeeper that she could leave, and called a taxi for her. "Tyra and I can make the coffee and serve it, you go on home"

"Thank you, sir. It's been a long day. Good night, all."

Tyra knew that Lewis had maneuvered it so that he could have a moment alone with her. "What kind of coffee are we making?" she asked him. "I expect Byron wants espresso. Can we make that?"

"I have a machine. What kind do you want, Nora?"

"Espresso will be fine, since it's still a few hours from bedtime."

Tyra followed him to the kitchen, a modern setting in royal blue and pale yellow and where cooking would be a joy. She was not going to be the first to speak. If he wanted to talk, he'd have to open the conversation. And he did.

"Byron is enchanted with you."

She didn't look at the man, but continued to rest her gaze casually over the kitchen. "Serves him right. He's got me stupefied."

"*What?* He's got you…" He put his hands on his hips and looked at her, and she couldn't help grinning. She'd put him on the spot. Suddenly laughter poured out of him.

"By gosh, he's got his match. By the way, have you met Andy?"

"Only by phone. We'll get around to that when Byron and I are both ready for it."

"You're protective of Byron, I see."

"Shouldn't I be?" Might as well go for broke. "I work at the Legal Aid Center, and I'm the only female among the professional counselors. I'm getting to know how unusual a man Byron is, and I have so much respect for him both for his qualities as a human being and for the way he treats me. He's very special.

"From the time I was seventeen, I was mother and father to my brother and sister. I didn't have financial problems, because our parents left us well provided for, but I was never a teenager or even a young adult. From age seventeen on, I was a grown up with adult responsibilities. My siblings have their degrees and their professional jobs and careers now, and I'm happier than I've ever been since I lost my parents. Byron is one of the main reasons for that."

While she spoke, Lewis focused intently upon her, seeming to digest every word she said. He leaned against a counter, folded his arms, crossed his ankles and narrowed his right eye, as if in deep thought.

"You're the first woman my son has brought home since he introduced me to the woman he married, and she's been dead a little over four years. That alone told me to expect an exceptional woman. And you are. I hope I have the chance to welcome you to my family as my daughter-in-law."

"Thank you, sir. And thank you for making me feel at home here."

"I couldn't have done otherwise. Let's get this coffee in there before Byron thinks I chased you off. I think I want some more of that key lime cake. Let's take it along." He added cake plates and forks to the tray.

"Say, I thought you two went to Colombia to get the coffee," Byron said and looked at Tyra. "I figured he wanted either to ask you some questions or to tell you something, and since you're not angry, I'm assuming it went well."

"Come now, you have a wonderful dad."

"I didn't mention this to Tyra," Lewis said, "but I'm sure you know I'd like some more grandchildren while I'm still young enough to enjoy them and you're young enough to raise them properly. That's not what we talked about, but it's the conclusion I drew from what we talked about. Have some cake to go with the coffee, Nora."

Byron looked at his father and grinned. "Well, I'll be damned."

Chapter 6

As he drove away from his father's house, Byron realized that he didn't want to take Tyra home, yet he couldn't take her to his home because no one there knew of his interest in her. Besides, he knew that, in the circumstances, she wouldn't go there. He needed to make love with her, but if she said he was rushing her, she could be right but not from where he stood. Looking at her all evening in the melon-red dress that caressed every curve of her body had amounted to what seemed like a prison sentence. Her luscious breasts with their protruding aureoles were a sight for any man, and his mouth had watered as he gazed at them. Never in his life had he wanted so badly to get something between his lips.

He glanced over at her, quiet before the storm that he would unleash in her the minute he kissed her. "How'd you get on with my dad?" He knew the answer, but he needed a conversation opener, and that was as good as any.

She'd been slumped in the seat, but she sat up. "Your father is charming. Serious, too. I think we got on very well. I can't imagine what I was afraid of. Do you mind if he teaches me the piano? If you do, I can find an easy way to get out of it. Since it involves your father, I readily accept and abide by your feelings about it."

"Dad usually has his own agenda. If he offered, he's serious about it, and he wants to do it, so why not?"

"But if you and I broke up, that could be a sticky wicket."

"You and I are not going to break up, and if you think we are, I'll park this car and prove it to you right now."

"You'd get a ticket for making out in a public place."

"You'd get one, too."

She rested her hand on his knee, and that was the wrong thing, because he was already about to incinerate. "What's the matter, Byron? Something's itching you."

What the hell! "Something definitely is. I want to…to be with you so badly that I'm about to explode. But you asked me not to rush you, and I'm trying to do as you asked, but baby, it gets more difficult by the second."

"I'm sorry. How does your father get along with your Aunt Jonie?"

"What? Great. She's his sister-in-law, and they always got along well. I wish I could take you home with me. Tell you what. Let's have a picnic at my house Saturday. Andy loves picnics, and I'll let him invite a couple of his friends. We'll blow up his tent for the children, and we'll have a real barbecue picnic."

"Sounds good to me. What does Andy like?"

"I'll give that some thought, and let you know." He wasn't sure that he wanted her to bring Andy a gift. The boy could be very manipulative and, once he got to know Tyra, he wouldn't be above calling her and telling her what to bring him. "If you're not accustomed to mischievous little boys, Andy will take advantage of you."

"I'm looking forward to meeting him. You sure you want to do this?"

"We need to see what we've got going for us, Tyra. What we feel for each other goes deep, and I think we're ready for the next step, because our expressions of what we feel aren't enough, never have been." He parked in front of her house and cut the motor.

"Leaving you right now is costing me more than I can tell you." The words "Come here to me" trembled out of him, and her soft, warm body moved into his hungry arms. She took his tongue into her mouth and sucked it feverishly. When his head began to spin or seemed like it, he set her away from him.

"We need some privacy, Tyra. Will you go away with me for a few days?"

"Let's see how it goes Saturday with the picnic."

"Are you saying you don't know whether you want to be with me?"

"That is definitely not what I'm saying, because I…it wouldn't be honest. But if I'm going to give myself a chance with you, I need to know what my chances are with Andy. He's the question mark in this relationship, and I don't want him to be that, because he's as important an ingredient in what happens ultimately between you and me as either of us is."

"I hadn't thought of it in precisely that way, but I agree with you." He eased her back into his arms. When she was close to him, she was all his, and he didn't want her to do too much thinking right then.

"When do you want us to go away, and where did you have in mind?" she asked, snuggling closer to him and giving his libido a fit.

"Think in terms of a short cruise in the early part of September."

She kissed his jaw. "You're so sweet. I…"

"What is it, sweetheart?"

"Nothing. Just be glad I can't have my way with you right now."

When he could get his breath back, he said, "My day will come, and when it does, I'll let you do anything to me that gives you pleasure."

"Sitting like this in a car at night is dangerous," she said, as if they hadn't just agreed that at a coming time, they would be intimate.

He gazed at her for a long minute. "I can't shift gears as fast as you can." He got out and went around to open the door for her.

As they entered her foyer, Clark came out of the dining room, evidently headed for the stairs. He stopped. "Say, man, how's it going. I didn't realize that you two are seeing each other on a regular basis."

Byron stepped forward and shook Clark's hand. "Good to see you, Clark. How are you?"

Tyra fastened her hands to her hips and stared at her brother. "You should be in your room by now with the door closed. Considering your age, I'd expect you to know that."

"Why? What do you mean?" Clark asked her, his face the picture of innocence.

Seemingly exasperated, she replied, "I wasn't planning to invite Byron to my room, but if that's the only way I'll have privacy to tell him good night, I'll do it."

Clark's eyes widened. "Well, 'scuse me. See you later, Byron." He ambled up the stairs, whistling as he went.

"That did the trick, but wasn't it a little heavy-handed?"

"Clark forgets that I practically raised him. From time to time I have to remind him."

But the encounter had dampened his fire, and when she moved into his arms, the tenderness that welled up in him nearly overwhelmed him. He needed to take care of her, to protect and shelter her, and the feeling hit him with such force that he knew he'd never felt it before.

He kissed her eyes, her cheeks, her nose and the corners of her lips. "You're so precious to me. I don't remember what I was like before you came into my life." He squeezed her to him. "I'll call you. Good night, love."

Tyra turned out the downstairs lights, climbed the stairs and knocked on Clark's room door. "Hi," she said. "I didn't know you were coming home tonight. Did you get some dinner?"

"Maggie didn't tell you? I called her this morning. She left me crepes filled with crab meat in a fantastic sauce, and a salad. I ate until I thought I'd pop. She and Darlene went to a movie. Say, what's with you and Byron? Is this thing serious?"

She sat on the edge of his bed and rested her forearms on her knees. "More serious than I've ever been."

"That's pretty fast, don't you think?"

"No, I don't. It began the minute I opened the door the night you brought him here."

"Get outta here! I didn't notice a thing. You'd better be careful. He's a good looking guy, and I imagine he's popular with women."

"That doesn't bother me, Clark. I'm popular with men. He and I had dinner tonight at his father's home. Wait 'til you see his dad." She doubted that her brother heard the last part of the sentence. With his lower lip hanging, he was probably still focused on her dinner with his father.

"You ate at his father's house? I've heard that the old man is a big shot surgeon."

"He certainly lives like it. He's only seventy-two. I know for a fact that he's every bit as good looking as Byron. They look like brothers. Byron's parents divorced when he was seven, and his father raised Byron and his younger sister as a single parent. Byron is doing the same thing."

"Wait a minute, Sis. You lost me. You talking about Byron or his father?"

"Both. Byron is a widower, and he has a four-year-old son who I'm meeting Saturday."

"I hope you know what you're doing, Sis. Maybe he's looking for a woman who'll take care of his child."

"If that were the case, I doubt he'd have waited four and a half years to start looking. He's never introduced a girlfriend to his son, and he wasn't anxious to take me home with him. So don't rush to any faulty conclusions. Byron Whitley is an honorable, straightforward man."

"So they all say. He's got a helluva reputation."

"That doesn't surprise me. At first I thought you and Darlene were trying to set me up with him, and I nearly did something stupid."

A sheepish expression flashed across Clark's face. "I'm ashamed that I didn't think of it. Not once did it cross my mind that the two of you would hit it off. You have to confess that you're a little more glamorous than you used to be."

"Not really. My hair's longer. I wear earrings and, some-times, high heels."

"Yeah, and your clothes are more fashionable. Whatever!"

She may as well tell him and get over with it. "Clark, sometime during the first part of next month, I'm going away for a weekend with Byron."

"What? You can't do that!"

"Why not? You wouldn't hesitate to do that if you wanted to."

He jumped up and towered over her. "But I'm a man."

"Really! So's Byron. And I'm a thirty-one-year-old woman. I'm not asking your permission. I want you to know how things are with Byron and me."

"*Good Lord!* You haven't gone and…" He ran his fingers through his hair. "You know what I mean."

"No, I haven't. Not yet. Are you suggesting that I should

wait and see if it works *after* I get married? Is that what you'd do? If I could, I'd push you back into the eighteenth century where you belong."

"Tyra, you're my *sister*."

"Yes, I know. Congratulate me on remaining uninvolved until you got grown."

She never knew what to expect when Clark began pacing the floor, running his fingers through his hair and rubbing the back of his neck. "Listen, Clark, if you're trying to turn me into a puzzle that has to be solved, don't bother. I am going to spend a weekend with Byron. If you can't resist behaving as if you're my father, next time, I won't tell you."

He stopped pacing the floor. "You planning to make a habit of this?"

Laughter poured out of her until she began to hiccup. "That's too personal. I'm going to bed. Good night."

"Don't you care that Maggie and our sister aren't home yet?"

"No, I don't. Maggie's sensible even if I'd be reluctant to say that about Darlene. Good night."

She got ready for bed and crawled in. Somehow, she had expected Byron to call and tell her good night. Why did he have to call all the time? She dialed his cellular phone.

"Hi, sweetheart. I wanted to call you, but I was afraid I might awaken someone."

"Same here, but I remembered your cell phone number, and I figured that it would probably be closer to you than the house phone is. I needed to know that you got home safely."

"And I needed to hear you say that you care for me. I…I'm in deep, Tyra….I've never cared this way. Never."

"Neither have I, Byron, and I've never been this happy before."

"Now you tell me when I'm here and you're there."

"Not to worry. We'll be together again soon. Good night, love." She hung up before he could question her having called him her love, and she knew he wouldn't call her for fear of awakening her family. Good, she thought. Now, he owes me one.

Picnic or not, she wasn't leaving her house in jeans, because she'd never found any that fit both her hips and her waist. She put on a pair of white slacks, a pale blue collared T-shirt, a double-breasted-linen navy jacket and a pair of navy-blue and white Keds.

"Little boys love the scent of a nice perfume," Maggie said, "just like men do. And don't kiss him first. A lot of children don't like that, and I don't blame them. Grown folks hugging and kissing children who don't know them is an invasion of children's privacy. I never let 'em kiss mine."

"Maggie, if this doesn't work out, what will I do?"

"You teach children to love you, and you do it mainly by loving them and showing them what love is. But if your feelings aren't genuine, a child gets it right away. If that boy's as intelligent as you say, he'll get the difference between what you offer him and what his father gives him. Small children love to cuddle up to a warm loving woman in a way that they don't cuddle up to their fathers. Now quit worrying. He'll be here in a few minutes."

Maggie answered the doorbell before Tyra reached the bottom of the stairs. "Come in, Mr. Whitley. Tyra'll be down in a minute. How y'all doing today?"

"Wonderful. What about you?" Over Maggie's shoulder, he saw her and a smile shone on his face so brightly that Maggie whirled around and looked in Tyra's direction.

"I'm just fine, Mr. Whitley. Y'all have a good time."

But Tyra doubted that he heard Maggie's words. He picked her up, twirled her around, kissed her and set her on her feet. "You beautiful woman! Kiss me, but just a little bit."

She grinned, opened her arms and held him close to her body. "I'll kiss you when we come back."

"What's that?" he asked of the package she carried.

"Something for the children. I figured on four including Andy. Was I right?"

"Right. And they are all boys. Andy thinks he should excel among girls. A real show-off, and I'm trying to rid him of that, but I suspect he gets that at his school."

"What kind of mood was he in when you left him? Does he know you're bringing me?"

"Yes. He's been looking forward to seeing you all week. He has sensed that you're special, although I didn't make a point of it."

"Thank you. I'm glad you didn't, because he could have decided to be obstinate. In any case, he has to make up his own mind. I only hope he thinks I'm special after I leave today."

"Not to worry, sweetheart. Given a little time, he'll be besotted with you just as his old man is."

She laughed at his attempt to lighten the conversation. Better not put too much weight on that. Crossing the city of Frederick on Court Street, he slowed down at First Street and pointed to a building at number 104 N. Court.

"Roger Brook Taney and Francis Scott Key shared an office in that building. With due respect to Francis Scott Key, I can't resist thumbing my nose at the building whenever I pass it. When Taney was a Supreme Court Justice, he wrote the Dred Scott decision, which ruled that no slave or descendant of a slave could be a US citizen and, as a non-citizen, Dred Scott did not have the right to sue in a court of law."

"I know. Here's Taney's house," Tyra said, "and I can't count the number of times I've spat at it. But Frederick isn't what you'd call the real South."

"Definitely not. You get southern hospitality and Yankee pride. That's why I like it."

When Byron parked in front of his house, Tyra closed her eyes and said a silent prayer. She looked up at the big, red brick corner row house that sat a stone's throw from Druid Hill and wondered what awaited her inside. A high iron fence, on the inside of which grew thick evergreen hedges that guaranteed privacy for it occupants.

Byron opened the gate, took her hand and walked up the steps. The door opened almost as soon as he pushed the buzzer, and she looked into the faces of Jonie and Andy. Her first impression of the child was that he didn't look at his father but at her.

"Hi, Miss Tyra," he said and they walked in.

"I've been looking forward to meeting you, Andy," she said, put the shopping bag on the floor, bent down and offered to shake Andy's hand. To her amazement, he shook hands.

"Me, too. Hi, Dad. Can we check my arithmetic before the kids come? I want to show Miss Tyra what I did."

"In a minute, Andy. Aunt Jonie, this is Tyra Cunningham. Tyra, this is Jonie Hinds, my aunt."

"And my aunt too, Miss Tyra."

After they exchanged greetings, Tyra said to Jonie, "May I help you with things for the picnic while they're doing arithmetic."

Andy looked up at her. "Daddy said you were coming to see *me*. Don't you want to see me do my arithmetic?"

"Yes, I do, but I didn't realize you would like me to be there. You and your dad always do your arithmetic together, and I didn't want to interfere."

"Oh, it's okay. Maybe next time, you can check my arithmetic. Dad says I'm messy, but I always get it right."

Tyra looked at Jonie. "Next time. Okay?"

"Of course. First things first."

She went with Byron and Andy to the boy's room and sat on the big red wooden elephant in the middle of it. "Don't try to lift my elephant, Miss Tyra. Only my dad can move it. Come look out the window, and you can see my tent."

Looking out the window, she decided that Byron's plot was extremely large for one in the middle of a big city, and she made a note to ask Byron how he'd managed to acquire it. She listened to the arithmetic exercise and decided that she was double glad she'd finished her formal education.

"How'd I do, Miss Tyra?"

"Your father told me that you're smart, so I'm not surprised. Congratulations on getting all of it right. You're a very good student."

He gazed up at her, his expression intense and his eyes—large with dark brown irises rimmed in light brown—so like his father's and grandfather's. "Do you have any little boys?"

"No, I don't. I wish I did."

"Gee, I'm sorry. You can come to see me sometime. That's the doorbell. I have to go downstairs." He ran out of the room and plowed down the stairs like an engine out of control.

She turned to Byron, who sat on the edge of Andy's bed. "He's a lovely child, and he is awfully good looking. What are you going to do when he gets to be a teenager and the girls find out about him?"

His grin suggested that she shouldn't be too concerned about that. "Not to worry, sweetheart. Cute little boys often grow up to be frightful looking teenagers."

She raised an eyebrow. 'Who're you fooling? You never had a day looking frightful in your life, and he's the image of you." She treated him to a long, slow wink. "I'm going downstairs and see what the kids are doing."

"Oh, no you don't." He jumped up and grabbed at her. "Flirt with me and leave me here to deal with it, huh?"

She dodged him. "You'd rather have a promise than nothing, wouldn't you?" she threw over her shoulder as she headed down the stairs.

"Witch! My day will come," she heard him grumble, and couldn't help smiling. He didn't know it, but she could hardly wait for their weekend together.

She removed a box from the shopping bag and went outside to the children's tent. "Andy, I have something here for you and your friends. Shall we give it to them?"

He ran over to her and looked at the box. "Colored bubbles? We're going to blow bubbles?"

"If you'd like. We can. I brought enough for all of you."

"Are you going to show us how?" Tyra said she would. "We'd better blow them out here or in the tent. Aunt Jonie will have a melt down if we mess up the kitchen floor."

"It's kind of windy. What about the back porch? If we mess that up, I'll mop it."

He stared at her. "You will? Okay." He called the children, and they gathered around her on the porch. She gave each of them a pipe, kept one for herself, and soon the boys were dancing, shouting and laughing as they tried to see who could blow the biggest bubble.

"Look, Daddy. I just blew a blue one, and I already blew two big red ones."

"Seems like a lot of fun," Byron said. She glanced up at him and asked if he wanted to try one. He blew several, but she could see that his mind wasn't on it. "I've got to make the fire in the pit so we can roast these hotdogs and marshmallows. They'll be starved in a few minutes."

"No, we won't," a chorus of voices disagreed. "We have to see how big a bubble we can blow."

However, by the time the hotdogs were done, the boys had bounced around until they exhausted themselves. Byron gave them each a long stick with marshmallows on the end and let them roast their own. After filling up on hotdogs, marshmallows, lemonade and strawberry ice cream, the boys wound down like tops.

"I'm going to take the boys home. I'll be gone about twenty minutes." He leaned over and kissed her lips. "Andy will keep you company."

She saw that Andy watched the two of them closely, but she couldn't figure out his reaction to seeing his father kiss her. But after Byron left, the boy confronted her.

"Why did my daddy kiss you?"

"We're friends, and we like each other." He rubbed his eyes with his knuckles. "What's the matter?" she asked him. "Are you sleepy?"

"He didn't have a nap," Jonie said. "I'm surprised he can stand up. They loved those bubbles so much they didn't even want to eat, and they used up a lot of energy. Don't you think you should go upstairs and lie down, Andy?"

"No, because Miss Tyra came to see me."

Tyra took Andy's hand. "I'll go up with you, and I'll sing you to sleep."

"But I don't want to sleep while you're here."

"Then we'll both sleep. Come on."

She sat in the big leather reclining chair in Andy's room. "Andy, do you think I could have a hug?"

He rubbed his eyes. "I guess."

She held out her arms, and he reached up to her, but her ruse didn't work, so she said, "If you crawl into my lap, we can both go to sleep." She pulled him into her lap, and he rested his head on her breast and snuggled up to her so quickly that it stunned her.

"Gee, Miss Tyra, you smell so good," he said, and before she could reply he was fast asleep.

After delivering Andy's playmates to their parents, Byron headed home, deep in thought. He hadn't expected that Tyra would get on so well with four rambunctious four-year-old boys, but she interacted with them as easily as if it were her life's calling. Andy hadn't misbehaved, but he knew that could happen at any time and he was eager to get back home.

"Aunt Jonie, this house is too quiet. Where are Andy and Tyra?"

"She took Andy up to his room to get a nap. When she insisted, I thought he was going to kick up a storm, but they went up there, and I haven't heard a sound since."

"Thanks, but I'll believe it when I see it."

He bounded up the stairs and went to Andy's room, tiptoeing on the chance that the child might actually be asleep. He got no further that the door. A gasp escaped him and his heart constricted to such an extent that he leaned against the door jamb. Winded. He'd never seen a woman holding his child that way, almost as if he were a baby. It was a picture that would remain in his memory and in his heart forever. Tyra asleep with Andy in her arms.

Suddenly, he wheeled around, went to his office and got his camera. Nearly a dozen times, he snapped pictures of the scene with his child asleep and nestled in the arms of the woman he loved. Unable to resist longer, he knelt beside the chair, gathered the two of them in his arms and kissed them. Her eyes opened, then closed and opened again. Then she recognized him.

"Oh dear, I…shh." Andy snuggled to her still asleep and unaware of the drama around him as Tyra gazed into Byron's eyes and saw in them, more plainly than words could tell her, that he loved her. She reached out, caressed his cheek and parted her lips for his kiss.

"Do you want me to put him in his bed?" Byron asked her.

"Please don't. He'll think I didn't want him here. Besides, I'm enjoying this. It's the first time I ever held a child this way, and he's so sweet."

"Wasn't he too heavy for you to lift?

She nodded. "Yes, so I asked him to crawl into my lap, and

he did. The next minute, he was asleep. I don't know when I dozed off. I didn't realize I was sleepy."

"If I wasn't looking at this, I probably wouldn't believe it. What did you do, wave a magic wand?"

"You told him that I was coming to see him, and he tried to be a little gentleman toward his guest. He didn't want to take a nap because I was here to see him, so I told him we'd both take one." She kissed the boy's head, and he turned and moved his head to her other breast.

"He'll wrinkle your pants."

"So what? Maggie will be glad to press them. She claims she doesn't have enough to do."

Andy turned again, and then he opened his eyes. "Daddy? Did Miss Tyra go home?"

"She's holding you in her lap."

"Oh." He put his head back on the sweet spot and went to sleep.

He could see that she didn't plan to put the child in his bed, and he didn't want to interrupt their bonding, because it was important to him. He got a chair and sat beside them. He wasn't comfortable, but he figured that his comfort was of minuscule importance compared to the miracle of his son asleep in Tyra Cunningham's arms.

That didn't mean Andy would accept and love Tyra and he could therefore relax. As a father, he had learned that children could shift with the wind and that Andy was not an exception. But he had hope now, and though she hadn't said she loved him, she would after their weekend together. He bolted forward. She hadn't agreed to it.

"Did you agree to our weekend?" he whispered.

"Clark got his back up when I told him I was going away with you for a weekend."

He was certain that his eyes grew to twice their size. "You told him?"

"Why not? I'm grown. I never dreamed he was so old-fashioned. If he mentions it to you, you have my permission to poke him in the snoot. I wouldn't go out of the country without telling a member of my family. I applied for my passport. Did you?"

"Mine's in order." He could only stare at her. She'd just told him that she agreed to something that was going to change both their lives, and she did it with all the casualness of one friend knocking knuckles with another. He let out a long breath and decided he better get used to it.

He realized that she wasn't going to budge about putting Andy in his bed, so he put a CD of easy-listening music on his stereo recorder, sat down beside them and took her hand. Was she aware of that scene's domesticity? He could definitely get used to it and to others of that ilk.

"Byron, I'm going… Mercy be. Will you look at this?"

He released Tyra's hand and went to the door where Jonie stood looking as if she'd seen an aberrant phenomenon. "How'd she get him to do that?"

"I don't look a gift horse in the mouth, Aunt Jonie, and I don't question Providence. I don't know how she got him to climb into her lap, but he certainly likes it there."

She rubbed her hands together. "I guess I don't baby him enough these days, but I don't want him to take me for his mother. I hope you're considering something permanent with her, Byron, because she's really a fine woman. I got that when she shook my hand. She isn't a glamour girl or a party hopper."

"Thanks. You're right. She's as solid as they come. I'd take you downtown, but I'd rather not leave them."

"It's okay. I'll take the bus around the corner and get off half a block from the store. Do you need anything from Macy's?"

"No, thanks."

He hadn't planned to take Andy with him when he drove Tyra home, but he obviously wasn't running that show. He sat down, and as he looked at Tyra and Andy, the boy crawled up higher, rested his head on Tyra's shoulder and put his arms around her neck. Although she didn't awaken, she adjusted her hold on him. It was too much. He got up, walked to the window and looked down at the tent. Andy loved that tent, but he'd hardly spent half an hour in it.

She's the one. He wheeled around to see who had spoken those words. He'd swear that he heard them, but except for Tyra and Andy, both of whom were asleep, he was alone.

Half an hour went by, and he sat in the silence, enjoying a peacefulness that he often wished for. "Daddy. Miss Tyra, where's my daddy? I have to go to the bathroom." Andy scrambled from her lap and, still half asleep, started toward his father's bedroom. Byron patted her shoulder as she sat up, took Andy's hand, led him to the bathroom and went back to Tyra.

"Both of you were sound asleep. Andy thinks he's too big to take a nap, though he gets one anyway. But I could see that he enjoyed that. Would you like some lemonade, tea or coffee? Aunt Jonie went shopping, but I can get it. Andy will want ice cream."

"I'd love some lemonade. You know? I haven't taken a nap in years. I feel like a million dollars." He leaned over, teased her lips with his tongue, and when she would have sucked him into her, he released her and straightened up.

"Daddy, can I have some ice cream? And can Miss Tyra have some too?"

"Yes, you may, and so may she if she wants some."

As they sat at the kitchen table eating ice cream, he made up his mind to wait until Jonie came back. He didn't want to take Tyra home, kiss her on the cheek and leave her. Every molecule of his body rebelled against the thought.

"Daddy plays the piano, Miss Tyra. Do you want to hear him play?" He looked at Byron. "You promised to play me the 'Barcarolle.'"

"Okay. Wash your hands and we'll go in the living room."

Byron sat down, flexed his fingers and began to play. It was a piece in which he could lose himself, and soon he did. When he finished, he saw that Andy had taken a seat on the sofa beside Tyra.

"Play something else, Dad."

"What would you like to hear, Tyra?" She asked for Rachmaninoff's second piano concerto, one that he knew well and loved, and soon he let it carry him away.

"I never dreamed that you played so beautifully. It's surprising that you didn't become a concert pianist," she said. "That was exquisite"

"I chose law, because I wanted to be able to support myself."

"That sure was beautiful, Byron," Aunt Jonie said, as she entered the living room. "I haven't heard you play in years. Not since… Oh, excuse me. I didn't know Miss Cunningham was here."

"I was waiting for you to get back, because I'm not taking Andy with me."

"But I want to go, daddy."

"I can't get back by your bedtime, so you won't go with me this time. Tell Miss Tyra goodbye."

"Are you coming back to see me?" Andy asked Tyra.

"Yes, I will. You're a sweet, darling little boy, and I'm so glad we met. Do you think I could have a hug?"

He hugged her and kissed her cheek. "I'll ask my daddy to bring you back to see me."

Byron didn't put too much emphasis to the long embrace between Tyra and Andy at his front door, because he knew how capable Andy was of grandstanding to prolong their departure. Still, he was much happier than he would have been if his son had disliked Tyra.

Tyra wasn't in a daze. Overwhelmed described more precisely how she felt about her experience at Byron's home.

That she liked his son did not surprise her, because she liked well-mannered children. But the little boy hadn't only crawled into her lap and made himself at home there, but he had made his way into her heart. Of course, his stunning resemblance to his father could have been the reason, but it went much deeper, far beyond her feeling for Byron. For the first time she had felt maternal, almost as if Andy belonged in her arms.

"Does the weekend following Labor Day suit you for our time together?" Byron asked her as he parked in front of her house.

Wondering why he chose a time so far in the future, she frowned. "Okay, but why so far away? That's ages from now."

He took her hand and squeezed her fingers. "I'm glad you feel that way. It's exactly two weeks from yesterday."

She didn't back down. "It still seems like forever. Okay. I'll tell my boss that I'll be away that Thursday and Friday. When and what time will you come for me?"

"Thursday morning around eight o'clock. Dress as if you're going to Miami Beach, and bring two dresses for evening wear. If you'd like to change now, we could go to the jazz festival or the Weinberg Center, but I think we ought to have supper first."

"Let's go inside." She glanced up at him and the expression of need on his face sent shivers plowing through her body. He wanted what she wanted, but her experience with sex didn't make the wanting so urgent for her. It was when she was in his arms that she felt she'd die if she didn't have him.

It had been a long time since she'd prayed. Really prayed, but as she headed up the stairs to change her clothes, she whispered, "Lord, I don't ask for much, so please give me Byron Whitley. I need him."

Chapter 7

Tyra watched Byron until he got into his car and drove off, gathered her reserves and made her way up the stairs to her room. Shaken and troubled. In five minutes he had destroyed her will, weakened her resistance and reduced her to putty. Standing in her foyer, she would have given him anything that he asked for, but he had asked only that she let him love her. She had wanted so badly to make love with him right then and right there. The immediacy of it still rocked her as she dropped down on her bed. Did she want him or any man to have such power over her?

The minute he'd closed her front door, he went at her as if he wanted to devour her. "Love me, Tyra. I need you. Do you hear me? I need you," he said, his voice urgent and demanding, but sweet and seductive. His big hands encircled her waist, moved up to her back and locked her to him. "Kiss me. Baby, open up to me."

She parted her lips and he thrust into her, grasped her

buttocks with one hand and the back of her head with the other
and pressed her to him, as he dipped in and out of her mouth,
showing her what he intended to do to her, heating her to
boiling point.

Her blood raced to her loins and her hard nipples began to
pain her. More. She wanted more. She had to have more.
Wild with desire, she undulated against him, giving him a
sample of what she'd be like when he finally got into her. He
bulged against her. And she grabbed his hand and rubbed her
aching nipple. He braced her against the wall, unbuttoned her
jacket, plunged his hand into her shirt and released her breast.
She held her breath until his warm and eager lips pulled the
nipple into his mouth and sucked it.

She bit her lip to keep from screaming. If only she could
strip and feel him against her breast to breast and belly to
belly. In spite of her efforts at control, moans escaped her and,
as if that were a signal, he straightened her clothes, pulled her
to him and stroked her with gentle caresses.

"I'd better go right now while I can," he said. "I'll call you
later. That's as close to losing control as I've ever been." She
couldn't look at him, so he nudged her chin upward. "What
just happened between us was sweet and sacred, so there's no
reason to fret over it. We'll talk later." He didn't say good-
night, merely opened the door and left.

Tyra sat up straight and tried to think. But after a few
minutes she told herself that what had just happened to her
with Byron couldn't be explained or dealt with logically, that
she loved him and maybe love automatically made a person
susceptible. How would she know? This was her first experience with it. She undressed, slipped on a housecoat and went
to the bathroom to prepare for bed. But as she walked, she
envisioned herself alone in a private place with Byron free
to do with him as she wished and just as free to accept
whatever he wanted to give her. She hugged herself and

skipped right into her brother, who bounced up the stairs and on to the hallway.

"You're very happy about something…or someone," he said, leaned down and kissed her cheek. "Did you see Byron today?"

"He brought me home a minute ago. I spent the afternoon at his house with his aunt and his little boy, and then we went to dinner and the jazz concert at Weinberg. It was a wonderful day."

"How'd you like his son?"

"He's a darling, sweet, but just as no-nonsense as his dad. We got on fine. What'd you do?"

"I took Darlene to a meeting in Washington. She was ready to drive and didn't have enough gas to start the engine. I told her she needs a nanny. You still planning on a weekend with Byron?"

"Absolutely. I'll let you know. Gosh, Clark. This business of being in love makes you so vulnerable. It gives the other person so much control over your happiness, even if he doesn't know it."

Clark rubbed his hand across his brow, and his expression was that of a wise and experienced man. "Look, Sis. Don't worry about that as long as you know he loves you. You'll learn that if the guy loves you, he may be a lot more vulnerable to you than you are to him. Byron's a tough guy, but I'll bet you've never seen that toughness in him. You probably won't, either."

How easy it was to love the whole world and everybody in it. She hugged him. "Thanks. I really needed to hear that. Good night." When she returned from the bathroom, her cell phone was buzzing, and she thought she'd fly out of herself. "Hi."

"I was just about to hang up. Surely you weren't already asleep."

"No. I was in the shower. I'll probably never sleep again. I'm on some kind of high, and it'll be a miracle if I settle down enough to fall asleep."

"Tell me about it. Did you ask to have your passport expedited?"

"Yes, so I should have it in a couple of days."

"Good. I'm not sure I could handle a disappointment in this."

"Byron, I'm sure you can handle anything that's given to you."

"Thanks for your confidence. You're good for a guy's ego."

Ego-building wasn't on her agenda. She wanted him to know what he meant to her, and she didn't want to come right out and tell him, at least not yet. "I didn't have your ego in mind, I was thinking of the way I see you."

"The effect's the same. Sleep well, darling. Good night."

"Good night, love." She hung up, wondering when, if ever, she would be with him always.

Byron had begun to feel uncomfortable in the role of advisor to Murphy Tate. He knew the man was within his rights in refusing his daughter's request, but he personally did not agree with the man's position. He had found in his years of law practice that what was legal and considered just by law was not always the humanitarian solution, and this was such a case. He'd do what he could, but his heart was not in it.

His two hours weekly at the Legal Aid Society had always given him pleasure in helping his fellowman, but he didn't feel that way now. Perhaps he was tired. He could have taken Tyra to his summerhouse on the Chesapeake Bay, but he didn't want either of them to have to do housekeeping chores. Besides, it would be too much like marriage or shacking up, and he had a way to go before he reached that point, if indeed he ever did. He could imagine himself married to Tyra and fathering their children, and if that happened, he'd be a happy man. But he could also imagine himself not doing it if their relationship failed to go smoothly over the next couple of months. For himself alone, he knew that Tyra was the one, but he had Andy to think about. So far so good, but time would tell the story. He answered the intercom.

"This is Whitley."

"Mr. Whitley, a Mr. Cameron is on the phone. He wants to consult with you about suing for divorce."

"Thanks. Put him on the phone." The phone light blinked, and he lifted the receiver. "This is Byron Whitley. What may I do for you?" He listened to a litany of accusations against the man's wife, and decided that he didn't want to hear more of it. "Mr. Cameron, I'm not an expert on divorce. Louis Chambers, one of my partners, handles divorce for us. If you'd like, I'll switch you over to him." He punched Louis's extension. "This guy's headed for a long and messy divorce. Take it or leave it."

"Thanks, Byron. That's the kind that pays the most money."

He answered his cell phone. "Daddy, can me and you and grandpa go fishing? Aunt Jonie said she wanted fish for dinner."

He couldn't help laughing. Andy always found easy solutions to every problem. He supposed the good thing was that, if things weren't as he thought they should be, the child always sought a solution. "We can't go fishing today, son, because I won't get home early enough, but tell Aunt Jonie that I'll buy some fish at the market on my way home."

"You will? Okay. I'll tell her. Bye."

He hung up, propped his elbows on his desk and cradled his head in his hands. For a little over four years, Andy had been his whole life, and when the pain of loneliness for a different kind of love began to bear upon him, Tyra came into his life, just the woman he needed. It had to work. He'd make it work. He'd teach them to love each other.

Her long and anxious wait over, Tyra put her suitcase beside her front door and went into the breakfast room to check the table settings. "You coming back Sunday or Monday?" Maggie asked her.

"Sunday night."

"That's good. Never wear out your welcome. I don't know what you're planning, and I don't have the right to ask, but I'll tell you this, if you don't come back here on cloud nine, honey, you'd better change gears."

"Thanks, Maggie. I look at it this way, I've never had a real vacation, never been out of the country, never been on a boat, never took a cruise and never spent a weekend with a man. I'm bound to learn something."

Maggie stared at her. "You can say that again."

The doorbell rang, and she made certain that nobody got to that door before she did. "Hi. I made you some Belgian waffles."

A grin spread over his face. "I love 'em. What am I going to put on them?"

"Well, you can have two. One with strawberries and cream, and the other with bacon and maple syrup. How's that?"

He picked her up, swung her around and hugged her. "You've got my number going and coming. Are you going to give me some coffee?"

She looked at him from beneath lowered lashes. "Sure, coffee and anything else that makes you happy."

He arched his left eyebrow. "Be careful. I may take that literally."

She put her hands on her hips and sashayed into the breakfast room ahead of him. "Suit yourself. You only get to live once," she said, parroting Mae West, the drama diva of the 1930s. "And even if you get another chance, I may not be here."

He put his arms around her and gently pulled her to him. "You are one fresh woman, but you suit me to a tee." He took a piece of paper out of his jacket pocket and handed it to her. "Andy asked me to give you this."

She looked at the drawing of a little boy and what she supposed was a room full of bubbles. "Oh, Byron. This is so sweet. Thank you. Do you have a picture of the two of you that I may keep?"

"Y'all better get to eating. That plane ain't gonna wait for you."

They sat down, and Maggie said the grace. "Tyra makes these fancy European waffles, and I admit they sure are good, but I'm not about to spend that much energy on a waffle. Hmm. Tyra, this is super. I never woulda thought of putting strawberries and cream on 'em."

"They're delicious. Say, where's Darlene?" said Byron.

"Darlene leaves for work at seven-thirty," Maggie said. "She just started driving, and she doesn't like to drive fast."

Byron savored a bite of waffle, and a smile of pure pleasure brightened his face. "Smart girl. Nobody should drive fast on that highway." He drained his coffee cup and looked at Tyra. "I think we should start, sweetheart. We'll be in rush-hour traffic."

"Okay." She leaned over and kissed Maggie's cheek. "Don't let Clark drive you up the wall. He's stuck in the Middle Ages. See you Sunday night." She had a right to do as she pleased, but still, Maggie wasn't only her housekeeper, but her surrogate mother, and walking off in her presence to spend a weekend with a man suddenly smacked of effrontery. She lifted her shoulder in a quick shrug. She wouldn't consider lying to Maggie about that or anything else.

Byron kissed Maggie's other cheek. "Clark's a good man. If he was taking my sister on a cruise, I'd behave precisely as he is, maybe worse. See you Sunday, Maggie."

She grasped his left hand, detaining him. "You take good care of my child. You hear?" Unshed tears glistened in her eyes. "She's been mine ever since I pulled her out of her mama's body. Before that, I didn't even know what a newborn baby looked like, but it was blizzard weather, Mr. Cunningham was stuck at his office, and it was just me and her. Fortunately her mama was a doctor and knew what to do. This child is precious to me, Byron."

He hunkered before her chair. "She isn't more precious to you than she is to me. I will protect her with my life if necessary. So don't worry."

Maggie patted his hand and blinked rapidly to hold back the tears. "Y'all gone before you miss that plane."

Byron sat beside Tyra in the back of the limousine he'd hired to drive them to the Baltimore-Washington International Thurgood Marshall Airport. Her quietness disturbed him. "Are you sorry you agreed to our taking this cruise?" he asked her.

She found his hand without looking at him. "Of course not. But there are times when you need your mother, because you think you could ask her things that you wouldn't dare ask another person."

"If it has to do with you and me, or any aspect of our relationship, share the problem with me, Tyra, and we'll solve it. I promise you that nothing will happen between us unless you assure me that you want it."

She moved closer and leaned her head on his shoulder. "I don't need any assurance about you Byron, I know who you are."

"Good heavens, with that kind of reputation, I can't act out even a little bit. What have I done to myself?" he quipped.

She snuggled closer. "I'm sleepy, and your shoulder isn't soft."

"Of course, it isn't soft. Why are you sleepy?" He eased his right arm around her. "Couldn't you sleep last night?"

"Sure. I slept like a baby. Every weekend, I go off with some guy, so this is nothing unusual."

"Those guys don't bend the frame, as they say. You can sleep from Baltimore to Fort Lauderdale." She had a way of saying things that made him feel like a giant.

"What time does the boat sail?"

"Five-thirty. We'll be there in plenty of time."

"You bought first class tickets?" she asked him when they were boarding the plane.

"What kind of man would I be if I invited you for a romantic tryst and gave you the cheapest accommodations? Give me credit for some class, sweetheart."

"This is all new to me. I feel like a butterfly in a garden." They took their seats, and he put their carry-on luggage overhead.

"Champagne, orange juice or wine?" the stewardess asked.

He looked at the woman who seemed tired before the flight began. "I'll have some coffee, ma'am."

"I'd like a comet," Tyra said. When he stared at her, she explained, "That's a vodka comet without the vodka. Gosh, I'm so sleepy."

"Take a nap. I'll awaken you when they serve lunch. I won't feel deserted."

"Why should you? If you hadn't fooled around in my head all night last night, I wouldn't be sleepy."

"Was I…uh…nice?" He gave her half of a chocolate chip cookie that he put in his pocket when he walked through his dining room that morning.

"Thanks for the cookie. That question's too personal. Try another one."

Her eyelids drooped, and he put an arm around her, a pillow beneath her head and a blanket across her lap. Within minutes she slept. Even as she slept, when she moved, she moved toward him. He gazed at the peaceful, relaxed contours of her beautiful face and had to control an urge to hug and kiss her. She was in him through and through, and in a few short months, he'd grown to need her as he needed his right hand. He bent over and brushed her forehead with his lips.

Because both of them lived with family members, and prudence dictated that they behave circumspectly, their passion had tested the limits of their capacity for restraint. And maybe that was a good thing; they had learned a lot about each other that they might not otherwise have known, and on at least two occasions recently, he was certain that, if they had had privacy, they would have made love. If they made love during that trip, and he hoped for it, it would not be a happenstance but something that they had both looked forward to and planned for.

"Will the lady be having lunch?" the steward asked as he handed Byron a hot towel.

"I'm sure she will," Byron said. "Give me a towel for her, please." He leaned down and kissed Tyra's forehead. "You told me to wake you up at mealtime." She stretched, and snuggled closer to him.

"Wake up, sleepyhead."

"Huh? Did they serve lunch yet?"

He handed her the towel. "Here. You were sleeping so sweetly, loving me and hugging me up, that I hated to awaken you."

"I was not. I was back in the Middle Ages flirting with a handsome Spanish picador."

He didn't believe he'd heard her correctly. "What? I didn't understand you." She assured him that he'd heard her correctly. He stared at her while she nonchalantly wiped her hands with the towel. "A picador in the Middle Ages?"

She nodded. "Uh huh."

"Well, I'll be damned." Suddenly, he could see the scene in his mind's eye, and laughter rolled out of him.

"What's funny?"

"Nothing. I guess, if you can't see the humor in sleeping in my arms and dreaming about some dude on horseback with a spear trying to take the wind out of a bull. That's funny as hell."

She sat up straighter, poked out her chin and said, "He wasn't anywhere near a bull. How long did I sleep, anyway?"

"Only about twenty minutes. The plane's just reaching

cruising altitude, so we'll get lunch shortly." He glanced from the approaching steward to her. "I'm not too hungry, but we won't get dinner until around eight, so judge accordingly."

"Thanks. I'll have the crab salad and cheese and fruit for dessert, please," she said to the steward. He chose filet mignon, parsley potatoes and asparagus with a salad.

After lunch, he removed the arm rest between them, made her comfortable, put his arms around her, reclined his seat and went to sleep. He'd hired a limousine to meet them at the airport, and, in view of the long line of people waiting for taxis, it proved to be a smart move. They arrived at the cruise ship an hour and forty minutes before sailing time.

He put her bags in her stateroom, looked at her and said, "I'm next door." He pointed to a door that opened into his stateroom. "If you want to visit me, here's the key. I don't have one. The other way to get to me is through the door that opens on to the deck."

A grin spread over her face. "You're kidding. What about my charms?"

"If you want to know how they get to me, I'll happily give you a demonstration right this minute."

"Okay. I was joking. I need half an hour. Then, I want to see the boat."

"All right, but before the boat sails, we get a talk about safety, use of lifeboats and that sort of thing."

"Can we stand on deck and watch the boat leave shore? Gosh, I'm so excited."

"We'll do whatever you want to do." He took a step toward her, but she backed away.

"If you start kissing me, I won't get to that safety lecture and probably not even to dinner." He didn't disagree.

"Do you like your room?" he asked her.

"It's lovely. Thanks for putting me on this level where I can see the water."

He stepped closer to her then, and took her in his arms. "I will always give you the best that I have. Always. Don't forget that."

"And I'll give you the same. That's a promise."

He gazed into her eyes, large, beautiful, long-lashed brown eyes that seemed to draw him as sweet clover draws bees. Eyes that promised him heaven on earth. Something quickened inside of him, and he knew right then that he was hers forever. "I'd better get out of here. Knock on my door when you're ready."

He went into his own stateroom, closed the door, dropped his luggage on the floor and himself on the chaise longue beside the window. He'd come within seconds of ruining all that he'd planned for them. Shaking his head in bemusement, he pulled himself up, took a shower and dressed in white pants, a blue, collared T-shirt and blue sneakers. Then, he stored his passport and valuables in the safe, locked his door and went out on deck.

Seagulls, herons, ibis, orioles, bulbuls and many birds that he couldn't identify flocked at the dock in such numbers that they covered the area. He gazed out at the vast water beyond, wondering what that trip would bring him, for he knew that in some way his life was about to change. He heard her door open, turned and saw her step out of her room dressed precisely as he. If he needed more evidence that he was on the right track, that had to be it. Happiness suffused him as she walked to him with a smile blooming on her face. He opened his arms and received her.

"Woman, you do something to me."

"Everybody must go to the auditorium," a voice said through a loudspeaker. "This safety drill is required by law, and everyone must attend. We sail in forty-five minutes."

He lifted his right shoulder in a shrug. "Let's go. I can't think of anything less encouraging than a lecture on the use of life vests and lifeboats."

"That's probably because you can swim. I can barely keep my head above the water."

He took from his pocket a map of the boat, checked it, took her hand and headed for the auditorium. "Have you ever thought about what you see in the future for us, Tyra?"

"Of course I have. What I hope to find out while we're on this cruise is whether you and I are on the same page," she said with her usual candor.

"I'll do my best to help you with that."

After the safety instructions, they explored the boat. "Gosh, that's a frozen yogurt dispenser," she said to Byron when the turned a corner to walk up the stairs. He asked if she wanted some. "Do they have strawberry or lemon?"

"Lemon." He piled a cone high with frozen lemon yogurt, wrapped a napkin around the bottom of it and handed it to her.

"You mean I can just come here and get it whenever I want it? Just like that? She snapped the fingers of her right hand. "Gosh. That's fantastic."

"You can find something to eat twenty-four/seven. So don't get carried away."

"Not to worry. I'm not going to gain so much that I can't get into my clothes." She savored the creamy delight. "This is so good. Where are we going now?"

"To the bar, and then to the top deck to see the boat pull away from shore." She could hardly contain her excitement.

"After dinner, we can do karaoke, line dancing to a country music band, see an old Sidney Poitier movie or sit in the lounge and talk, since I assume you're not interested in throwing your money away in the gaming rooms."

"Oh, I'm willing to give away five dollars, but not a penny more." He asked her how she managed that. "I change a five dollar bill. I go to the slots. If I win five dollars, I put the five dollars back in my pocket and play with what I won. If I lose all of that, I tell the slot machines bye-bye. I do not go back in my pocketbook for more money."

They sat at a bistro table in the corner of the lounge, and she became aware that she didn't have his full attention. After a while, she noticed that a man who wore the trappings of wealth had focused his attention on her. The man smiled. Simultaneously with her frown, Byron glanced at her.

"Have you ever seen that man before?" he asked her.

"No, I haven't. Let's go."

Byron crossed his left knee with his right ankle and leaned back in the chair. "I'm not ready to leave, Tyra, but don't get nervous. I can hold my own with any man, and if that one is smart, he'll find a woman of his own and ogle *her*."

He could tell her not to be nervous, but with that feral expression on his face, he had the bearing of a man ready to pounce. She knew that Byron's type of man wouldn't let another crowd his woman and that he wouldn't let another man fool around in his space. She hoped the man wouldn't challenge Byron, because she didn't think he'd back down.

"Byron, I'm getting sick. Come go with me to the women's room. *Please!*"

He stood, helped her up and put an arm around her. "I saw one around the corner." She went into the woman's room, leaned against the counter and her breathing came faster and faster.

"Are you all right?" a woman asked her.

"Just a little nervous. I'll be fine. Thank you." The woman left but was back in a minute. "A tall man standing outside, who's dressed like you, wants to know if you're okay. He seemed very worried."

"Thank you. Tell him I'm fine. I'll be out in a minute." She breathed deeply in and out until she was able to regain her equilibrium. Maybe the foolish man had gone. In any case, she wasn't going back to that particular lounge.

When she emerged from the women's room, he rushed to her. "Are you all right, sweetheart? If that guy upset you, I'll—"

She interrupted him. "It's all right. That man is not normal, and he obviously doesn't mind a fight. I'd be happier if we went up on the next level. I don't want to go back there."

"I admit the guy probably wasn't rowing with both oars, but—"

She grasped Byron's arm. "My dad always said that the certain way to avoid trouble was to turn and walk the other way when you see it coming. All right?"

"I don't want to make you uncomfortable. It's the last thing I'd do."

They walked in the direction of the stairs, and she saw that the gaming room had opened. "Let's go in here."

"I see you want to blow your five bucks right now. All right." He took her arm and walked with her past the roulette table to the row of twenty-five-cents-a-throw slot machines and handed her a five-dollar bill. She bought a five-dollar card with it, bet twenty-five cents and pulled the arm. It seemed that the bell would never stop ringing, and her eyes got bigger and bigger until, at last, she looked up and saw that she had just won sixteen thousand dollars.

She pulled the card out, put her arms around him and hugged him. "That's a good omen. I'm never going to leave you. Let's go cash my money and get out of here."

But he stood as if frozen, staring down at her. "Don't ever say a thing like that unless you mean it."

She frowned, trying to think. What was he talking about? "Like what?"

"That you're never going to leave me."

She stared right back at him. "I won't of my own accord. Come on."

At the cashier counter, she collected her winnings and the remaining money on the card. He put an arm around her as if to leave the place, but she didn't move. Did he think she was so selfish that she wouldn't share with him what his money won? She handed him the four dollars and seventy-five cents that remained on the card and then made him wait while she counted out eight thousand dollars.

"This is yours," she said when she handed it to him.

"I don't know how you figure that. You won it, so it's yours." He attempted to give it back to her, but she wouldn't take it.

"Byron, I have a conscience, and I know what's right. I believe in sharing, and especially in this case when I don't think I deserve any of it. If you don't want to ruin this trip for me, you'll put that money in your pocket. This eight thousand in my hand is going to be the down payment on a new car, a white one. And this will probably be the last time I ever go near a slot machine. I believe in quitting while I'm ahead. If you don't want to spend that eight thousand, but it in Andy's piggy bank toward his Harvard education."

"Good idea," he said. "I can definitely do that. We'd better change. It's almost time for dinner."

To her disgust, the man who eyed her in the lounge sat at the table next to theirs at dinner. "Do you see who that is over there?" Tyra asked Byron, nudging his knee immediately after they sat down to their assigned seats.

"Yeah, and if he can't keep his eyes off you, I'm going to ask him why. Don't get upset. I'll be as calm as the Pacific Ocean just before a storm."

She told herself to relax, that at least she'd learn who the real Byron Whitley was. "I'm only concerned because he seems much less a gentleman than you are."

The waiters served the elegant dinner in six courses, and it occurred to her that they had first class dinner accommodations when wines accompanied each course and liqueurs were offered with after-dinner coffee. She didn't know whether the intemperate stranger looked her way, because she didn't once glance toward him. While the guests enjoyed espresso coffee, the waiters sang "Boot Scootin' Boogie" and "Y.M.C.A." and gave the guests souvenirs.

Tyra didn't know when she'd had so much unexpected fun. She leaned against his shoulder, but he was rigid and pre-occupied. She looked toward the uncouth stranger and saw that his gaze was on her.

"Excuse me," Byron said without looking at her. He walked to the other table, and she held her breath.

He'd had it. No man was going to disrespect him to that extent and do it with impunity. He walked to the next table and faced the man. "Excuse me. Do you know that woman with me?"

An expression of alarm flashed across the man's face. "Uh…no. I mean she resembles someone I…met once."

"What was the name of that woman you met once?"

The man stared up at him, and the other five people at the table had stopped talking. "I…uh…don't remember. It must have been at least twenty years ago."

"Where?"

"Uh…San Francisco."

"She's never been to San Francisco in her life. Stop ogling her. You're making her uncomfortable, and you're getting on my nerves. I don't want to have to speak to you about it again."

"Sorry. No hard feelings, I hope."

He looked the man in the eye. "Not this time."

He wasn't satisfied that the man got the message, but he hoped he'd put an end to the blatant leering. He went back to his seat praying that Tyra wouldn't make him angry by telling him that he'd overstepped his authority. She surprised him.

"You promised me we'd dance after dinner."

"I asked if you'd like to line dance. Jazz dancing is scheduled for tomorrow evening. Would you like to leave?"

"Yes. If the moon's shining, can we walk along the deck for a few minutes?"

He stood, held out his hand, and she rose and took it. He put an arm around her as they strolled along the deck, but he only half listened to what she said, because he'd trained one ear to listen for footsteps or any unusual sound behind them.

"I didn't realize it would be so cool out here," she said. "Next time, I'll bring my shawl."

"Good idea. We'd better go in. I don't want you to get a cold." What he did want was a chance to check whether her admirer had left the table. He walked with her back to the dining room, looked toward their assigned table and saw that the man remained where they left him. So far so good. All he needed was to have a foolish man tailing them.

She surprised him again. "Don't worry. He's not foolish enough to take you on. The little runt is less than half your size. Besides, that kind of man is a coward."

"I hope not. Cowards will attack you from behind. I think his money usually talks for him, and he wants to see if he can turn your head with it."

"Poor fool. My heart's taken."

He nearly stumbled. "What? What did you say?"

"Honey, you have to keep your mind on where you're going," she said, showing her white teeth in a wide grin. "And if you don't listen carefully to what I say, you're subject to miss something important."

"You little imp. I heard every word you said. And if you aren't careful, I'll get possessive right here in this corridor."

She threw back her head and looked to the side. "Why would you want me to be careful? I thought you wanted me to let it all hang out."

"You're flirting with me. Keep it up. Remember I know exactly how to get you to let it hang out."

She lowered her lashes and her voice. "I'm counting on that."

Chapter 8

Exhausted from the long day that had begun at six o'clock in Frederick that morning and shifted to the world of cruise boats, slot machines and line dancing, Tyra leaned against Byron and stifled a yawn. Not that she was sending him a message, she wasn't. She made it a habit not to play games with men or to mislead them. She loved to line dance, although she'd rarely done it, and line dancing with Byron was such fun, and a revelation, too. He seemed to have put every muscle and sinew of his body into it, and she danced long after she became tired, because she enjoyed seeing him move. She covered her mouth in hopes of hiding another yawn.

"Are you sleepy?" he asked her. "If you are, I'm not surprised, since it's already eleven-thirty."

At a beverage fountain, he stopped and asked what she would like to drink, but she wanted nothing more than to get out of her clothes, put her head on a pillow and go to sleep. "No thanks, Byron. I just want to fall into bed."

With an arm firmly around her waist, he headed them to their staterooms. "What would you like for breakfast tomorrow morning? I'll put our orders in tonight. Want to watch the sunrise?" She told him she would and that she'd like to eat grits, sage sausage, scrambled eggs, a buttermilk biscuit, honeydew melon and coffee at around eight. He stared at her and nodded his head.

"I'm a big breakfast eater, and I often don't take lunch."

At her door, he put both of his arms around her. "I'll stand here until you're inside. Lock your door, and I'm not moving until you do it."

She reached up, put a hand behind his head and urged his mouth to hers. His kiss was light, without the explosive passion that she expected. She wanted so badly to go to sleep in his arms, but she knew that, exhausted as she was, that's all she would do. Fall asleep.

"You're so sweet," she said in a half-asleep, seductive voice.

He kissed her cheek. "Get in there before I lose my halo. I'll call you ten minutes before sunrise." He opened the door, pushed her inside, and closed it behind her. His light knock reminded her to lock it, and she did.

Ten minutes later, snug in her bed, she vowed, "Tomorrow night, I am going to sleep in his arms or know the reason why not." She buried herself between the covers, put the pillow on top of her head, closed her eyes and said a prayer. "Lord, please don't let me make a mistake with this man, and please let me know if he's the one."

Byron stood on the deck in their private balcony-like area and listened to the waves as they hit the side of the huge boat. As much as he ached to bury himself in her to the hilt, he knew and appreciated her gentle way of telling him that tonight was not the time. But she had given him many signals that she'd had minimal experience as a lover, so he knew he had better prepare her for it. He went into his stateroom, ordered their breakfast for eight o'clock and coffee for six-thirty, set his watch to alarm at six, showered and went to bed.

Knowing that she slept alone next to him should have kept him awake all night, but he awakened a few minutes before his watch alarm triggered the end of sleep. Feeling refreshed, he threw on a pair of shorts and went out on deck to let the fresh, salty air caress his body. He saw a gray streak edge above the horizon, went back inside and dialed Tyra's room number.

"Hmm?"

"Tyra, this is Byron. Do you still want to see the sun rise over the ocean?"

"Uh huh. In a minute."

"Try not to go back to sleep. It won't wait for you."

"Be there in a minute, hon."

Five minutes later, she came out wearing a pair of white shorts and a yellow tank top that didn't leave much to his imagination. He told himself to get it under control.

"Hi. How many times did you ring?"

"Once. You look as if you're still asleep."

"That's because I am. Where's the sun?"

He brought her into his arms and hugged her. "It seems to be a little sleepy, too, but it's getting there."

A waiter arrived with a container of hot coffee and a service for two. "Good morning, sir, madam. It's due to rise in seven minutes." He poured a cup for each of them. "Your breakfast will be here at eight." Byron thanked the man, put a five-dollar bill on the tray, looked at the red, blue, orange and gray streaks in the sky and turned to Tyra.

"For the remainder of my life, I'll think of you whenever I see a sunrise."

"Funny. I was thinking something similar, that whenever I see a setting like this, I hope I'm with you."

He sipped his coffee, eager to know if she loved him, but

unwilling to ask, for he wasn't ready to show his *own* hand. The weight of her hand tugging at his arm almost startled him. "What is it, sweetheart?"

"It's so…so awesome," she gasped. "I've never seen anything like it."

He concurred as they gazed at the great kaleidoscope of colors bursting on to the sky. "I'll bet every painter on this boat is out here with his canvas, paints and brushes. Or they should be. It's a phenomenal sight."

"I'm never going to forget this. In fact, I'm never going to forget this trip or you."

He shook her gently. "I hope the hell not, and I intend to do what I can to make sure that you don't."

Her soft hand eased into the palm of his left one. "With both of us working on it, I don't see much chance of that. Look! There it is, a big red ball. Oh, Byron. I wouldn't have missed this for anything."

He refilled their coffee cups. "Neither would I. Seeing it with you makes it special." He thought for a minute. "I want you to enjoy a weekend with Andy, Aunt Jonie and me at my house on the Chesapeake Bay. We spend a lot of time there in July and August. Andy and my father love to fish, though the fishing isn't as good as it used to be, and we catch crabs, too. We could have gone there this weekend, but I was in no mood to keep house and cook, and I certainly wouldn't have let you do it."

"We could eat lunch and dinner at a restaurant, couldn't we?"

"I suppose, but we enjoy that house so much that we almost never leave it. Maybe we can get there before mid-October."

"I'd like to see it," she said. "Thanks for the coffee and the show. I'm going inside to get dressed. My tummy is telling me it's about time to eat."

"All right. I'll see you back here in half an hour?" She nodded, blew him a kiss and disappeared into her stateroom.

He sat there gazing at the vast ocean. Could he possibly love her as much as he believed he did? He shook his head from side to side. Puzzled. He'd never met a woman so down to earth, unpretentious and candid, traits that he hadn't often seen in a female acquaintance. Good. But she was also beautiful with eyes that lured him like a magnet pulls in a nail. And her body...tall and shapely with those breasts that fit perfectly in his big hands. Add that to the fact that she was educated, intelligent and very moral. And she cared for him. He wasn't going to fool himself. Tyra Cunningham was perfect for him. But he had to give it more time. He had to be sure that she and Andy accepted each other without reservations and that she was his soul mate as a lover. He didn't doubt the latter, so that left Andy.

He went inside, shaved, did his ablutions, dressed in white shorts and a yellow T-shirt and got outside simultaneously with the arrival of their breakfast. Tyra joined him almost immediately.

"I could really get used to this life. Not all the time, mind you, but often enough to feel queenly."

"You're my queen," he told her, "so you can feel like one all the time, no matter where you are." He'd thought she'd smile at that, but instead, she stopped eating, put her fork down and looked at him.

"You've got me on a high, Byron. If you take the props out from under me, I'll never forgive you. Give a woman a taste of pure heaven, and then—"

"Hey, wait till I bomb. Then you can come at me swinging."

"I'm sorry. You know I'm not much of a gambler, and this time, I'm wagering all that I have."

"Ah, sweetheart." He stood, picked her up and held her close to his body. "I'll hurt myself long before I'd hurt you. I told you that you're precious to me, and each minute, you become more so. Come on, let's finish eating and see what's on this boat."

* * *

Tyra told herself not to dwell on the fact that he hadn't said he loved her. Some men had a hard time uttering that word. She put some money and a credit card in the pocket of her shorts, locked her valuables in the safe provided in her stateroom and joined Byron on the deck. They spent the morning at a lecture on international travel, played a game of tennis—their first with each other—ate double scoops of frozen yogurt instead of lunch and, at one o'clock in the afternoon, went to their respective rooms for a nap.

She awakened at two-thirty, resisted using the key that connected her room to his and set her mind to planning his surrender. She phoned his room.

"Hi. Feel like checking out the gift shop?" He said he did. "Promise not to buy anything for me, and we can go." She hung up and dialed his number again. "Hi. And oh, yes. I'll be ready to leave in five minutes. That suit you?"

"Woman, what are you up to?" When she replied, "Nothing," he said, "I'm telling myself to believe you. I'll be out in the five minutes you've given me."

In the gift shop, she went directly to the perfume counter. "Those are for men," a saleswoman said.

"I know." She watched Byron from her peripheral vision as she pretended to look at perfumes for women. He fingered a bottle of YSL cologne, ran his hands in his pocket, evidently discovered that he didn't have with him the means to buy it and put it back.

"Would you wrap a bottle of YSL for me?" she whispered to the clerk. "But I'd prefer he didn't see you do it. It's a gift."

The woman selected a bottle from beneath the counter, giftwrapped it and handed it to her. She paid, took the tiny shopping bag and tapped him on the shoulder. "What do you think I can buy for Maggie?"

"One of those nice totes with the ship's logo on it. What did you buy just now?"

"Perfume," she said truthfully.

"I hope you bought the kind you were wearing last night. I loved that."

"Thank you. I feel good wearing that." She looked up at him, aware that her countenance showed her alarm. "Why is this boat rocking?"

Holding her close to him, he steadied her. "A big wave can cause that. The Atlantic is known for its unfriendly waves. Some of them can wash up on deck, but the captain will usually give plenty of advance warning for that. Want to see a movie?"

After the movie, they sprawled out beside each other in two deck lounge chairs. Oh, oh, she thought. Here comes trouble. Unfortunately, she didn't have a book or newspaper with which to obscure her face. She thought for a moment that the overly attentive stranger from the night before would pass without noticing her, but when he paused, she knew he had seen her.

Like a rocket-propelled mannequin, Byron sat up straight. But the man had moved on after only a half-second pause. "I don't trust that guy," she heard him murmur, but she said nothing, merely reached over and brushed her hand slowly over his warm and hard washboard middle. Nobody and nothing was going to interfere with her plans.

"I think I'll get in the pool," she said, "and since I'm not much of a swimmer, you have to come in with me. Will you?"

"Of course, but we have to change, don't we? I mean, you brought a bathing suit, didn't you?"

"Uh huh. Come on."

He jumped up, reached for her hand, and they strolled hand-in-hand to their staterooms. She supposed he wondered if she ever planned to use that key. Well, let him wonder. A surprise would be good for him.

"I only need fifteen minutes," she said as he unlocked her door.

"Considering what you'll probably put on, it shouldn't take you half that long," he said without the semblance of a smile.

"Not really," she said, airily. "The smaller they are the more careful you have to be putting them on." His eyes nearly doubled in size, but she pretended not to notice. He didn't have to know that she'd never worn a bikini swimsuit, and that she was embarrassed to wear the one in her drawer.

"All right. I'll be out in fifteen minutes."

She looked at herself in the red string bikini, which amounted to four patches, two covering her nipples, one covering her mound and the other at her hips, all held together with strings. *Lord, I can't walk out there looking like this*.

But it's a part of your plan, her conscience prodded. She put on the red, fishnet tunic designed to wear with the bathing suit. And though it covered nothing, she felt more modestly clad. She stuck her feet in a pair of red flip flops, got her bathing cap and rushed out. She had expected to see him pacing the floor or looking anxiously at his watch, but he leaned casually against the railing as if he didn't have a care.

"Sorry if I took longer that fifteen minutes. I had to—"

"You're going to wear *that*? You can't wear *that*."

"Why not? It's a standard swimsuit. Ninety-nine percent of the women lounging in those deck chairs had on skimpier ones than this."

"I don't like it." He grumbled. "What about those men? I know exactly what they'll be thinking."

She took his hand. "But you didn't think er…anything bad about those women, did you. Tell me you didn't."

"I don't remember what they looked like."

"You see? And those men aren't going to remember what I look like, either."

"You must be out of your mind."

At the pool, he pulled off his linen shorts and prepared to take off his shoes. Her lower lip dropped, and she had to talk herself out of rubbing her hands over his perfect body. Thinking that she may have bitten off more than she could chew, she kicked off her flip flops, removed the fishnet top and started toward the pool, but he grabbed her. "Baby, these guys are having a field day."

She winked at him. "What do you think the women sitting around here are looking at? Get the beam out of your own eye before you go after the one in mine. You're practically nude."

He winked back at her. "Like what you see?"

"Damn straight, I do." Now, if only she could manage to fool around in the water without wetting her hair. She said as much to Byron.

"There's a hairdresser upstairs. Charge it to your room."

"Why should I spend a couple of hours in a hair salon when I could spend it with you?"

He swam with her on his back, and she didn't think she'd ever had so much fun. "Did your hair get wet?" he asked her as they climbed out of the pool.

"I don't think so. Thanks for the ride." He rushed to get her top and held it for her as she put it on.

"It doesn't hide a thing," he said, "but at least it's a stab at modesty."

"You should talk. You're not even pretending to be modest."

"I almost swallowed my tongue when you walked out of your room," he said, not a little exasperated. "You should see how you look in that thing."

"You mean it didn't look nice? I wanted to look nice."

"Nice? We'd better drop this subject."

"I think I'll doll up tonight," she said, though she wasn't warning him, because she knew he'd dress for dinner.

"The big night's tomorrow night," he told her, "so save the thunder for then."

"Thanks. I've got it covered."

Inside her room, she took the gift-wrapped bottle of YSL cologne out of the little shopping bag, and knocked on the door between their rooms. Still dressed for swimming, he opened the door and stared down at her with a strangely expectant expression on his face.

"I know it isn't your birthday, but I've missed too many of them already, so I decided I'd better start catching up." He looked at the package she held in her hand. "Aren't you...I mean, don't you want it?"

"You bought that for me?" She nodded. He picked her up, locked her to him and flicked his tongue over her lips. She opened to him, greedy for it and sucked his tongue into her mouth. For the first time, she felt his skin against her skin. His large hands rubbed her naked hips, and her taut nipples pressed against his hard pectorals. Heat flashed through her from her toes to her core, and her blood began to race. Excited beyond reason, moaning his name, she straddled him and rocked. As if she triggered something wild in him, he pulled her breast from the skimpy bra and sucked her nipple into his mouth, and when she felt him hard, heavy and within an inch of penetrating her, she let out a keening cry of surrender.

But that must have brought him back to his senses, because he eased her down to the floor and, still holding her, whispered, "I want more for us."

"Me, too, but being with you this way was more than I was prepared for."

"I know. Thanks for my present."

"I uh...I think I'll take a nap so I won't be sleepy tonight. What time are we going to dinner?"

"Seven-thirty."

She reached up and teased herself with a quick kiss on his lips. "I'll be ready."

"Should I phone you at six-thirty?"

"It wouldn't hurt." She blew him a kiss, closed the door, and skipped across the room. She didn't see how she could wait until they got back to their rooms.

Byron showered, shaved and set his clock to alarm at a quarter of six, although he didn't expect to need the alarm. He sat up in bed with his cell phone and dialed his home. He called Andy daily, but didn't allow the boy to call him because, given the circumstances, Andy would call him five or six times a day. He wasn't poor, but he wasn't about to throw away money at the rate Andy could make it vanish.

"Hello?"

"This is your father. How are you and Aunt Jonie?"

"Daddy! Did you catch any fish yet" He couldn't help laughing. If that question had been put to him as intentionally ambiguous, it wouldn't have been more appropriate.

"No, son," he said, answering with a truth that would have applied no matter the meaning of the question. "I'm not fishing. I'm having a short vacation with Miss Tyra."

"Can I talk to Miss Tyra?"

"She's in her room, but I'll tell her that you wanted to talk with her." He hadn't planned to tell Andy that Tyra was with him, but it wouldn't hurt for the child to know that Tyra was special to him, and the sooner he knew it, the better.

"When you coming home, Daddy?"

"Day after tomorrow." They talked for a while, after which he spoke with Jonie and confirmed that his family was fine. Now, he could concentrate on Tyra and what was to come that evening. She had casually informed him that she wouldn't be sleepy—as she'd been the previous night—and after what had passed between them minutes before she said it, he understood that she had, in effect, made him a promise.

And it was past time for them. If he hadn't summoned the strength to terminate the hottest session they'd had to date, their first mating would have been far less than it should and could have been. Time enough for extemporaneous lovemaking after they knew each other's needs, but today was certainly not the time.

He unwrapped the package she gave him and shook his head in wonder. How had she known that YSL was the scent he wore? He had intended to buy a bottle of it when they were in the gift shop but except for forty dollars, he'd left both his money and his credit cards in the safe in his room. It was her first gift to him, and he'd have that bottle long after he emptied it. What a sweet, tender and loving woman, he thought. And how can she be like that and, at the same time, have such strength, fortitude, honor, and compassion for other human beings. If he told her how much he admired her, she wouldn't believe him. He wanted his son—and his other children, if he were fortunate in having more—to know the love and nurturing of such a woman as Tyra.

Byron looked at the goose bumps on his arms and slipped beneath the cover to ward off the chill from the air conditioner. But, in his heart, he knew the true source. He told himself that he had no reason to be anxious, because she loved him, pulled the cover up higher, and was soon fast asleep.

He awoke minutes before his watch alarm rang. If he'd had privacy, he would certainly have let the salty Atlantic air cool his loins. Something in him seemed hell-bent on bursting free. He thought about that for a minute and released an uproarious laugh. He was forty, and he should damned well know what was wrong with him.

When Tyra stepped out of her room at seven-twenty that evening, looked up at him and smiled, he knew that if she hadn't already sunk into him, he could be sure of it then. She glowed in a pinkish kind of color, a soft-delicate fabric that clung to her curves the way bark clings to a tree, and advertised the prettiest legs he'd ever seen.

She blew a kiss to him and took his hand. "Hi," she said. "You look good enough for dinner."

"Thanks. I knew that if I didn't shape up, I'd look as if I were your gardener. Tyra, you're so lovely. I'm a proud man."

"That's my line, Byron. You make any woman proud. How'd you sleep?"

"Like a baby. I phoned home, and Andy wanted to talk with you. I hadn't planned to tell him that you were with me, but I did, and I'm glad. He needs to know that you're special to me."

"But, Byron, he may become jealous. Then, he won't like me."

"He will be jealous, because he hasn't had to share me with anyone. But you will ease him out of that when he realizes that he's special to you."

Tyra didn't know what to make of their conversation. Speaking of Andy and her relationship with him in that way presupposed something that they had not discussed, or so it seemed to her. She pushed it to the back of her mind and reminded herself that she shouldn't allow anything to hamper her plans for their evening. They reached their table minutes before service began.

"My, but you look nice," the woman who sat across from them said to Tyra. "You make a mighty good-looking couple too, very nice together. Enjoy it while you have each other. My husband's gone now, and every year, I go to the places we went together and do the things we did, but it'll never be the same. I had no idea how happy I was."

"How long were you married?" Byron asked her.

"Fifty years. I was eighteen, and everybody said it wouldn't last a week. He's the only man I ever knew, and it was the same for him. We had a wonderful life together. Y'all take care of what you got. Love's the most precious gift you can have."

He leaned back in his chair and appraised the woman

gently. "What in your view is the basis for a happy marriage…other than love?"

"Well," she said, warming up to the topic, "you know love is important, because that determines how you treat your mate. But even more important is commitment. My husband and I were totally committed to each other and to that marriage. Breaking up was never an option for us, and each of us did little unexpected things to please the other." She took a deep breath and looked away from them. "He was like sunrise and sunset. I could count on him like I could count on the passing of time. In fifty years, not once did he let me down, and he was always there for me." She covered her face with her hand. "I loved the ground he walked on."

Tyra watched in astonishment as Byron got up, walked around to the woman and put his arms around her. "I'm sorry that I awakened those memories, but I'll cherish every word you said." He took his handkerchief from his pocket and wiped her eyes.

"I forgot your name," he said.

"Lydia Coston. I'm glad we met. You two be good to each other."

"We will," Tyra heard herself say. Byron had been married, so she wondered in his interest in what made a good marital union. But she had no intention of prying into what must surely be sacred to him.

"You have a wonderful man," Lydia said to her. "It's written all over him."

"I know," Tyra told her. "He's precious." She didn't look at Byron then. She couldn't for she knew he'd locked his gaze on her, and that his eyes reflected the questions he must have about her statement. He called the waiter.

"Would you bring a bottle of Dom Pérignon and three glasses, please."

When the champagne arrived, the waiter poured some in

their glasses, bowed and left. Byron raised his glass. "To one of the loveliest women I've ever met. I'm glad we made your acquaintance, Mrs. Coston." They drank to the toast, and Tyra gave silent thanks that Byron poured only a small amount in her glass. She'd learned that champagne played tricks with her head. After a sumptuous meal, they followed the sound and strolled into one of the smaller ballrooms where a jazz band played "Round Midnight." She wanted to dance, but Byron seemed more inclined merely to listen.

"I've never liked 'Round Midnight' for dancing," he said when the band struck up "Sleepy Time Down South." "This is my style."

She found that she got carried away when she danced with him. He moved with abandon, yet with such grace that he mesmerized her. He stared into her eyes and swung his hips suggestively, teasing and tantalizing her. The music ended, and the band moved into "When You're Smiling" with an old Louis Armstrong arrangement that Byron clearly loved. He danced close to her in a fox trot, then swung her out for a few fast steps, all the while sending her unspoken threats and promises proclaiming his intentions later that evening.

"You've exhausted me," she accused when the music ended. "How can you dance like that, never missing a beat, for half an hour? If you did this every night, I could understand it."

His grin would have put any woman off balance. "The last thing I want to do is exhaust you here," he said in a tone that projected a significant meaning. "How tired are you?"

Suddenly alert and aware that he was about to commence an agenda of his own, she smiled her sweetest smile. "Let's get a glass of something or other and take it to our balcony. I love dancing with you, but I'd also like to sit with you and look at the stars."

"Works for me," he said. "But we can order something to

drink from our staterooms, and you won't have to carry it. You're too elegant for that." She had a feeling that she'd played right into his hand, but she didn't suppose she cared. No matter what, when she went to sleep, she'd be in his arms.

They strolled arm in arm to their staterooms, and when he put her key into her door, she gave silent thanks that they had not encountered the ubiquitous stranger. Byron stood statue-like beside her and handed her the key to her door.

As if she didn't know why he behaved that way, she said, as casually as she could, "It's early. Come on in."

"Sure you don't mind?"

"Of course not. Have a seat, unless you really want to look at the stars."

"You're the one who mentioned stars," he said, settling himself into the boudoir chair that left half of his thighs off the seat.

"You're my star," she shot at him over her shoulder. "Excuse me a minute." She went into the bathroom to brush her teeth and freshen up. What a woman wouldn't do for love! All evening, she'd thought her feet and legs would freeze, since she hadn't worn stockings. Clark always said that panty hose were about as sexy as a wet rat, and since she didn't own a garter belt she went without them. In any case, the less she wore, the better, at least for tonight.

"Right. Room 739," she heard him say, as she walked back into the room. He hung up the phone.

"Come over here and sit down?" he said. She didn't see any place over there to sit, except on him, and she wasn't sure that was what he meant. So she hesitated. He stood and opened his arms, and she dashed into them. Then he sat down with her on his lap. His hand held her bare thigh, and she wished he would do more with it. She slid her arms around his neck and kissed his ear.

"Go slow, honey. The waiter should be here in a few

minutes, and I wouldn't like him to return with the order because he didn't get an answer."

"Why wouldn't we answer?" she asked, playing the innocent.

"Since I know you're pulling my leg, I don't feel compelled to respond."

The waiter arrived with a bottle of Moët & Chandon champagne, two champagne glasses, fruit, cheese, crackers and petit fours, opened the champagne and recorked it. "Have a pleasant evening, sir, madam."

"Let's take this over to my place. I've been anxious to get you in my lair, and you seem to have lost that door key."

She gazed at him with her hands on her hips and her feet bare. "Men have no imagination. It's such a pity."

His grin displayed a tiny dimple that she hadn't seen previously, because he was sitting down and she was standing, looking at him from an unusual angle. "We do the best we can with the little intelligence we've got," he said. "Did you have something else in mind?"

"Yes, I definitely did. Are you going to wear that jacket all night? Not that I mind, 'cause you look fantastic in it. But it's so formidable-looking that I can't uh…play with you."

He jerked out of the white linen jacket and tossed it across the room. "For heavens sake, don't let a little thing like that stop you."

How did you seduce a six-foot-five-inch jewel? "I think I'll have a sip of that champagne," she said.

"I'll join you." He splashed a small amount of champagne into a glass, handed it to her and poured his own.

"Is this all I get?" she pretended to pout, but after having spent the last three weeks looking forward to that moment, she was suddenly scared to death.

"That's enough." He took the glass from her hand, picked her up and sat her in his lap. "Are you nervous?" She shook her head in the only lie she'd ever told him. "Scared?" She nodded. "Nothing will happen that you don't want to happen."

"But I want it to happen," she blurted out and buried her face in the curve of his neck.

"You may as well get used to me, Tyra, because I don't see myself letting you go."

"Same here," she said, feeling as if her command of the language had deserted her.

He kissed her lips, and when she parted them, he moved to her cheeks, kissed her eyes, the tip of her nose and pressed his tongue to her throat. She wanted one of his mind-blowing kisses, but he ignored her mouth and kissed her bare shoulder.

"Kiss me," she whispered.

"I am," he said, and suddenly his hand went into the top of her off-shoulder dress, released her right breast, as he bent to it and sucked the nipple into his mouth. His hand stroked the inside of her bare thigh until she thought she'd catch fire. When she rubbed her thighs together, trapping his hand and began to moan, she knew her self-control had abandoned her, and she didn't care. His hand moved further up her thigh, and he suckled as if he'd been starved for weeks.

Heat spiraled through her veins, and an aching emptiness settled in her vagina. "Byron, honey, do something. I'm aching." He kissed her lips, and when she parted them, he gave her his tongue and she sucked it greedily into her mouth. With one hand he pinched her nipple while his other hand inched closer to its ultimate target. She shifted in his lap and felt him bulging against her. Then he stopped his ministrations.

"Are you using a contraceptive?

She shook her head. "I haven't needed one."

He glanced at the table beside the chair in which they sat, saw the key lying on it, picked it up and stood with her in his arms. "I want you in my bed." He handed her the key, and she opened the door. Seconds later, her dress lay beneath her feet and he stood staring at her. She covered her erect breasts with her hands, but he moved them.

"You're so beautiful," he said in seeming awe, pulled back the bedcovers, picked her up and put her on the bed. "I've dreamed so many times of putting you in my bed."

He loosened his tie, threw it over his head and got out of his shirt. Then, he kicked off his shoes, stood and slipped down his pants.

"I want to do that," she said, when he reached for his skimpy, jockey shorts.

He stepped closer to the edge of the bed and she reached over, pulled them down, and let his hard penis spill out into her hand. She stared at it as one does when charmed by a snake. Then she bent over and kissed it.

"What does it taste like?" she asked, fascinated by the first penis she had ever touched and seen up close. Her previous sexual experience hadn't covered that.

"I don't know," he said, grinning. Then he rolled her over and got into bed with her. "I asked you once if there was another man in your life. You said there isn't. I don't want you with any other man. You're in this bed with me because you're mine." She didn't agree with that, but right then she'd give him anything he wanted, including her silent accord. She spread her legs and shifted her body in anticipation.

"Don't rush it, sweetheart. We've got all night." He kissed her lips, her forehead and every inch of her face until she felt that her skin was alive. His teeth nibbled at her shoulder until she thought she'd scream for what she wanted.

"Byron, stop playing with me and kiss me. You know what I want."

"What? Can't you tell me?"

"Please. I…" His hand toyed with her belly and she undulated against it. "Please…my breasts ache."

"What do you want me to do? Tell me, baby."

"I want you to suck them." He pulled the nipple of her left breast into his mouth and she let herself go, moving, undulating, begging with her hips for what she longed for. He left her breast and moved down her body, kissing her navel, the insides of her thighs, and then he stopped, teasing her. She spread her legs, as if air would cool her, and when he hooked her knees over his shoulders, she held her breath. Was he going to… He parted her folds, kissed her and then plunged his tongue into her. Her scream pierced the air while he possessed her.

"Byron! Honey, something's happening. I feel like I want to burst. Please. I can't stand this."

"All right, love." He kissed his way up her body, handed her a condom and helped her put it on him.

"Look at me, Tyra." She stared into his eyes, nearly dumbfounded by the love she saw in them. She raised her hips for his entrance, and shrunk back from the brunt of his penetration, but slowly he eased into her. "It will be easier when you get used to me," he said. "Are you all right?"

She didn't care if it had hurt. It felt good. He was hers at last. He began to move within her slowly at first. "Am I in the right place. Tell me when you feel that I'm there." Almost at once, as he let her have the onslaught of his passion, she could feel herself trying to explode.

"Oh, my lord, Byron. Something… Honey, I think I'm going to die."

"You aren't." He put one hand under her hip and began to thrust rapidly, unleashing his power. "I want you to love me, Tyra. I need you to love me."

"I do. I do love you, Byron. Oh, lord, I'm going to…" The heat seemed to swell from the soles of her feet through her trembling thighs to her sexual core. And then the pumping and squeezing began. "Do something, Byron, I'm…I want to burst."

He moved faster still. His body trembled against hers as

her perspiration melded with his. She locked her legs around his hips and rocked to his rhythm.

"That's right, love. Give yourself to me," he shouted and she felt her body gripping him before he ejaculated sending them both into ecstasy and then collapsing in her arms. He placed his head on her shoulder, wrapped his arms around her and let his forearms take his weight. And when he shifted his hips, aftershocks plowed through her. He looked down at her and grinned.

"That's like cheating, baby. I get it once, and you get it twice." But immediately, he sobered, and his face took on a serious expression. "I don't want you to have any doubt that I'm in love with you. I knew it when I met you. Do you think you can love me, Tyra?"

She stroked his shoulder and at the hairs on his chest, investigating his body. "I wouldn't have left home with you yesterday morning, if I hadn't been positive that I love you. Yes, I love you, and I'm glad that you love me."

"This is it for me, Tyra, and there's no going back."

Chapter 9

Tyra and Byron spent much of the following day in Nassau, Bahamas. She bought a dancing monkey dressed in red and black and a white, lacey accordion fan. Although she shopped along with Byron, he made his purchases discretely, and she didn't know what he bought. Except when eating, he hardly took his hands off her, and whenever she looked at him, he was already looking at her. He smiled easily and hugged her frequently. His every move said, I love you. She'd never been so happy.

That evening, she dressed in an off-white floor-length sheath that draped over one shoulder and left the other one bare. She had practiced walking in the three-inch heel sandals and was confident that she wouldn't fall because of them. When he tapped on her door at seven twenty-five, she opened it and gasped at him in a black tuxedo with royal blue accessories. Her hand went involuntarily to her stomach. *What was she doing with a man who looked like this?*

When he kissed her cheek, she realized that he didn't want to ruin her makeup, but she didn't think it was the appropriate time to tell him that she didn't wear any, only mascara on her upper lashes. She sniffed. If he was wearing YSL, she'd hit the jackpot.

"Thanks for my wonderful cologne," he said. "It's my favorite. I've been using it for years, ever since it came out. I waited till now to tell you, in case you liked the way it smells. I really love this scent. How did you happen to give it to me?"

"Just another one of my clever traits," she said, more coyly than she'd intended. "Everything about you interests me."

A smile flowed over his face. "Did I talk in my sleep last night?" Her eyes widened. "If I didn't, how'd you happen to choose this dress? You wear it like a queen. I was afraid you'd wear a red one, and my accessories would clash with it. I didn't think about that when I packed them."

"You look great in it," she said, "and you'd match any dress that wasn't green."

He tested the lock on her door, took her hand and headed for the dining room.

"We're sitting at the captain's table tonight," he said, and she heard the pride in his voice. "I met him this afternoon while you were napping, and I was stunned to get a call from him about an hour ago, inviting us to dine with him. It seems that his dad and my dad were at Ohio State together. They were both on the football team, and they're frat brothers. Dad will be delighted to know about this. The captain's parents are on this cruise. I guess he mentioned me to his dad, and you can guess the rest."

"What a wonderful coincidence."

"Yeah. I used to wonder if my dad did any studying when he was at the university. He was really popular."

"Of course he studied, or he wouldn't be a first-rate surgeon. With his charisma, to be popular he only had to show up. Besides, he's a very serious person."

"That's true. Have you ever felt as if you had the world on a string?" He hugged her to his side. "Right now, the whole world is mine, and I just started living. Ah, sweetheart, you're so…I don't know."

She understood his feelings as well as his inability to articulate them, for she'd been on a high since she awakened that morning with one of his arms around her and his other pinning her to the mattress. "If you feel like I feel," she said, "it's unexplainable. I just don't want anything to happen that will bring me down out of these clouds. I didn't know I could be so happy."

He squeezed her fingers. "This is one of those times when I'd give anything if I had my piano. I express myself best when I'm sitting at that grand."

"You didn't do badly last night," she said and bit the flesh on the inside of her right jaw.

He pushed the button at the elevator that would take them to the captain's dining room. "You make a man feel ten feet tall and bullet proof." The minute he said it a cloud descended over his face. Who should join them at the elevator but the stranger who had shown an interest in Tyra.

Visibly annoyed, Byron spoke to the man. "Good evening. Are you going to the captain's dinner?"

The man appeared frustrated. "Is that where this elevator leads? I thought I was going to dinner in that restaurant where we usually eat. I just followed you."

"That elevator is in the bank to your left."

"Thanks. Good night," the man said as he hastily fled the elevator.

"My common sense tells me to believe him, but that was just too bloody convenient."

"Let it go. That little man is no match for you, and you know it."

"Well, at least he didn't leer at you. I don't blame him for wanting you, only for being foolish enough to think I'll tolerate his insolence."

"Honey, he's not important," she said as the elevator arrived. "Gosh, the captain even rides an elegant elevator. Get a load of this ceiling," she said of the twinkling stars that lit the elevator. He looked up, and that seemed to restore his former mood. With his arms wrapped around her, he kissed her seconds before the elevator came to a halt.

"Good evening, sir, madam," a uniformed attendant said. "Right this way."

Shortly after midnight, as she strolled with Byron to their quarters, Tyra began anticipating the night to come in Byron's arms. She wondered if she was possessed by memories of the way he'd loved her the night before, of his hot passion and the way he'd rocked her time and time again to mindless oblivion, teasing her, possessing her and telling her without words that she belonged to him and him alone.

At her stateroom, he took the card key, opened the door and gazed down at her. She had noticed before that he took nothing for granted, and he didn't now, but didn't move until she said, "Aren't you coming in?"

He smiled, splayed his hand in her back and walked in behind her. "What's this?" She gasped. A large bouquet of red roses in a crystal bowl sat in the middle of the coffee table. A platter containing miniature sausages, dips, finger sandwiches, grapes, crackers, cheese and fresh figs rested beside the roses, and a cooler with two bottles of white Burgundy wine stood beside the table. On her dresser, she saw wine glasses, napkins and chocolates.

She stared at Byron, her face a question mark. "I didn't want you to get hungry. It's been almost four hours since we ate dinner."

"But that was a seven-course banquet," she said, as she placed her silver mesh purse, which had belonged to her mother, on the bed. "Thank you for these beautiful roses. Truth is, I didn't eat much dinner. The occasion, the breath-taking ambiance, all of it practically overwhelmed me."

"It was an exceptional evening," he said, "but I thought it was because you seemed so perfect for it."

If he'd voiced his true feelings, he would have betrayed himself, and the time for that hadn't come. Neither the atmosphere nor the opportunity to meet an old and dear friend of his father's had affected him as she did. He'd been too proud to eat, proud of her and proud that he was his father's son, so he'd only gone through the motions.

She twirled around with her arms high and her face toward the ceiling as if she were embracing the sun. "If we had some of our favorite music, it would be perfect."

"We'll make our own music," he said, though it surprised him that he'd said it aloud. She walked up to him with her arms open, and like nail to magnet, he walked into them and lost himself. Hours later, exhausted, drained and as happy as a man could be, he sat up in bed, reached over and poured two glasses of wine.

"Here's to us," he said, and without warning something akin to fear gripped him. The feeling startled him, because he wasn't used to it. Did he deserve such happiness? He put the glass down and gazed at the woman beside him, a woman who held within her his happiness, his hopes for a future, a home with a loving wife and children. He let out a long, harsh breath. Suppose it didn't work out. Suppose she and Andy didn't get along.

She inched closer to him. "What is it, Byron? What's the matter?"

He thought for a minute. He'd loved before, but not like that, and not with more than himself at stake. "It amazes me how well you can read me," he said. "For a minute there, I doubted that I deserved such happiness."

She startled him when she said, "Don't worry. You mean everything to me. I'll never let you down. Never." If she was a mind reader, he didn't want to know it.

"I believe that," he said, clinked her glass and drained his.

He felt her elbow nudge him. "What are we going to do when we're back in the States, and you're living with your family and I'm living with mine?"

"We can always make out in the back seat of my Cadillac, in your foyer and other places that teenagers love. I used to babysit for our neighbors, and as soon as the couple left, I'd call my girlfriend."

"Shame on you. That was very bad."

"Yeah. As I think of it, I was lucky." He enclosed her in his arms turned out the light and tucked her nude body, spoon-fashion to his. "Good night baby." She wiggled against his arousal, and he took them both on a fast ride to ecstasy.

The next evening, Sunday, after they reached the Baltimore-Washington Thurgood Marshall International Airport, he picked up the car he'd rented and headed home. "I hope you don't mind if I stop for a minute to see Andy. It's been so long since I saw him, and it's the first time we've ever been separated. I need to see how he is. Then, I'll take you home."

"Of course, I don't mind. It's what I expected you'd do."

When Byron unlocked the front door, Andy barreled down the stairs at a neck-breaking speed. "Daddy! Daddy!" He launched himself into his father's arms. "Gee Dad, you were gone so long."

He had missed the child, and he had to control the fierce hug that he longed to give him. Kissing the boy's cheek, he said, "You actually grew in the short time I was away. Have you been good to Aunt Jonie?"

"Yes, sir. I didn't give her any trouble, Dad, but I got real tired of grits. She loves that stuff. I like it, but not every single morning." He looked toward the door. "Hi, Miss Tyra." Byron put the boy down to see if he'd go to Tyra, and to his surprise, the child walked over to her and held out his hand for a handshake. But Tyra ignored it, opened her arms, and Andy settled into them.

"I don't know if you have one of these," she told him, "but I saw it in Nassau, and I thought you'd like it." She handed him the bag. He opened it and looked at the monkey dressed in red and black.

"He walks, dances and jumps," she said.

Andy pushed the button and fell out on the floor laughing when the twenty-four-inch-high monkey bared his teeth and jumped up and down. "I'm gonna name him Nassau," he said, hugging her. "Look, Daddy. Isn't he cool?"

"Yes. You get acquainted with Nassau while I take Miss Tyra home. I'll be back in a little over an hour."

Andy kissed them goodbye in an absentminded way for only Nassau had his full attention. "Hurry up and come back, Dad. Bye, Miss Tyra, and thanks for Nassau."

"That boy is my life," he said to Tyra as he drove her home. "Since he was two weeks old, he's had only me. Aunt Jonie bends over backward to avoid his thinking of her as a motherly figure, although she loves him as much as I do. But she's a super realist. She claims that, because of her age, which is seventy, she probably won't live until he no longer needs a mother and that he should look to a younger woman.

"She's both right and wrong, but she tried to be a mother to me, and I suppose that was enough for her. Dad didn't let her assume that role fully, and I guess he was wise. He always said his children were his responsibility, and he wasn't handing it over to anybody."

Darlene greeted them as they entered Tyra's home, her face alight with a know-it-all expression. "Hi, you two. I thought you were having too much fun to come home."

"Hi, Darlene," Tyra said, hugging her sister. "We were due back this evening, and we're here, so cut the drama."

"Hi, Byron." She looked at Tyra. "How was it?"

"Awful," Byron said, moving to within inches of Darlene and towering over her. "You never saw such weather, such waves, such lousy food and so many sick people. What else can I tell you?"

"Oh," Darlene said, clearly disappointed. "Gee. I thought you'd come back on cloud nine. Too bad. Come on in, and I'll get you some tea. Maggie made a caramel cake that's to die for. Want some?"

"Wrap a slice for me," he said. "I promised Andy I'd be back in around an hour, and I try to keep my word to him."

Darlene wrapped the cake and gave it to Byron. "See you again soon, I hope."

"You bet."

Tyra looked at Byron, unaware of her threatening stance. He grinned. "Don't worry. I'd kiss you if she was sitting on my shoulder." He wrapped his arms around her and singed her with one of the hottest kisses he'd ever given her.

"The weather couldn't possibly have been all that bad," Darlene said as she passed on the way to the stairs. "I sure wouldn't mind being made that miserable."

"Nobody said we were miserable, Darlene," Tyra said after Byron left. "Also, it didn't rain one drop, the food was out of sight and there was plenty of it twenty-four/seven."

"But he said—"

"He was telling you to mind your business."

"By the way, who's Andy?"

"Andy is Byron's four-year-old son. Byron has been a widower since Andy was two weeks old."

"Hmm. Did you have a good time? Clark doesn't like the fact that you went away with Byron, but I think it's so romantic. And after the way he kissed you, I guess you two are on the same page now. I can see that you love him, 'cause you don't even look the same."

"Honey, you love drama. If Maggie tells me that, I'll believe it."

"Humph. Maggie's such a realist that she's negative half the time. You look glamorous and radiant. You don't have to tell me about it. I can guess. I'm almost thirty, remember?"

"You're twenty-seven and nosey. But I did have a wonderful time, and I can't wish more for you than a man like Byron. All right?"

"I'll definitely buy that."

"Maggie's at Sunday evening church service, and she'll eat with some of the sisters there. Let's defrost a pizza, have a glass of wine and call it supper."

Darlene readily agreed. "Works for me."

Byron returned home to find Andy engrossed in the monkey's antics. "Daddy, he even grunts and sings. He walks, jumps, dances and says yes and no. I have to call Miss Tyra and thank her again. And I'm not going to let any of the kids play with him 'cause I can't get another one unless you and Miss Tyra go back to Nassau. How far is Nassau, Dad?"

"Several thousand miles. Where's Aunt Jonie?"

"In the family room watching reruns of *Matlock*. She said we're having lasagna and a lettuce and tomato salad for dinner."

He went into the family room and greeted Jonie. She turned off the television and looked at him. "Was it all that you wanted it to be, son?"

He sat in a chair opposite her, braced his elbows on his thighs and cupped his chin with his palms. "That and so much more. Thank you for keeping Andy for me."

"I'm glad. Soon as I saw her, I knew she was the one. Supper's ready and the table's set, so we can eat."

They finished eating, and he cleared the table, put the

dishes in the dishwasher and tidied the kitchen. After playing Scott Joplin's "The Entertainer" for Andy, he trudged up the stairs. When a piece of music settled in his son's head, the boy could listen to it repeatedly for hours, but the monotony of "The Entertainer" got to him, and after playing it the third time, he quit, telling Andy that the monkey was bored with it.

He noticed the red light flashing on his phone and sat down to check his messages. "It's real urgent, Mr. Whitley, otherwise I wouldn't call you on the weekend."

"What is it, Mr. Tate?" he asked. Murphy Tate was forbidding his sixteen-year-old daughter to marry the boy whose baby she carried, yet he claimed he couldn't provide for her and the child.

"Mr. Tate, I cannot force Social Services to take care of your daughter's expenses when you say you're going to sue the child's father and his family for money. Social Services will expect you to use that money to care for your child and grandchild."

"They can't do that. I'm gonna sue for damages and for…for humiliation and things like that."

"But what about your daughter? She needs medical care, and you say that's not your responsibility."

"It ain't. It's that boy's responsibility."

"Look. I have to put my son to bed. I'll call you tomorrow from my office. Good night."

He read a part of "Hiawatha" to Andy to satisfy the boy's current craving for Native American lore, tucked the child into bed and went to his room. He could hardly wait to hear her voice.

"Hello, sweetheart," he said when Tyra answered the phone. "Did you have dinner?"

"Darlene heated individual frozen pizzas. Maggie's at church, and neither of us wanted to cook or go out." Her voice softened. "What about you?"

"We had lasagna and a salad. After all those calories I took in the past few days, I didn't even need that."

"I know. After four days of leisure and being treated like a queen, among other things, I dread being back at work tomorrow. I can't think of anything but our…nights together."

"If I think about that, I'll be in Frederick as fast as that Cadillac will get me there. In any case, work was waiting for me when I got back home. I had a message on my business cell phone. You know I volunteer at the Legal Aid Society. The guy is self-centered and a beer guzzler to boot. His daughter's pregnant. He refuses to let her marry the child's father. He wants Social Services to take care of her, and he's planning to sue the boy's parents because having a pregnant teenage daughter humiliates him. It's the damnedest—"

"Wait a minute. Is that drunk's name Murphy Tate?"

He had a premonition that he wouldn't like what came next. "Yeah. You know him?"

"I've never met the jerk," she said in a decidedly cooler voice, "but I certainly know about him. His daughter's boy-friend is my client, and that man won't allow him to do one thing for that girl nor will he do anything for her himself."

"Wait a minute. You mean you're counseling one side of this case and I'm counseling the other. This won't do," Byron said. "Turn it over to one of your colleagues. The man may be a jerk, as you put it, but he has the right to decide what happens to his daughter, and he thinks she's too young to get married. Besides, that boy is misguided. He's underage, and that means he hasn't the right to marry. Neither does she."

"Sure. But she's not too young to have a baby. How can you go along with such stupidity? That girl doesn't even get checkups, because her father won't let her out of the house to go to a clinic. You're counseling that man to deny that boy his rights."

He had phoned her because he needed to hear her voice, but he did not need to hear her ice-cold lecture. "Look. We'll discuss this another time. Sleep well." He hung up, stretched out on the bed and wondered if what he remembered of the past few days amounted to hallucination.

Tyra stared at the phone. How dare he! She didn't care what kind of magic powers he had in bed, damned if she was going to take that from him. Hang up on her, would he? She dialed his house phone number.

"What do you mean by hanging up on me?" she said without preliminaries when he answered. "That was rude."

"I did not hang up on you. I said good night, and I am not going to argue with you about that or anything else. If you think I did, I'm giving you the chance to hang up on me, and you'll be even."

She stared hard at the phone, getting madder by the second, dropped the phone into its cradle and burst into tears.

When she reached her office the following morning, it did not surprise her to find that she had three calls from Jonathan. She phoned him at once. "What's going on, Jonathan?"

"Miss Cunningham, we have to do something before Becky starts showing, and she needs to be seeing a gynecologist. If we could get married, she could stay with me and my folks till I finish school. Dad said he'd take care of her medical bills. Her old man's ignorant. He doesn't care what happens to the baby, but what about Becky? She said he's going to sue my folks for punitive damages, because she's pregnant and because that humiliates him. He humiliates *her* with his boorish behavior."

She thought for a few minutes. "The first thing we have to do is ensure that she has proper care. Then, we have to see what your rights are. I suspect that means getting a lawyer."

"Miss Cunningham, you know I can't afford a lawyer."

"I won't expect you to. Just leave that to me, and I'll do my best." But what lawyer would she get? In Byron, Murphy Tate had one of the best lawyers around, and he didn't even have to pay him. Surely Byron didn't countenance the man's position; it was inhumane. She resisted the urge to call Byron. *I ought to chew him out, but that would only make things between us worse than they are, provided they can get any worse.*

Thinking of the way in which their relationship had plummeted to a halt, she feared sinking into depression. "Damned if I'll let it kill me," she said to the gray wall that faced her. *I know I love him, and he loves me, but he's a stubborn as I am, and he's as loyal as I am. So he'll do everything he can for his client, and I'll do everything I can for Jonathan. In the meantime, we'll grow farther and farther apart. What did I do to deserve such a blow to my psyche?*

She wrestled with the problem for most of the morning, and by noon a decision began to take shape in her mind. She phoned Darlene and gave her an account of the problem. "It's a matter of human rights and women's rights, straight down your alley."

"Let me get this straight," Darlene said. "You're telling me that you're going to fight Byron over this?"

"I am not fighting Byron, Darlene. This is not time for drama or for rose-colored glasses. We're talking about a girl's rights and maybe her life, not to speak of the well-being of that baby."

"I'll be delighted to take it on. Apart from granting permission for those kids to marry, that man doesn't have a leg to stand on. In fact, if he prevents her from getting health care, I could guarantee him a vacation in the slammer. I can't see Byron going along with that."

"He may be unaware of it. As Tate's counselor, he's only getting one side of it, and maybe not even the whole truth."

"And you're not even going to straighten him out?"

"Darlene, you know that would be unethical."

"Unethical my foot. If he was kissing me the way I saw him kiss you, I'd straighten him out. Heck, I get weak in the knees thinking about it. You seeing him tonight?"

"I haven't spoken with Byron since last night when I hung up on him."

"You did what? Have you lost your mind?"

"Probably. But when he suggested that I turn the case over to one of my colleagues, I saw red. He didn't consider doing that. Why should I?"

"Gosh, Sis. I'm beginning to think I don't know you. You hung up on Byron Whitley? Whew! Girl, you got guts."

"Cool off. He may look like Adonis incarnate, but he's a man, and you should never let a man walk over you, not matter how much you love him."

"Yeah. Well, I'll ask my supervisor if I can handle this case gratis. If you've got any more shocks, wait awhile with them, I'm not sure I can handle any more surprises today."

"Thanks for helping my client. Dad would be proud of you."

"I know. He was always doing things for others. See you tonight."

Tyra hung up and began preparing a brief for her sister. She was confident that Darlene's supervisors would allow her to take the case gratis, for its merits would be as clear to them as to her. She wished Byron would call and apologize for suggesting that she turn the case over to one of her colleagues. How could he ask her to do so unprofessional a thing? She went to the closet-size nook that she and her colleagues referred to as the coffee room to get a cup of coffee and encountered Matt, who slouched against the door jamb drinking coffee.

"Hi, Tyra. How was your long weekend? Go any place interesting?"

If she told a little, she'd have to tell all. "Yep. I had a bang-up weekend. It's good to do that at the end of summer. Kind of prepares one for the coming cold weather. How was your weekend?"

"Fantastic." The memory of it seemed to brighten his face.

"Never before in my life have I spent two whole days doing absolutely nothing. I put peanut butter and jelly on some bread, got a glass of milk and had my breakfast. When I got hungry again, I duplicated that. For dinner, I added a tomato and an apple. That was Saturday, and I was so happy with the way that day went that I did the same thing Sunday, with one exception. I found a piece of cheese in the refrigerator and added that for lunch. I feel de-stressed, rested and rejuvenated."

She enjoyed a good laugh. "Where did your body hang out while the time passed?"

"On the hammock in my back garden for most of the day. I had my radio, and that was all I needed. Try it sometime."

"I may do that, although I think my siblings would have me committed. They think I'd never do anything frivolous."

"They're probably right, Tyra. By the way. My ex-wife met someone, and she's been spending some time at his place. So I may be a free man earlier than either of us thought."

Her eyes widened. "You're going to charge her with adultery?"

"She's still married to me, and we are not legally separated. My mom always said, 'The Lord Will Provide,' and looks like she was right."

Tyra walked back to her office deep in thought. How quickly one's fortunes could change. In the week since she last saw him, Matt had gone from despair to hope, and in the meantime, she'd gone from euphoria to misery. She shrugged. "It was great while it lasted, and I don't intend to shed another tear over it," she said aloud as she walked into her office.

Her grandfather's words pounded like drums in her head. "Talk's easy done, it takes money to buy land."

Why couldn't she talk with Byron and have some assurance that they still meant everything to each other? She needed evidence of the love he'd lavished on her the previous weekend. But Byron didn't call her, and each time she reached for the phone to call him, she hung up without dialing, telling herself that he had started the problem and he should straighten it out.

Tired of waiting for Darlene's call confirming that she could take Jonathan's case, Tyra took the brief on which she was trying to work and went to the staff lounge in the hope that a change of scenery would alter her mood.

"Don't tell me the princess deigns to join the common folk," Christopher Fuller sneered. "What's the matter, your weekend didn't pan out?"

"What do you know about my weekend?"

"Plenty. Not that anything you'd ever do interests me."

"Of course not," she sneered right back at him. "That's why you're always sniffing around." She went back to her office and got busy. Anger always seemed to energize her, and a couple of hours later, she completed the brief, e-mailed it to her sister and received an immediate answer that Darlene would take the case.

"Byron is a heavy-duty attorney," Darlene said when she called Tyra. "I'll do my best, but I'm not in his league."

"Your best is all I need. Both the law and human decency are on Jonathan's side."

"Not about marrying the girl, but about everything else. You hang in there, Sis. I've got to get busy on this. Imagine me tangling up with Byron Whitley! I must be dreaming."

Tyra telephoned Jonathan. "I've engaged a lawyer for you, Jonathan. She's attorney Darlene Cunningham, and I want you to call her right now at this number." She gave him Darlene's phone number.

"Is she your sister or your mother?"

"She's my sister. Go on and call her." The boy thanked her and, for the first time, she heard hope in his young voice.

Her feeling of relief about Jonathan was short-lived when she saw on her desk calendar that she had an appointment with Erica

Saunders. Dealing with that woman was surely payment for her sins. Half an hour with Erica was nothing less than torture.

Byron read the letter for a third time. Tyra had declared war and enlisted the firm of Lawson, Myrtle and Coppersmith as an ally. Furthermore, her sister was representing that powerful firm. But hell! He'd handle it. A man had the lawful right to say what happened to his underage children. Still... He threw up his hands, then leaned back in his chair. Should he phone Darlene or Tyra?

He didn't admit to himself that he'd use any excuse to talk with Tyra. She was furious with him, and he couldn't understand why. He'd offered a practical solution to a sticky situation, but it had twisted her lid. He loved her so much that it pained him to think that he may have lost points with her. To prevent her caller ID from giving her the upper hand, he blocked his number and dialed Tyra at her office.

"Hello, Tyra," he said when she answered. "This is Byron. We need to talk. I just got an e-mail letter from Darlene, and she's suing my client for child abuse and child endangerment. Is she serious?"

"Hello, Byron. For the answer to that question, you have to ask Darlene. She is representing her firm as Jonathan's lawyer and, incidentally, they didn't hesitate to take the case gratis. You'd better make sure your client isn't misleading you."

"I know the law, Tyra."

He waited for her comment to that, but the silence pierced his ears. Now what? He hated loose ends in his life, and he especially didn't want them with her. Not after having experienced perfect union with her. He decided to try, but he was not going to let her or any other woman bring him to his knees.

"Tyra, are you content to let our relationship peter out without telling me why?"

"If y...you don't know why, it would be useless to tell you."

"I'm trying to get an understanding here, Tyra, and I'd appreciate it if you'd refrain from getting high-minded."

"Getting what? Why…" She seemed to check herself. "I have a client coming in a few minutes. Can we talk this evening after work?'

"All right. I'll call you at six. Bye for now."

"Bye."

Chapter 10

Telling herself that she needed to discuss Jonathan's problems with Darlene before her sister went out for the evening, Tyra rushed home from work, although she had not shared her intentions with her sister. When five o'clock arrived and Darlene hadn't come home, Tyra faced the fact that she'd lied to herself, that she had dashed out of her office and scrambled for a taxi—though she more often traveled home by public transportation—in order not to miss Byron's six o'clock call.

More subdued now, she changed into black jeans, a yellow, cowl-neck, cotton knit sweater and black sneakers and went into the kitchen to help Maggie. Instead of the housekeeper, she found a note that Maggie had attached to the refrigerator.

"Tyra, dearie, since it's just you tonight, I made your favorite—chicken and dumplings and string beans with smoked ham hocks. You can have ice cream and caramel cake for dessert, provided you have any room left. Darlene phoned and said she has a date, though she didn't say with who, and Clark called to say he's still in Washington. I'll be home around eleven. Maggie."

She went over to the stove. Lifted the pot lids, looked down at her dinner and licked her lips. Having gotten used to wine with her dinner during her weekend with Byron, she looked for the wine that Clark kept in one of the refrigerators, found a bottle of Chardonnay and set her mind on enjoying her favorite meal.

"Oh, gosh," she said aloud, glancing at her watch, "now who on earth could that be just as I'm expecting Byron's call?" She took her time getting to the door, aware that her entire demeanor bespoke annoyance. Why couldn't the high-school students aiming to get college scholarships pick more reasonable times to sell their magazines? She looked through the peephole and saw only what looked like the back of a gray-clad shoulder. She slipped the chain and cracked open the door.

"Byron! What a surprise!"

"May I come in?"

Her heart began a wild thudding in her chest. He seemed taller, bigger, more handsome and…had his eyes always been that dreamy and seductive? He stood there, like hot quicksand, sucking her into him.

"You going to make me stand out here?" he asked her as a grin spread over his face.

"Oh, no. Sorry. It's just…you surprised me." She took his hand, as if to pull him inside, walked in with him and closed the door.

"I was hoping you'd have dinner with me," he said, the famous grin no longer there to mesmerize her. "And I made the trip over here to lessen the chance that you'd turn me down. Will you…have dinner with me?"

She opened her mouth and closed it without uttering a word.

"Did I make a mistake?" he asked. But with his charisma

once more in full bloom and that grin splashed across his face like summer sunshine, she knew his question was merely rhetorical. Not even he believed she'd turn him down.

"Thanks for the invitation," she said doing her best to keep a straight face. With effort, she creased her brow into a slight frown as if musing over some problem. "Tell you what, Maggie left some good stuff on the stove, she and Darlene are out, so why don't you eat here with me? We can talk because it'll be just the two of us, and Maggie left enough for four people. It'll be ready as soon as I heat it up."

"Sounds good to me," he said, "but if I'd known I was eating here, I would have brought wine for the table and flowers for you. What can I do to help?"

"We'll have to settle for Clark's taste in Chardonnays," she said and put her hands behind her where they couldn't touch him and ease their itch to caress him. After all, she was supposed to be mad at him, wasn't she? His showing up unexpectedly and looking like a brown Adonis had shaken her to the core and undermined her resolve to keep a distance between them. She told herself to get her act together.

"We can…er…s-set the table," she said, annoyed at herself because her childhood stammer seemed to have returned.

When she started toward the dining room, he stopped her. "Why can't we eat in the kitchen?"

"Because…look at you. You're dressed for the White House. I can't—"

The man didn't plan to play fair. He gathered her to him, wrapped her close and brushed his lips over hers. "I'll remove the jacket. I just want to be with you. I don't care what we talk about or if we talk at all. I missed you, Tyra. Kiss me, baby, and let me feel that I'm still important to you."

He was honest and open, and she could be no less. "You *are* important to me. Oh, Byron! You are."

She parted her lips, and he went into her. Frissons of heat

plowed through her as his hands skimmed over her body, heating her, sending her blood on a mad dash to her loins, possessing her and reminding her of the pleasure he gave her when he lay buried deep inside of her.

"Baby, I don't want us to lose what we've found together."

"Me neither," she said in a voice muffled against his shoulder. "But if we talk about it right now, we probably won't eat together. I was mad at you. I'm not right now, but I know how tenacious you can be."

He moved her away from him, his smile luminous. "I don't plan to leave here with you angry at me. What time will Darlene and Maggie be home?"

"I'm not telling. Come on. Let's set the table. Aren't you hungry?"

His left eyebrow shot up. "For what?"

She looked at him through partially lowered eyelids. "Behave yourself. The flatware's in that drawer over there, and if you look straight ahead, you'll see the wine glasses. Since we're eating in the kitchen, the silver can stay where it is, and paper napkins can suffice."

"I don't like paper napkins," he said, giving the impression of a pout. "They're too small."

She whirled around to get a linen napkin, and when he reached out to stop her, his hand brushed against her breast, its nipple still erect from their caress. He stared down at her. "You're as sensitive to me as I am to you, and I am not going to let this tiff we're having wreck what we feel for each other. Is that clear?"

"Then I take it you know how to compromise," she said, moved away from him and opened the drawer that contained napkins. "Now, we can keep your Neiman Marcus trousers free of foreign matter." She ushered him to the kitchen and pointed to the table.

"Have a seat wherever suits your fancy." She filled one

large serving dish with the chicken and dumplings and another with string beans and smoked ham hocks. "No first course tonight, because we're going to eat all of this," she said, reaching for the serving spoon.

He took her hand, "Lord, we thank you for this food and for the love we have for each other."

A little of the steam went out of her, and when she looked at him, she realized that her annoyance at him must have dissipated. "Thanks for saying grace, Byron. I'm ashamed to say that when I'm real hungry, I tend to forget it."

He tasted the dumplings first. "Hmm. This is good stuff. I once drove all the way to Lancaster, Pennsylvania, to get some of this. Give Maggie my compliments. No. I'll do that myself. Aunt Jonie's effort at this didn't go over well with either Andy or me."

"Want me to send her a recipe for it?"

"I'd rather you came over and made it. Aunt Jonie resists learning what she doesn't have to learn. This is wonderful, Tyra."

"Wait 'til you taste her string beans."

"I'll get to that in a minute. Where's that Chardonnay?" She nodded toward the refrigerator. He opened the wine, filled their glasses and lifted his in a toast. "The ineffable joy of forgiving and being forgiven forms an ecstasy that might well be the envy of the gods.'"

"Quoted from…"

"Elbert Hubbard in *The Note Book*."

She raised her own glass. "According to William Blake, 'It is easier to forgive an enemy than to forgive a friend.'"

He put his glass on the table. "I think we're talking serious now, so let's forget about the quotes. Does that mean you can't forgive whatever I said that upset you? You haven't even told me what it was."

"You suggested that I turn my case over to one of my colleagues in order to avoid conflict with you. You didn't suggest that you would turn the case over to one of your colleagues, although you're doing that on a volunteer basis, and it's my job. I'm a trained professional, Byron, and I approach my work with integrity and honor. I'm not doing it for fun. I want to make a difference in the lives of people who need what I have to offer, and I suppose that's why you're doing it. I've been hurt that you think I'd do such a frivolous thing."

He stopped eating, leaned back in the ladder-back chair and ran the fingers of his left hand back and forth over his chin. She knew him well enough now to expect that he wouldn't comment until he'd given the matter reasonable thought. So she served herself another helping of string beans, cut a piece of the pork hock and continued eating. To her astonishment, she had no anxiety as to what his comment would be.

He picked up his fork, continued eating for a bit and then said, "I can see how that would ring your bell. It wouldn't have annoyed me, I suppose because I wouldn't have taken it seriously."

"But *you* were serious, Byron."

"You're right. I was, and I apologize. From the way you related it, it smacks of male chauvinism, and I like to pride myself on not being guilty of that. Just don't walk out on me if my client wins."

"He doesn't have a chance, and you know it. I can't figure out why you'd waste time representing him. He's unprincipled."

"I'm his counselor, as in social advisor. If I represent him, it will be because Darlene forces me to."

She served herself more chicken and dumplings, looked at him and asked him, "Don't you want some more?"

"Yeah, but the way you're going after that, I was hesitant to ask, for fear there won't be enough for you."

"Have you seen how much is in the serving dish, not to speak of what's in the pot. I'm not a pig."

Laughter poured out of him, almost as if in relief. "Of

course not, but I can testify to your love for chicken with dumplings and string beans." He refilled their wine glasses. "Not bad. Tell Clark I said he knows his Chardonnay. I'll clean the kitchen."

"Not yet. We have to have dessert."

He stared at her. "You're kidding."

"Would I pass up homemade caramel cake and vanilla ice cream?"

"Probably not. I sure won't."

After enjoying the dessert and the remainder of the wine, they cleaned the kitchen together, laughing, touching and teasing each other.

"Want to go fishing with Andy, Dad and me tomorrow morning? I can be over here at about six-thirty, and we'll be on the lake by seven. Early bird catches the worm."

"Do I have to wake up, or can I do all this in my sleep like a somnambulist?"

"If Andy's willing to sacrifice his sacrosanct sleep to go fishing with his granddad, surely you'll do the same for the company of the man you love. Uh…ahem. Right?"

"That's below the belt. I can't do breakfast for four that early."

"Not to worry about breakfast. We'll cook by the lake. What about it?"

"Okay, but call me forty minutes before you get here."

"Gladly. Now, tell me this. Is everything straight between you and me?"

She removed her rubber gloves, placed them on the counter to dry and looked at him. "Am I mad at you, you mean?"

"That's one way of dicing it. Yes."

"I'm not mad at you, and I'm getting over being hurt, because you said you were wrong."

"I'm serious, sweetheart. I want us back where we were when I left you here at your foyer Sunday night."

Why did he insist on reasoning through their problem…

that is, if they had one? She wished men wouldn't have to be logical in everything. Couldn't he just… Irritated all of a sudden for no reason, she said, "You were very adept at getting us to that point. Doing it again ought to be easier."

He stared down at her. "I could take that two ways."

She didn't give quarter, but stared right back at him. "Take it the way that suits you best."

His gaze didn't waver, and when his left eye narrowed slightly, goose bumps popped out on her arms. Her head said, Don't toy with him, but her body reminded her that she could do with him as she pleased. "You're a quick study," she said, getting bolder, "and if you know what you want, what's stopping you?"

Like a streak of lightning, his arm shot out, and he pinned her to his body, so tightly that air couldn't get between them. "If *you're* a quick study, this will teach you not to play with me." He picked her up and carried her up the stairs. "Where's your room?"

"I'm not telling you."

He didn't put her down. "You want it right here?"

She eased her arms around his neck, rested her head on his shoulder and said, "Down the hall to your right." She told herself that she'd have to find other ways of getting what she wanted.

Beside her bed, he set her on her feet, and looked at her. "May I undress you?"

What a time for gentle behavior! She itched to see him without his famous control, open and as passion-driven as she, with some rough edges showing. "You could at least kiss me."

With his arms tight around her, he whispered, "I may be putty in your hands, sweetheart, but be careful not to remind me of that fact." His tongue slid over the seams of her lips, and she opened to him, greedy and anxious to suck him into her. Knowing what to expect of him now, she locked her hands to his buttocks and gripped him to her as he teased her with the feel of his tongue streaking in and out of her mouth, promising, telling her what was to come. She sucked it and squeezed it in pulsing motions, telling him in return what lay in store for him. He spread his legs and brought her closer, flush against his erection. When she moaned, he put his hand on her breast, thrust his hand in the bodice of her sweater, released her breast and sucked its nipple into his mouth. Her keening cry seemed to encourage him, and he suckled vigorously as if he'd hungered for weeks.

The moisture of her desire dampened her and she begged shamelessly, "Honey, put me in the bed and—"

"You're not going to challenge me again. You hear?" He rubbed against her, heating her to boiling point.

"I won't promise. I want you in me right now. I need you, Byron."

He pulled her sweater over her head, threw it on a nearby chair, unzipped her jeans, dragged them down and flung them over his shoulder, pulled back the covers, lifted her and put her on the bed. But she sat up and worked at getting rid of his trousers while he removed his shirt.

She stared at the treasure before her—big, hard, ready and all hers, leaned forward and eased him between her lips. Liking the taste, she took more of him, but he quickly moved away. "Are you angry because I did that?" she asked him. "I figured if you did that to me, I could do the same." He settled her in bed, and when she opened her arms to him in a gesture every woman understands, he nearly fell into them.

"Angry? How could I be? It's the most delicious feeling. But I couldn't afford to make a mistake, and I'm already about to burst."

He bent to her breast, licked the valley between them, and moved with maddeningly slow pace to her left breast, frustrating her until she held her nipple to his mouth. When he sucked it, heat flooded the bottom of her feet and she spread her legs in invitation. He ignored the gesture and charted his own course, skimming his fingers over her flesh as he eased his way down her body. His tongue sampled her navel, and her hips began their slow dance, as he licked and nipped his way to his goal. He'd taught her what to expect, and she thought she'd go mad waiting for the thrust of his tongue. And then he had her, sucking, probing and plunging until he found that spot at which he could drive her wild.

She cried out. "Byron! Honey, give it to me. It's so good. I can't stand it. I think I'm going to die. *Please!*"

Near completion and straining for control, he eased his way up her body, licking and enjoying the taste and scent of her delicate flesh. Her woman's scent excited him, and he wanted to suck her sweet nipple again, but he knew that if he did, it would be over.

"Take me, sweetheart." She raised her knees, took his penis into her hands, caressing and stroking as if she didn't know she could make him lose it. "Baby, easy. Take me in."

She positioned him at the entrance of her vagina, thrust her hips upward, and he sank into her sweet tunnel. He kissed her lips, saying without words that he loved her. Almost immediately, that maddening way she had of pulsating around him rhythmically commenced and became stronger and stronger with each move, until… Oh lord, she'd started squeezing him, and he had to hold on. He couldn't desert her now. What was she saying?

"Byron, honey, I need to burst. I can't stand this. It won't… Oh, lord, I'm…"

Screams poured out of her as she squeezed him so tightly that he could hardly move. "I love…Byron. I…I'm dying."

He heard her words. "Are you straight, baby? Tell me. I—"

"Yes. Yes." Her voice was barely a whisper. Then she accelerated her thrust, tossing her hips up to him in sync with his rhythm, and his whole body shook as he splintered in her

arms, moaning her name. Strung out, vulnerable and practically helpless, he doubted he could move a finger.

At least five minutes had passed when he raised his head,
looked down into her face and said, "I love you. Are you all
right? I mean, did it work for you? Are you satisfied?"

Her hands stroked his back. "Will it always be like this? It
was even better this time than when we were on the cruise,
and I didn't think that possible."

"The more we're together and the better we understand
each other's needs and preferences, the better it will get. Do
you feel sore? I couldn't muster as much control as I needed.
From the minute you took me in your mouth, I was ready to
go." He released a long sigh. "You're so perfect for me."

"And you definitely suit me. I wasn't challenging you
when we were in the kitchen. I just didn't know any other way
to get what I wanted. It didn't seem feminine to blurt out,
'Byron, would you please take me to bed.'"

He couldn't help laughing. "Maybe not that, but if we're
in the right place, you know how to touch me and how to kiss
me, don't you?"

"Suppose we're not in the right place? Oh, well."

"Not to worry, sweetheart. I've begun to recognize your
little moves. If you want me, you'll find a way. We'd better
get up and remove the evidence, because Maggie or Darlene
could come home at any time. People have been known to
change their plans."

She jumped up. "Right. Maggie is famous for precisely that."

Shortly before eleven, standing in her foyer, he stroked her
back, keeping as much distance between them as he could,
because he didn't want to spend the remainder of the night
hard and fighting the sheets. Clearly unaware of his dilemma,
she tried to get as close to him as she could.

"Why don't you want me to hug you?" she asked him, not
bothering to hide her annoyance.

"Because I don't have the option of going back up those stairs with you to your room. As it is, I'll probably be staring at the ceiling most of the night."

"You mean?"

"I mean."

"Oh. I'm sorry, darling. I'll fill a thermos with coffee, and you can drink it on the way to the lake. Cream, no sugar. Right?"

"You're kidding. That's fine for tomorrow morning, but it won't get me through the night." He kissed her on the mouth. "Stay sweet."

He had to get out of there, and quickly. He drove off just as a blue Chevrolet slowed down in front of the house and turned into the garage. Just in time to avoid Maggie's knowing eyes. He hoped Tyra got back into her room before Maggie entered the house, because it would surprise him if anybody could hide the effects of what he and Tyra had just experienced. She didn't know how lucky she was. No. Tyra was blessed. He'd known a few women, but not one, including his wife, who could let herself go and experience mind-blowing ecstasy with him as Tyra could. A woman without pretense or guile, and who didn't have to fake. She took him where he'd never been and gave him feelings that he didn't know he could experience. How had he been so fortunate?

If she thought he would allow a court case to ruin their relationship, he'd show her. He didn't intend to allow anything or anyone to take her from him.

Tyra grabbed the alarm clock and raised her arm to throw it across the room when she remembered why she'd set it. Byron would call her at a quarter of six, but that wouldn't give her time to shower, dress and make the coffee before he arrived. She dressed in her black jeans, a red, cashmere, cowl-neck sweater and black boots, combed down her hair and, as she ambled down the stairs, inserted silver hoops into her ears.

The phone rang as she reached the bottom step, and she raced to the dining room to answer it.

"Hi."

"You sound as if you're wide awake."

"I am. I gotta make your coffee, so I got up a little earlier. What can I make for Andy?"

"If you have any cocoa, he'd love that. I'll bring along a two-cup thermos to put it in. See you shortly, sweetheart."

She made the coffee, filled the sixty-four-ounce picnic thermos with coffee, heated the milk and made the cocoa. She poured some milk into a small thermos, put sugar in a zip lock bag and looked in the foyer closet for her knee-length pea coat. When the doorbell rang, she opened it and looked down at Andy.

"Gee, Miss Tyra, you don't live close to us, do you?" He handed her the thermos, and she took his hand and walked with him to the kitchen. He looked at the large thermos. "If you're bringing that, I'd better go get my dad." Before she could answer, he ran to the door, opened it and raced down the walk. She filled Andy's thermos with cocoa and waited, though she'd begun to get warm in that coat and sweater.

"I'll take my thermos," Andy said, calling attention to his presence.

"Where's your daddy?" she asked the boy.

"Right here, sweetheart. How much coffee did you make?" He kissed her on the mouth, and she glanced down to see an expression of bewilderment of Andy's face.

"Why'd you kiss her, Daddy?"

He put the strap of the thermos over his shoulder and took Andy's hand. "I kissed her because I like her."

"Oh. Don't you like Aunt Jonie?"

She wondered how he'd get out of that. "There are different kinds of like," he said, locked her door and took her hand with his free one.

"Good morning, sir," she said to Lewis Whitey, Byron's

father, who had gotten out of the car and waited for them beside the back door of Byron's Cadillac. She kissed his cheek.

"How are you, Tyra? I'm happy to see you again."

"Grandpa didn't kiss her in the mouth, Daddy."

"You bet he didn't. Did you thank Miss Tyra for getting up early and making cocoa for you?"

"She put cocoa in my thermos? Gee. Thanks, Miss Tyra. My daddy and my granddaddy love coffee, Miss Tyra. Is that why you brought so much?"

"I like it too, Andy."

"It's gonna be cold," the boy said. "Daddy, did you tell her to put on long underwear? I'm wearing too many clothes."

Neither of the men answered him, and she was glad the boy hadn't directed the question to her. She turned so that she could see Andy and his grandfather in the back seat. "Do you usually catch any fish, Andy?"

"Yes, but sometime I need help when the fish is big. I hate to put the worms on my hook. Who's going to put the worms on for you, Miss Tyra?"

If he wanted her to stay in the car while they fished, he'd just given her a good reason. "I haven't thought about that," she said, cast a side glance at Byron and had an urge to punch him. She didn't see anything funny about the boy's question.

They arrived at the lake around seven o'clock as planned. Lewis built a fire under his twin hibachi, dumped a bag of charcoal on it, baited his hook and went over to where Tyra sat on a huge boulder wondering if she had bitten off more than she was willing to chew. She definitely was not putting her hands on any worms.

"I'll bait your hook, Tyra. Byron's waiting for you to ask him to do it, so that he can tease you. I see your relationship has taken a giant step, and nothing could make me happier."

She looked up at him. "How do you know that?"

"I'm seventy-two years old, been there, seen that and done

that. Don't let Andy's smart-alecky behavior get to you. As soon as he's sure you love him, he'll be sticking to you like a tick."

"So far, we get on well," she said, although she didn't think their relationship had been tested.

Lewis confirmed that when he said, "Andy is clever and accomplished beyond his years, and he likes to show off. Don't accept nonsense from him the first time, and it won't be a problem a second time. Do you understand? No matter how cute it seems, correct it."

She looked at Lewis Whitley for a long minute, taking in what he'd said and what he'd left unsaid. "Thank you, sir. I appreciate that more than I can tell you."

"You're welcome. Do we understand each other?" She nodded. He wanted his son to marry her, and if she needed help, he was there for her. However, she refused to join in cahoots with anyone against Byron, not even his father. If she got into trouble with Byron, the two of them would have to work through it together. Still, knowing his father approved of her was like a shot of adrenaline, and she got up, walked out on the edge of the pier, where the wind ripped through her, and cast out her line.

Lewis caught the first fish, a four-pound pike, and immediately cleaned the fish and prepared to coat it with cornmeal and fry it. Andy ran over to Tyra, "Is anything pulling on your line? Daddy's is way over there pulling in a bass, and I don't have a thing."

"I don't have anything on my line, either, Andy. I think I'll go get some coffee."

"I'm going with you, Maybe the fish don't bite when four people are trying to catch them. I always catch them when there's only Daddy, grandpa and me."

She got that undercut, but she didn't plan to comment on it. At the campfire, she handed Andy a paper cup and unscrewed the top of his thermos.

"This is good, a lot more chocolate-like than Daddy and Aunt Jonie make. I love chocolate and caramel. Thanks for the cocoa, Miss Tyra."

Lewis patted Andy on the shoulder. "Tell your daddy we're ready to eat, son."

"When did you make the cornbread?" Tyra asked Lewis.

"Last night. It's cracklin' bread. Byron's fishing for catfish, and this goes great with them. How about a taste of that coffee?"

She poured a cup for him and one for her, sat down on a nearby stump and sipped it, warming her hands with the cup. "Have you caught anything?" Byron asked when he arrived bringing three good-size catfish.

"Not yet," she said. "Right now, I am happy to sit here close to the fire."

Byron walked over to her, bent down, kissed her forehead and whispered, "Andy's right. I should have told you to wear your long johns." She didn't laugh although he enjoyed a good guffaw. He poured a cup of coffee, sipped it and stretched out his legs. "This hits the spot, sweetheart. Don't worry, you'll catch something before we leave."

"Sure," she said. "But I won't enjoy having pneumonia. It's freezing out here."

He brushed her cheek with the tips of his finger, as lightly as if he feared bruising her. "Sorry I can't warm you up the way I'd like to. Be back in a minute." He took a nail from his pocket, nailed the tail of the largest catfish to a nearby tree, made a small incision, and pulled the skin off the fish. He took it to his father. "I did my job with this, but I have no idea how to clean a fish."

"I'll do it. Serve Tyra and Andy some cornbread and a piece of this pike, while I fry the catfish."

"When are you going to eat?"

"When I finish frying this catfish, I'll have some of all of it." Lewis took a long sip of coffee. "This coffee is delicious.

Take good care of her, son. I don't think you'll be able to duplicate her."

"Neither do I, Dad. She's very special."

After enjoying the kind of breakfast he'd loved since early childhood, Byron longed to stretch out with Tyra in his arms and go to sleep, but neither the weather nor the presence of his father and son would permit that.

His dad looked at him and laughed. "Self-control is good discipline, son, and the sooner we learn it the happier we'll be."

"I'm glad you're having such a good time," he said, but Lewis only laughed harder.

"I've known since I was Andy's age that the longer I wanted something, the better it was when I finally got it. Where did he and Tyra go?"

"Andy wanted to help her catch a fish, because she didn't catch anything, and we did."

"How are they getting along?"

"Hard to say. Andy didn't want her to come with us, but she made cocoa for him, and he's delighted she's here. He doesn't like sharing me with other people."

"That's understandable. I wouldn't worry, though. She doesn't chase him, she draws him to her. They'll get on just fine."

Byron stood and looked at his father. "You're talking as if this is a done deal."

Lewis looked into the distance. "No, but I've seen you with a lot of women and not one who could hold a light to Tyra. I knew that when I met her. If she's loving—and I can see that she is—and if she's a good lover, you've got a gold mine. My last word on the subject."

"I'm not arguing with you, Dad, but we've got a few steeples to hurdle."

"They can't be too high."

"You're right. They're not, but they're troublesome."

"Let me tell you something, son. If you're not stubborn, and she's not stubborn, you should be able to sit down together and work it out. Choose a time when no one is likely to interrupt you, when you're totally alone and likely to be for some time."

He understood what his father said and what he hadn't said, but he doubted that talking about it would solve it. He had to tread carefully to avoid crushing her spirit. He looked up and saw that his father watched him like an eagle watches a hawk.

"Does she love you?"

"Yes. She loves me, and I love her. That is not the problem. It has to do with our work, and she and I didn't create the problem."

"I see. So we're dealing with professional pride. If I were you, I'd enjoy losing. Remember that you're famous in these parts. Well, let's clean up. If they don't come back soon, I'm going to check on them."

Byron got a pan of water from the lake and put out the fire, dumped the hibachi, cooled it in the lake, cleaned and dried it. He was putting it in the trunk of his car, along with the thermos jugs, when his father returned dragging a recalcitrant Andy.

"We only caught two fish," Andy cried, "and I'm not ready to go home."

"What's the problem, Andy?" Byron asked the boy. "Have you forgotten that you do not disobey or disrespect your grandfather? Have you lost your mind? Apologize to him this minute."

Andy wiped his eyes and handed the fish to his father. "I'm sorry, Granddaddy, but I want to stay and fish with Miss Tyra. She hasn't caught any fish."

"She can catch some next time," Byron said. "We're ready to go." He looked at Tyra. "Did you at least get a bite?"

"Not that I know of, but Andy and I were singing so loudly that we may have frightened them off."

He stared at her, not believing what she'd said. "No doubt about it."

"Daddy, can I spend the night with Miss Tyra? I'll be good. Honest I will."

"Maybe sometime in the future, son, but not tonight."

"You let me stay with granddad, so why can't I stay with Miss Tyra?"

"We'll discuss this at home, Andy. Miss Tyra will not be home this evening, for one thing. In addition, you must wait for an invitation."

Tyra paused in the act of getting in the car and stood inches from him looking into his eyes. "Who said I won't be home this evening?"

"I've hardly been near you. Either Dad or Andy has been pushing me out. I want to see you tonight. We can go to a movie or just sit in the park or on my back porch. I want to be with you."

"Why not," she said without the semblance of a smile. "Next week, we'll probably be at loggerheads, and I'm going to hate every minute of it."

He helped her into the car and fastened her seat belt. "Have no fear, Tyra. I will never do anything intentionally to hurt you."

"I hope you're right," she said. "From the bottom of my heart, I hope you're right."

Chapter 11

After arriving at court a few minutes early, Tyra stopped at the cooler and drank a cup of water, mainly to calm her nerves. She didn't want Byron to see her jittery and lacking her usual composure. She sat on the front row between Jonathan and Darlene, perspiring in spite of the perfect, late October Indian-summer weather. Byron walked in, elegant and sure of himself, giving the impression of a man who was lord of all he surveyed. He spoke a few words to a man who looked as if he'd drunk too many cans of beer, glanced in Tyra's direction and smiled. Although she felt as if she'd been tied into a knot, she smiled in return.

"This is just the first hearing," Darlene told Tyra and Jonathan. "I'm almost certain that there'll be at least one more. Getting a final judgment in Family Court isn't easy, and if Becky is at odds with her father, it may be especially difficult in this case."

A few minutes later, Darlene stood, addressed the judge

and presented her case. At the end, she questioned why the state should pay for Becky's care and confinement and for the child when Jonathan wanted to do it and had the support of his family. She also asked why Murphy Tate should be allowed to deny a child its father's nurturing and care.

Tyra watched Byron intently throughout Darlene's argument and Jonathan's testimony, and noted that Byron's eyebrows shot up repeatedly while Jonathan spoke. She couldn't understand why Byron didn't put his client on the witness stand, but instead, asked the judge for a recess, stating that he wanted Becky's testimony. Murphy pulled at Byron's coat, evidently hoping to prevent his putting Becky on the stand, but the judge ruled that since her well-being was the issue, she should be allowed to testify.

As they left the courthouse, Jonathan told Darlene, "My big brother—he's my half brother—thinks this whole thing stinks. He's willing to help me take care of Becky until I finish school. He's an airline pilot."

"Tell him to call me at work today," Darlene said.

In the afternoon, three days later, when the case reconvened, Edward Hathaway—Jonathan's half brother—sat with Darlene, Tyra and Jonathan. Darlene called Edward to the stand, and he testified to his younger brother's good character and to his own willingness and ability to help Jonathan support Becky and her child. "Our mother wants to take care of Becky and insure that she receives proper medical treatment, and both our parents want her to stay with us until she is of age and can marry my brother or has the court's permission to marry."

Byron faced the judge. "Your Honor, a father is legally entitled, right or wrong, to deny the marriage of his underage daughter for whatever reasons he chooses. However, because of Jonathan Hathaway's testimony as well as Edward's, I want to call Becky Tate to the witness stand."

He examined the girl on every point that Jonathan had made, and on each, her response agreed with his. "This is not what I've heard from Becky's father, my client, and I am resigning from this case, because I have been misled."

After questioning Becky, the judge removed her from her father's care, made her a ward of the court and sent her to live with Jonathan's parents until after the birth of the child at which time she should return to court for further resolution of the case.

Byron walked over to Darlene and shook hands with her. "If you get tired of that gang you work with, consider Whitley, Chambers and Jones."

"What? You're serious? It'll be months before I get my feet back on the ground. Me in an outfit like that?"

"Think it over," he said and turned to Tyra. "I'm happy for Becky and Jonathan, but I feel a bit wounded, not to speak of furious with Murphy Tate for lying to me."

"He's an awful person," Jonathan said, "and she doesn't have a mother to stand up for her. Well, we'll take care of her now."

Byron's gaze swept over Tyra, drawing her to him the way a flame entices a moth. "May I speak with you?" he asked her.

"Of course," she said, hoping that no hard feelings remained between them. "When do you want us to get together?"

"It's a quarter of four. Do you have to go back to work?" She didn't. "If you'll go home with me, we can pick up Andy, have dinner somewhere, and then Andy and I will bring you home. I divide my time away from work between you and Andy, but I prefer to put him to bed as often as possible. It's a time he particularly enjoys, and so do I."

"Okay. I'll call Maggie and tell her I won't be home for dinner." *So something still bothers him. He's not totally at ease with me. Surely, he isn't sore because he lost.* He shook hands with Darlene, Edward and Jonathan, winked at Darlene and, as he kissed her cheek, he said, "You two make a fine-looking couple. Get to work."

Tyra raised an eyebrow. If she heard him, Edward probably… She didn't finish the thought for, at that moment, Edward took Darlene's arm and said, "There used to be a place around here where you could get the best ice cream in Maryland. Let's check it out."

As Tyra and Byron walked to his car, he said. "I hope Edward Hathaway isn't married."

"Darlene said he isn't, and if I know her, she asked him point blank."

"Good for her. That isn't a thing to guess about."

"You're still a little peeved with me, Byron, and I'd thought that when this case was settled, we'd be over this thing."

"I thought you and Darlene got a little heavy-handed. It's appropriate for an attorney to get the best witnesses possible, but she filed letters from a dozen citizens, some of them very distinguished, attesting to Murphy Tate's blighted character and, particularly, to his mistreatment of Becky. She should have made that information available to me. I didn't raise it with the judge, because I didn't want to hurt her. Besides, I was already having a hard time counseling Tate. He's an immoral man and makes no excuses for that fact."

"Then it's Darlene you should be angry with, not me." Whenever she reasoned with Byron, he managed to win, and he should, considering the cost of his legal education, she told herself. She tried a different tactic. "Are you going to kiss me, I mean really kiss me when you bring me home tonight?"

A grin spread over his face, and he tilted his head to the side and glanced at her. "I can pull over at the next rest stop. What do you say?"

She hadn't expected that. "I say I don't want the highway patrolman to take me in for indecent behavior."

He stared at her, although his eyes twinkled with mischievously. "Indecent behavior? What are you planning to do to me besides kiss me?"

"You're making something out of this that… You know I didn't mean anything like *that*."

"Anything like what? Sweetheart, if the problem is that you want to have your way with me, I can definitely arrange that"

"You're poking fun at me."

"Am not. You're so easy to tease. The answer to your question is that when I take you home tonight, I'm going to kiss you until we blow a fuse and ignite a fire in the furnace."

"Which furnace?"

"Yours, baby. If I light one in any other woman's furnace, you'll have my head. Why do you think I'm peeved with you?"

"'Cause you are, or were. I'm not sure about right now."

He stopped in front of his house, checked to determine whether he could squeeze that big Cadillac into the one available parking space, and backed in. "Let's enter through the back."

Away from public view, he stopped walking, stepped close to her and stared down into her eyes. "You're sweet, soft, feminine and warm, and the way you respond to me makes me feel like a king. But when I see that you're strong, independent, competent and my intellectual equal, I become a giant of a man." His arms went around her. "Open your mouth for me." She did, and he slipped his tongue into her, claimed her and sent shivers plowing through her body.

Get your act together. You can't let a man have this much power over you, and you definitely can't let him know it. But thrill after thrill streaked through her as he stroked her back and whispered, "Yes, I was hurt, but I know you love me. It's all right now. You're my whole world."

"And you're everything to me, Byron. Everything."

Arm-in-arm, they walked into the house. "Byron, lord, I didn't know you were bringing Tyra home for dinner. How're you, Tyra?" Jonie asked. Tyra hugged the older woman. Jonie seemed frantic over not having dinner prepared. "I'll run out and—"

"Not so fast, Aunt Jonie. We're going out to dinner and taking Andy with us."

"You'll have to let him bring along that monkey Miss Tyra gave him, because he hasn't been two inches from it all day. All of a sudden, he's gotten real pensive. I don't know why."

"I've been away a good deal these past couple of days. He'll be fine." His arm tightened around Tyra. "Let me run up and see why he's so quiet up there."

Andy's fierce and clinging hug shocked Byron. The boy ordinarily enjoyed exercising his independence. Knowing that his son had missed him, he didn't ask what was wrong but, instead, tried to make up for it.

"Take a shower and get dressed, son, we're going out to dinner."

Andy's face brightened. "Are we going to Miss Tyra's house?"

That question surprised him, and it also pleased him. "Not this time. You, Miss Tyra and I are going to have dinner in a nice restaurant."

"Oh! Can I take Nassau, and can I wear a suit like you?"

He looked down at the pleading expression on the boy's face and wondered what had gotten him down. "Yes to both, but we have to leave Nassau in the car while we're in the restaurant." Andy's bottom lip poked out. "None of that. We do as I say, or you stay home."

A brilliant smile lit the child's face. "Okay, but can I go with you when you take Miss Tyra home? Can I, Daddy?"

The little rascal. "Yes, we're going to take her home, because we'll be eating at a restaurant in Frederick, where she lives."

"I know she lives in Frederick, Daddy. She told me when

she and I were fishing for catfish. I also know she has a sister and a brother, and that she doesn't have any little children."

That took him back a bit. "Well, if you want to eat dinner with her, you'd better get a move on."

"Yes, sir." Andy loved dressing like his father, so Byron laid out the boy's navy blue suit, the same color as his own, white shirt, red and blue striped tie, black shoes and navy socks. *That ought to get him out of the dumps.*

A short time later with Nassau in his arms, Andy charged down the steps ahead of his father, raced to the living room and launched himself into Tyra's arms. "I'm going to dinner with you and Daddy, but I can't take Nassau into the restaurant. Miss Tyra, I love Nassau." He stared at her. "What happened to your hair? Daddy, what happened to her hair?"

Byron laughed. "Boy after my own heart. I've been wondering the same thing for most of the day."

"Oh, all right," Tyra said. "I'll be back in a minute."

"Where's she gone, Daddy?"

"I suspect we'll see when she comes back." He knew she went to comb out her hair, and he also knew that she was doing it for Andy. He wouldn't have dared to complain about a woman's hair, and he hoped she knew that.

"Gee," Andy said in awe when Tyra returned with her hair hanging around her shoulders. "How did you do that?" She explained that and answered several more of Andy's questions as they headed for Frederick. He decided not to interfere. Tyra had to learn to deal with the child. However, he sensed the understanding between them and drew a considerable measure of satisfaction from it.

"I guess Jonie and I have done a pretty good job with him," Byron said to himself in the restaurant, as he watched Andy take great care to use his knife and fork correctly, chew his food slowly—something he didn't do at home, though he'd been taught repeatedly, and to finish chewing before he started to speak. He didn't know when he had enjoyed an evening out with Andy so much. The child mimicked his every move, even saying thank you and no thank you to the waiter.

He nearly choked when Tyra said to Andy, "You are so precious. If I had a little boy, I'd want him to be just like you."

"Gee," Andy said. "I didn't know I was being that good."

She stroked the child's cheek in a way that told him that she wanted badly to hug Andy. *Yes, she will love him and teach him to love her.* He didn't know when he'd been so happy.

They left the restaurant with Andy holding their hands and dancing between them. Maybe he would finally get his life in order. He didn't want to raise Andy as an only child, and it was time he got busy on the next one, unless he planned to crawl around on his knees at age sixty with a couple of children on his back. During the coming weekend, he intended to have a serious talk with Tyra about their future together.

Similar thoughts stirred in Tyra's mind. She knew he was observing her relationship with his son, and she approved of it. She also knew that seeing each other occasionally was no longer enough for either of them. And since she had no intention of letting him have his cake and eat it, too, if he wanted her in his bed every night, he had to give up his single status.

"How much for your thoughts?" he asked when they approached his car. She hadn't said a word since they left the table.

She couldn't help grinning. "Not even gold is sufficient to tempt me to incriminate myself like that."

His eyes gleamed with a knowing look, and she knew she might well have painted it on canvas and hung it up for him to see. "Don't worry, you and I may not be far apart." Her pulse shot forward at a dizzying rate, and she grasped him for support. He held her, gazing down into her eyes, with all that he felt for her blazing in his face.

"Are you going to kiss her, Daddy?"

"I've been trying to catch up with you, buddy." A man in a chauffeur's uniform stepped up to them and said, "You owe me for escort services, and I want my money, or I'll splash it all over the tabloids that you're my customer, and you owe me."

Icy marbles rattle for space in Tyra's belly, and she thought she was about to lose her dinner. She watched at Byron's lower jaw sagged seconds before his eyes narrowed, and he advanced toward the man. "What the hell are you talking about?" He turned to Tyra. "Put Andy in the car while I straighten this out, will you."

She opened the back car door, put the boy in his car seat, hooked the seat belt and went back around the car to where Byron stood. On an impulse, she noted the license plate of the stretched-out limousine, turned her back and wrote it in the palm of her left hand. Then, she moved closer to Byron in order to be sure that she heard what she thought she heard.

"You're lying," Byron said to the man, flexing his fists. "I've never had any dealings with you or any other escort agency. What's the meaning of this? Did Murphy Tate put you up to this?"

"Who is Murphy Tate? You're the one who's lying, Attorney Whitley," the man said. "I can produce records of calls from three of your phone numbers, including your cell phone." He told Byron the numbers, as well as his home and office addresses. "I wouldn't embarrass you in the presence of your friend if you'd pay your bills."

Byron stepped closer to the man. "I don't know who you are or what your game is, but you'll pay for this and dearly." He walked to the front of the limousine and wrote down the license plate information.

Tyra thought she had never seen such anger on anyone's face as on Byron's as he knocked his right fist against his open left palm., rhythmically and furiously, clearly itching to throttle the man. However, seeing the danger to himself, the man turned toward his stretched-out limousine, then looked back at Byron and said, "You'll hear from me, and wait till the boys get hold of you."

Byron's hand on her arm unsettled her. How could such a man as Byron patronize an escort service, and why would he need to? Did he have a dark side that he hadn't exposed to her? Angry and humiliated, she jerked away from him, got into the car and buckled her seat belt. She realized the magnitude of her error when Byron got into the car, started the motor and said, "Thanks for your support. You can't imagine how much I appreciate it. I'll take you home."

Alarmed that she hadn't given Byron an opportunity to defend himself and that she had accepted the circumstantial evidence from someone she didn't know as proof of a character flaw in the man she knew and loved, she slumped in her seat. "I'm sure there's a mistake, Byron. That man did seem unsavory and, besides, what he accused you of isn't your style."

"Too late. I don't need a woman who doesn't believe in me and who needs evidence before she can trust me. I'm glad the guy showed up. He did me a colossal favor."

He parked in front of her house, glanced to the back seat and saw that Andy was asleep. "Good night, Tyra. See you around."

Tyra sat still, unable to move. He'd practically told her to get out, and he wasn't going to walk to the door with her. She was wrong, and she knew it, but that didn't mean she would accept rudeness from him. "Thank you for a most informative evening," she said, digging a deeper hole for herself and in a tone iced with bitterness, opened the door, got out and didn't look back.

She heard his car drive off before she reached her door, and as she fumbled for her key, she tasted the brine of her tears. In the foyer, she slumped against the wall and let the tears come. She heard the key turn in the front door lock, but she had no will to move, and didn't try.

"What the… What's this?" Clark grabbed her. "Sis, what happened? I just saw Byron at the stop light. Did you two have a fight?"

His questions exacerbated her pain, and sobs poured out of her stronger than before. He put his arms around her and walked with her to the living room where he sat with her on the sofa.

"I'll be back in a minute," he said, and she struggled to calm herself. He returned with a cup of instant coffee, and put it to her lips. "Sip this." She did and slowly returned to normal.

"Can you tell me what happened?"

Between whimpers and sniffles, she related the charges that the man in a chauffeur's uniform lodged against Byron and described her reaction.

Clark bounced up and faced her. "I don't believe what I'm hearing. You mean to tell me you accused Byron of that on the basis of some jerk's word, a guy you knew nothing about. Sis, you can take one look at Byron Whitley and see that he does not need to pay for sexual favors, and I mean no matter what his tastes are, a guy who looks like him can get what he wants for free.

"And another thing, didn't it occur to you that when sex is for sale, the guy pays in advance. Nobody gives credit for that, and if it's not satisfactory, you don't get your money back. Honey, you laid an ostrich egg. He'll never forgive you."

"I know. He as much as said so. What am I going to do?"

"I wish I could say something encouraging, Sis, but it beats me. I know how I'd feel in his place. If you're in an intimate relationship with him, I don't see how you could have slipped up like that."

"I came to my sense right away, and I told him it wasn't true, but he said that was too late. Clark, he didn't even walk to the door with me. I've never been so humiliated."

"Think how humiliated he was when you believed he used an escort service, and frequently at that. If you want him, you're going to have to crawl."

"I know, and I'm not going to crawl. Period."

"Don't say what you're not going to do. You love him. You don't know what you'll do. Take it from one who's been there."

She couldn't focus right then on Clark's reference to himself, her heart was so filled with agony. "I don't know what I'll do, Clark."

"I've never known anything to beat you down, and this won't either. Whatever you do, don't use his physical attraction to you as a means to bring him to heel, because he'll give in, and then he'll despise you."

She wouldn't have dreamed that Clark's personal experiences had made him so wise. "I wouldn't stoop to that, Clark. I may be miserable, but I will always respect myself."

He went to the pantry, poured two glasses of Chardonnay and gave one to her. "Dad used to say that when Jack Kennedy was assassinated, he thought the world had come to an end, but the next day, the sun rose and set as usual. You will survive."

"I know. I just don't care for the idea of surviving without him. Please don't mention this to Darlene."

"Of course not. She'd probably call him and chew him out. Say, I saw her Sunday with a guy named Edward Hathaway at the Great Blacks in Wax Museum in Baltimore. She said he's an airline pilot."

"That's right. I met him this afternoon at court. He testified for my and Darlene's client in our case against Byron's client." She told him about the judge's ruling. "Hathaway's a great looking guy, and he speaks extremely well."

"Yeah," Clark said. "He impressed me, too. Let's hope this signals the end of Darlene and those guys who never put anything on their feet but Reeboks. I'll say good night now. Chin up."

"Good night, Clark. Don't worry. It definitely won't kill

me." She could say that, but the way she felt gave the lie to it. She plodded up stairs, undressed and went to bed without turning on a light. When dawn broke, she was wide awake.

Byron drove home at an unusually slow speed. He had his child in the back seat, and he could not afford to have an accident. Still, for most of the trip home, he was unaware that he drove. His world had just been shattered. Blown to smithereens. He'd never been so glad to get home as when he finally parked in front of his house, rested his head on the stirring wheel and gave thanks that he'd gotten there without having an accident.

He took Andy from the back seat, locked the car and, with his precious child asleep in his arms, made his way up the steps to his front door. A man wasn't supposed to seek solace in his child, but right then, he needed love, and the only love he could count on was the love of his son. He put Andy to bed and told himself not to let his mind dwell on the day's events. But how could he not do it? Less than an hour after he'd made up his mind to ask her to marry him she let him down and all that she had become to him crashed around him, into pieces, unrecoverable like shivers of broken glass.

"I'll get over it," he told himself, but he hardly believed it. Somewhere between furious and disconsolate, he looked at himself in the bathroom mirror. "Fool," he muttered and stopped himself just before his fist rammed the mirror. He slept fitfully, arose early and went into Andy's room where the boy, who usually slept as long as he was allowed to do so, sat up in bed playing with Nassau, the monkey that Tyra gave him.

"Daddy, why didn't we take Miss Tyra home last night?"

"We did, but you were asleep."

"Why didn't you wake me up? I wanted to tell her good night."

He did not want to begin the day with a discussion of Tyra.

"Get up, son. Get dressed and be downstairs in fifteen minutes, and brush your teeth thoroughly." Andy didn't see the value in day school, because he was farther advanced than most of the other children. "Can I take Nassau to school with me?

"Leave Nassau on the bed and step to it. I put your clothes in the chair."

"Yes, sir."

He should be happy that his four-year-old could dress himself perfectly and tie his shoes, and that he often was able to tie his tie, though he was more likely to need help with it. The boy loved his school uniform and wore it proudly. He drove Andy to school and escorted him to the door. Some parents let their children out of the car, sat there and watched until they were safely inside, but he walked the boy to the front door and waited until he passed the guard. His father always counseled that an ounce of prevention was worth a pound of cure, and he also believed that.

He got to his office earlier than usual, opened his computer and began a search for the license plate number that he recorded during his confrontation with the man who falsely accused him the night before. When he could find nothing for that number, he made a note to call the stated office responsible for license plates. Chances were that he knew someone there. A call from a client took his mind off the escort service, and he was soon busy revising his brief for his morning court appearance.

Tyra had less success at diverting her attention from the events of the previous night and, at eleven o'clock when she had nothing to show for the two-and-a-half hours she'd sat at her desk, she got up and went to the coffee room hoping that a shot of caffeine would help. She didn't feel like talking, and when she saw Matt leaning against the door jamb and holding a paper cup to his lips, she turned to go back to her office.

"Hi," he said. "Haven't seen you since last week. What's up?"

She walked back to him. "Nothing special."

Matt stared at her. "What's come over you? Say, are you all right, Tyra?" He put his drink down, poured a cup of coffee and handed it to her. "What's the matter, friend? Can I help?"

"Thanks, Matt, but I'll be fine. Things are a little rough right now, but as you know, 'This, too, shall pass away.'"

He patted her shoulder. "If I can help, you know how to reach me." She nodded listlessly, sipping coffee without tasting it, unaware that he'd gone and she was alone.

One week of detachment from all around her invited the constant solicitousness of Maggie and her siblings, and she had begun to tire of it and to spend increasingly longer hours at her office.

On a Thursday morning, one week and two days after she last saw Byron, she got to work at seven-thirty, made the coffee, got a cup for herself, sat down at her desk and opened her computer. To her surprise, the door opened, and Christopher Fuller stood before her with a cup of coffee in his hand.

"Thanks for the coffee. I was wondering who got here so early. What's the matter? Can't sleep?"

"What do you want, Fuller?" She didn't bother to keep the sneer out of her voice.

A smirk sufficed for the smile around his lips, but his eyes flashed hatred. "How are things going with you and the big shot?"

A frown altered her face. Where was this going? "Who're you talking about?"

"Whitley. Is your thing with him still hot?"

Her antenna shot up. "What do you know about my relationship with Byron?"

The "gotcha" expression on his face reminded her of a teacher who'd caught a student cheating. "I make it my business to know how my competition is faring," he said, closed the door and left.

"What competition?" she thought. She'd never given Christopher Fuller an iota of encouragement. In fact, she'd let him know that she disdained his advances. Deciding to top off her coffee, she headed back to the coffee room and stopped mid-way there. How did Fuller know about her and Byron? Wait a minute. He was just the type to use an escort service. With bells ringing in her head, she went on to the coffee room and got there simultaneously with Matt.

"You're looking a lot brighter," he said. "How are you?"

"I may be better by the minute." When he raised both eyebrows, she said, "Would you say Fuller is the type of man to use an escort service?"

"Probably. Why?" Asking for his confidence, she told him of Byron's encounter with the unidentified chauffer and related her suspicion because of her conversation with Christopher minutes earlier.

"You gotta be kidding. Of course. I hope you didn't believe that. It's as thin as onion skin. Prostitutes take the money in advance, and there are no refunds. I hope Whitley gets at the bottom of this. Fuller has hit on every woman who works here. He's just the type to do something like that."

"Please don't mention it."

"I won't, but you dig into this and report it. If you need any help, let me know. I imagine this cooled things off between you and Whitley. Sure. That would put any woman in the dumps. Get busy on it."

She thanked him, and went back to her office, her heart lighter than it had been in weeks. She called the taxi commissioner's office, reported the limousine's number, said she wanted to file a suit against the driver, whose name, she learned, was Rodney Fuller. The man was said to drive a private limousine for parties of individuals on such special occasions as weddings, funerals, graduations, but when she dialed the phone number given her, the operator replied, "Pamela speaking. What service is this?"

"Well, well," she said aloud. "Somebody is going to catch hell." She told herself not to do anything in a hurry, and a niggling impulse wanted her to call Byron and tell him. But she wanted Christopher Fuller to pay heavily, and she didn't know whether Byron would see to that. She decided to think about it until after lunch.

She sat alone in the staff cafeteria eating a tuna fish sandwich. "Mind if I join you?"

She glanced up and saw Matt, though she would have recognized his voice even if she hadn't seen him. "Any progress with that little mystery?" he asked her.

"You bet. Fuller is our man. His brother has a tie to more than one escort service."

"I'm sure Whitley will be glad to get that cleared up. What did he say when you told him?"

"I haven't told him yet."

Matt stopped in the process of cutting a piece of cheese. "What's the matter? Couldn't you reach him?"

"I wanted to think it through. I'll call him when I get back to my office."

Matt have her a long and bemused look. "Yeah, but don't tell him you've known this all day and waited till two-thirty to tell him."

"What? You're right. In my anger, I wanted to sock it to Fuller myself, but I realize I should let Byron take care of it. Thanks."

"I'm sure he'll do a good job of it. Good luck."

Byron watched his junior partner leave his office crestfallen. He'd been hard on the man, harder than necessary perhaps, but he was in a foul mood, and Ben's sloppy handling of that case had done nothing to brighten his outlook. When his phone rang, he ignored it. But after a lengthy ring, his secretary answered it.

"Byron, Ms. Cunningham is on line one." He did not want

to speak with her, didn't want to hear the voice that would trigger in him reminders of his dried up dreams. "She says it's urgent, Byron."

"Hello, Tyra, what's up?"

"Hello, Byron. I have some information that may interest you." She began by telling him of Christopher Fuller and his interest in her, and he was on the verge of telling her that the matter was of no interest to him when she said, "The driver of that limousine was Rodney Fuller, and among other jobs, he transports workers and their clients for different escort services."

His antenna shot up. "If you have a pen handy," she continued, "this is the phone number, and I've checked with the Taxi and Limousine Commissioner's officer."

He sat forward, "Are you sure your colleague is behind this?"

"I am absolutely positive. He came by my office this morning to gloat, asked me how things were going with you, and I had no idea he knew you and I had a relationship. He said he made it a point to know what his competition was doing. He's hit on every woman who works here, and if you check, I'm sure you will discover that he uses that service. I'm sorry about that and about a lot of things, Byron. I sincerely hope you'll make certain that Christopher Fuller gets what he deserves. Here is the information for the person you should contact here at LAC. Good luck with it."

"I'm going to follow this up today, Tyra, and I'll let you know the outcome. I want you to know that I…I appreciate your taking the trouble to dig into this. It tells me more than words could have. I'll be in touch. Uh…Tyra, thank you."

He sat back in his chair, flicking his fingernails. If she had believed that guy, she wouldn't have gone to the trouble to find out why the limousine driver made the accusation and the name of the person with whom he was in cahoots. It was something to go on, and he cherished it. Maybe…

Chapter 12

Byron propped his left elbow on his desk and supported his chin with the palm of his left hand. In the practice of law, he'd met a lot of unprincipled people, but he didn't think any surpassed Christopher Fuller, a man who made a living counseling others. He didn't believe in "an eye for an eye and a tooth for a tooth," but he did believe that criminals should pay for their unsavory deeds. He could sue the man for defamation of character, but he didn't want the guy's money; no amount of it would compensate for the pain he endured at Tyra's lapse of trust and belief in him. He lifted the telephone receiver and dialed the Taxi and Limousine Commissioner's office.

"Hello, Ken. This is Byron. Can you verify this for me, please? It's a personal matter, and it's very important." He related in detail the purpose of his call. "What? The guy misrepresented me." He took notes while his friend and fraternity brother talked. Fifteen minutes later, he hung up, satisfied that he had the information he needed. So officials suspected

Rodney Fuller of being a part of a prostitution ring, and of covering it with one general transportation vehicle used for parties, weddings and other occasions. But he used his other cars to transport girls to and from their johns. Mr. Fuller had given himself the task of embarrassing him in order to destroy Tyra's confidence in him. Christopher Fuller would rue the day he conjured up that scheme.

Using his official stationery, Byron wrote letters to the Legal Aid Center and to the Taxi and Limousine Commissioner in which he accused Christopher of orchestrating the deed, explaining the man's motive for doing so and pointing out that he had never seen, spoken with or met Christopher Fuller. He had the letters notarized and mailed them. If he didn't get satisfaction, he'd take the matter to court.

He should have felt better about it, but the pain remained. He still went home to his four-year-old son every night to explain why he hadn't brought Tyra back to see the child or taken him to see Tyra, and he still tossed in his bed nightly aching for her. He knew she didn't think that of him, but trust in him hadn't been paramount in her thinking about him. It was now, he knew, because that incident had forced her to think, but she'd already delivered those awful scars. He tried to edit a brief he'd prepared for a court session two days hence, but he pushed it aside. Dammit, he loved her. He packed the brief in his briefcase, telling himself he'd get to it later, told his secretary that he was leaving for the day and went home.

He opened the door. Not a sound. Momentarily alarmed, he relaxed and slumped into a dining room chair. For a moment, he'd forgotten that at two-thirty, Andy hadn't come home from school and in fact Jonie had gone to pick him up. He went to the kitchen, looked first in the refrigerator and then in the freezer, didn't see anything interesting and decided to take Andy and Jonie out to dinner. He wrote a note to Jonie, taped it to the refrigerator, got his brief and a bottle of beer and went out on the back porch to work. His cell phone rang.

"Byron, can you speak with Clark Cunningham?" his secretary asked him.

If anything had happened to her, he'd... "Sure, put him on. What's up Clark? It's good to hear from you." He said the latter as an afterthought.

"I'm fine, I hope. I'm trying to track down Tyra."

He bolted upright. "Tyra? Man, what are you talking about?"

"Maggie said she left home this morning at the usual time, dressed as if she was going to work, but she's not at her office and she doesn't answer her cell phone."

"She called me around ten-thirty this morning, but she didn't mention leaving her office." He thought for a second. "But I can't see any reason why she should have mentioned it. What's going through your mind, Clark? Is that all Maggie said? Did you call Darlene?"

"Naw. I'll call Darlene as a last resort. She is so full of drama that she'd alert the White House. Maybe I'm overdoing it, but while I can understand her leaving work early— I've done it myself plenty of times—I can't see why she doesn't answer her cell phone. I'll be in touch."

After checking Tyra's office phone and her cell phone and being unable to locate her, Byron contemplated his next move. Now what? How was he supposed to work when Tyra could be in danger or worse...? He didn't want to think of alternatives. He went on the Internet, found the Legal Aid Center's Web site, and checked its roster to see whether he knew any of the staff members. When he saw Matthew Cowan's name among the volunteers, relief spread over him the way water spreads over even land. He wasn't bosom buddies with the man, but he knew him well enough to call him.

"Cowan speaking."

"Matt, this is Byron Whitley. I'm calling you for a favor. Have you seen Tyra Cunningham today?"

"Why, yes. I spoke with her at length shortly after ten this morning, and I saw her in the staff cafeteria at lunch time. She must be in her office."

"She doesn't answer there nor does she answer her cell phone."

"Wait a minute. I'll walk around there." A minute later, Matt said, "She isn't in her office, the coffee room or her supervisor's office. I'll check the staff lounge." He returned a minute later. "The guard said he hadn't seen her since she came to work this morning, and she's not in the lounge. The women's room is empty, because the light is green. I don't know what else to tell you. Wait a second. This may take a minute longer."

After two full minutes, Matt spoke to him. "I checked the one place I knew she wasn't likely to be, but these days, you can't tell. She's not in this building. I won't mention this unless she's missing from home tonight. Okay?"

"Okay, Matt, and thanks. I'm in your debt."

"Not at all, man. Tyra's been a good colleague to me, and I appreciate your interest. Good luck."

Byron hung up with a suspicion that Matt Cowan knew how Tyra felt about him, assumed it was mutual and had done his best to put him at ease. Had she confided to Cowan her unhappiness about the break in their relationship? He'd said he would check the one place he didn't expect her to be, and logic said that meant he checked Christopher Fuller's office. Hmm. So Fuller had a reputation among his colleagues. He rubbed his forehead. Where was she? He had to wait until her family's dinnertime, and he didn't see how he could stand it.

After her conversation—if you could call it that—with Byron, Tyra paced from one end of her office to another, pushed papers around on her desk, went to the coffee room and decided that coffee wasn't what she needed. On the way back to her office, she tapped on Lyle Riddick's office door.

"If it's urgent, come in, if it's not, you know the rest."

She opened her boss's door and went in. "I'm washed out. I have one routine appointment this afternoon, and I'm going to postpone it and go home."

"I've noticed that you haven't seemed yourself for the past couple of weeks, although I haven't found any problems with your work. Go someplace where you can be alone and think through whatever's bothering you. And turn your cell phone off."

"Thanks, Lyle, but I can't think of such a place."

"Sure you can. It's not cold today, somewhere in the high sixties, so why not trek over to the river. There some nice views in Gambrill Park over near Hamburg Road especially around Pal's Ridge. I've sat there many times so peacefully that I fell asleep. With so many joggers and women pushing baby carriages around there, it's safe in the daytime."

"I think I will." She looked down at her feet, saw the heels and grimaced. She went to her office, changed into flat heel shoes, locked her briefcase in her desk and left the building. She rode the bus to about a block from the park, bought a magazine and a bottle of ginger ale from a newsstand and strolled along until she found a park bench. She thought that she couldn't have chosen a more beautiful afternoon on which to sit outside in the sun. She looked in her purse for a Snickers bar, her comfort food, saw her cell phone and remembered Lyle's advice that she should turn it off. But she saw that she'd never turned it on, and that she had calls from Clark, Byron, Maggie and Matt.

She phoned Byron.

"Where are you, Tyra?" he said with the urgency of a desperate man.

"I'm up in Gambrill Park. I…uh…nothing was going right,

so I…I forgot to turn on my cell phone." Her heart began to race as hope surfaced within her. "Did you want to speak with me?"

"Clark didn't know where you were, nor did anyone else, and I've been out of my mind with worry about where you could be or what could have happened to you."

"It's been too much for me, Byron, and after speaking with you this morning, and dealing with your cool detachment, I…it was too much for me."

His long silence didn't bother her; they couldn't get much farther apart than they were. "It's been too much for me, too, Tyra. Where are you in that park?" She told him. "Stay there."

Was he coming to the park to be with her? She had a clear head, and she was not confused, but nothing made sense right then. She checked her cell phone. Yes, she had just spoken with Byron. He'd said wait, so she would. But each minute seemed like an hour, so anxious and flustered, she phoned Clark.

"Did you tell Byron that you couldn't find me?"

"Where the heck are you?" She told him but added that Byron was on his way there and he shouldn't come. "I'm fine. I needed some time alone. I guess I ought to thank you for telling Byron that you couldn't find me. Maybe we'll get back together."

"I should think so. He was out of his mind when I told him I didn't know your whereabouts."

"I'm sorry if I caused you alarm, Clark. Would you please phone Maggie and tell her I don't know what time I'll get home, so she shouldn't wait dinner for me."

"Good idea. Pull out the stops, Sis. And remember that your pride won't make you happy, but he will." After hanging up, she tried to develop an interest in the magazine, gave up and said a prayer.

"Hello, Tyra."

She hadn't seen or heard him approach. Without knowing why she got up, she stood and smiled. "I'm glad to see you,

Byron. I missed you." Should she have let him say it first? She'd never been in such a situation, and she had no idea how to act.

"If I was allowed to do what I want to do," he said, "I'd take you in my arms and hold you as close as possible. I have lived in hell since that night. We were both wrong. You didn't have enough trust, and I didn't have enough compassion. I learned something. Did you?"

"I had it reconfirmed that you are my morning sunrise and my evening shade, Byron, and that I'd trust you with my life."

"I knew that I needed you, but I didn't know how badly." He opened his arms, and she walked into them, back home where she belonged.

"I'd suggest we go to dinner, but Andy is expecting me at home. He's asked repeatedly why you didn't come to visit us or why we didn't go to visit you. You're the only woman I've introduced him to, and not only does he like you, but he senses that you have a special role in our lives. Let me take you home, and perhaps tomorrow evening we can be together."

"I'd like that," she said, and they started hand-in-hand to his car, which he'd parked at the edge of the park.

"Would you like to come in?" she asked him when he parked in front of her house. He walked with her to the door, opened it with her key and a second later, she had the comfort of his loving arms around her. More. She wanted and needed more of him. All of him. Like a starved animal getting its first meal in weeks, she clung to him, taking all that he gave her as he reminded her of the fire they built together. Heat roared through her body, and when she attempted to wrap her leg around his upper thigh, begging for what she wanted, he broke the kiss, panting for breath as he did so.

"Honey," he said, "we are not alone in this house."

"I forgot." Depleted of energy, she backed to the opposite side of the foyer and let the wall take her weight. His gaze was soft upon her, the eyes of a man in love. She told herself to straighten up and lighten the situation, and a way to bring them closer together began to form in her mind.

"Byron, could you…would you, your aunt and Andy have dinner with me and my family Thanksgiving Day?"

He didn't hesitate. "That would be wonderful. Aunt Jonie wants to go to Virginia to be with her daughter and sister, but I'll tell her that you invited her. Andy will be ecstatic."

"What shouldn't I cook? I mean what does he dislike?"

"He dislikes broccoli, but he eats it, because he has to eat whatever we give him. Not to worry. I'd better head home." He cupped her face with his hands. "I love you. I love you deep down inside at the pit of me."

Her arms went around him. "And I love you, Byron. I haven't ever loved any other man. See you tomorrow." He brushed his lips across hers and left. She skipped toward the stairs, stopped and said a word of thanks that she hadn't ruined the most precious thing that had ever happened to her.

Two days later, Lyle called her into his office and showed her Byron's notarized letter. "This is disgusting," he said, "and I have a mind to fire Fuller. I have eleven full-time professionals and half-a-dozen volunteers, and Fuller is the only person on my staff who gives me problems. But if I terminate him, he'll attempt to defame both you and Whitley. I am going to censure him and put it on his record. I suspect that since Whitley sent a letter to the Taxi and Limousine Commissioner, Christopher Fuller and his brother will pay heavily, and if I get a chance to fire Fuller for something relating to his work, I'm going to do it. I don't want such a person around me."

She thanked Lyle and stood to leave. "I hope he didn't impair your relationship with Byron Whitley. He's a fine man, and he's contributed a lot to the Legal Aid Society."

"At first, it was touch and go, but I think we've weathered that storm. Thanks for your concern."

A telephone call from Andy that evening surprised her.

"Hi, Miss Tyra. This is Andrew Whitley. My daddy said I could phone you and thank you for inviting me to eat dinner at your house Thursday. When are we going to your house, Miss Tyra?"

"You can come Wednesday if you want to, but it's up to your father."

"Oh. Is my granddaddy going to be there? He loves turkey, too."

"Andy, that's a good idea. Do you have his phone number?" He recited it from memory. "Thanks. I'll see if he's free."

"He's free, Miss Tyra, because he always eats with me and my daddy."

"My daddy and me. I'm going to call him."

"You are? I love you, Miss Tyra. Bye."

"Andy, darling. I love you, too. See you this weekend." She hung up and dialed Lewis Whitley's number.

"Whitley speaking. Good evening."

"Mr. Whitley, this is Tyra Cunningham. How are you… I know you're surprised to hear from me, but Jonie will be in Virginia Thanksgiving Day, and Byron and Andy are having dinner with me and my family. I'd love for you to join us."

"Well, it's wonderful to hear from you, Tyra, and I'll be absolutely delighted to join you for Thanksgiving Day dinner. I hope we'll spend many Thanksgiving Days together."

She gave him her address. "We eat around two in the afternoon, and at seven-thirty, we're ready for a light supper. Thank you for accepting my invitation."

"Thank you for inviting me. I should tell you that Andy called to say you were going to invite me and asked me to be sure and accept. He's a kid who dots every i and crosses every t, Byron incarnate. I'll see you Thursday around noon. Thank you again."

She went to the lounge where she knew she'd find Maggie watching television. "Maggie, I've invited Byron, Andy and Byron's father for Thanksgiving, along with Clark's and

Darlene's dates, we'll be ten for dinner. So I think I'll hire a caterer, because that's too much work."

"It's just three more than we've usually had in recent years. We'll just cook more of everything, but you can get someone to serve the meal and clean up, if you want to"

"That's a fair compromise. Would you please make out the grocery list? I'll take Wednesday off and help with the cooking."

Byron telephoned her several times a day and every night just before he went to sleep. "Can't you and Andy spend the weekend with us?" she asked Byron when he called her that Tuesday evening. "Andy can sleep in Clark's room and you can have the guest room. Take Friday off, and we can have a mini-vacation right here."

"Won't Clark need his room?"

"He's taking his friend to Bermuda Friday morning and returning to Baltimore Sunday evening."

"All right. I'll let you know about that tomorrow. I like the idea. Kiss me."

She made the sound of a kiss. "This tease is getting to me."

"I consider it my nightly punishment," he said. "I love you, woman. Good night."

"And I love you. Good night, sweetheart."

Thanksgiving Eve finally arrived, and Byron would discover what it was like to live in Tyra's world. He could hardly wait to experience her home, her family and the aura she would create. "Can we go now, Daddy? I'm taking Nassau. Can I call Miss Tyra and ask if we can go fishing?"

Byron looked at his child, so eager to attach himself to this woman. He couldn't understand it, accustomed as he was to Andy's standoffishness with everyone except Jonie and him. He sat down, pulled the boy between his knees and said, "I'll take the fishing rods and tackle, but if she has other plans, we'll do as she likes, because we'll be her guests."

"Yes, sir. But she'll do what I ask her to do. Let's go, Daddy."

Tyra opened the door, and he looked down at her, hoping to see in her eyes the love that he needed, but Andy dashed past him and into her arms.

"Gee, Miss Tyra, I thought Daddy would never get us here. I could hardly wait."

She hugged the boy and then, as if she feared what she'd do next, she brushed his cheek with her lips. To Byron's delight, the boy took the initiative and kissed her, looked her in the eye and said, "You always smell so good."

She thanked Andy, then she stood, opened her arms to him and he walked into them. "It's like coming home," he told her and he meant it.

He and Andy followed Tyra to their rooms. He hadn't realized that the house was so big. Andy would get lost or worse, get into something he shouldn't. He asked her, "Could you give Andy a tour, tell him where he can go and where he can't go?"

She walked them through the house and out to the back porch and deck. "We're having a cookout, a barbecue supper. I thought Andy would like that. Tomorrow, there'll be ten of us for Thanksgiving dinner. Clark and Darlene will have their significant others with them and—"

"And Granddaddy's coming, isn't he, Miss Tyra?"

Byron stared at her. "Since when?"

"Since she asked him, Daddy."

"You two, go put on something casual," she said. "I'll start the fire in the barbecue pit, and then I'll wake up Maggie."

Andy reached for Tyra's hand. "Don't you have a mommy either?" She shook her head. "Do you have a daddy?"

"Both of them are in heaven," she told him.

He hugged her thigh. "My mommy's up there, too." How had his child developed an affection for Tyra? He didn't know when it happened, but it was there, and it was solid.

"We'll be back in a few minutes," he told her.

She grabbed his hand, detaining him. "Whenever you get tired of people, you're welcome to go to your room and close the door. I want you to feel at home, and that means having privacy whenever you want it. Okay?"

"Thanks. It's something that I need from time to time, but I doubt I'll need privacy from you."

She started the fire in the big, aluminum barbecue grill and covered it with charcoal briquettes. "Tyra, what are you doing?" Byron asked her. "Don't you have any wood chips?"

She stopped, looked up at him, dressed in a red turtle-neck sweater and dark-navy jeans, and resisted licking her lips. "I wanted to get it started in a hurry," she said, explaining her reason for not using wood chips.

"Sweetheart, the wood burns just as fast and releases less impurities. Let me help you."

"What y'all doing down there? All you have to do is grill the meat and shrimp and roast some potatoes. Everything else is in the fridge," said Maggie.

"I know, Maggie, but do you know it's already five minutes to seven. You slept forever."

"Five minutes to seven? Lord, I slept away the day. I'm coming down."

Tyra lighted the garden with lanterns and built a fire in the pit to keep them warm. Maggie had hotdogs and marshmallows for Andy, steaks and shrimp for the adults and assorted vegetables and potatoes that they grilled along with the meat and shrimp.

"Gosh, this is fun," Andy said, and she made a note to invite other children for a picnic with Andy when he visited her again. She answered the house phone and heard her sister's voice.

"I…er… Okay, you're grown, Sis, so this shouldn't shock you. I'm going to spend the night with Edward. Be home tomorrow around twelve."

"I hope you at least prepared yourself for it."

"I did. See you tomorrow." Well, that was a surprise.

After the barbecue supper, they sat in the living room, and she nestled herself in Byron's arms. To her amazement, Andy stopped reading his book, came over to her and sat on her lap. She eased an arm around his waist and held him close to her. She'd been leaning against Byron's chest, and she felt his breathing change. Since she wasn't sure whether that was a positive or a negative sign, she twisted enough to see his face.

He bent over and kissed her mouth, but his lips trembled against hers. "It's Andy's bedtime. I'm going to put him to bed, but you stay here. I'll be back in half an hour."

"I want Miss Tyra to tuck me in and kiss me good night."

"In that case, ask her nicely." He did, and she climbed the stairs with them, feeling like a character in a real-life drama. Game playing. Yet she knew that what they did then could well be a preview of their lives in the near future.

The child changed into pajamas and crawled into bed. He asked her to tell him a story, and she told him the story of *The Little Engine That Could*, dramatizing the sound as the engine plodded up the hill. He raised his arms for a kiss and was soon fast asleep.

She could see that the scene undermined Byron's composure, for he blinked rapidly and turned his back to her. "I'll be downstairs," she whispered, leaving so that he could have privacy.

"Please don't go, Tyra. Maggie's asleep on the other side of the house. Is there a reason why we can't be together for a few hours? I'm about to boil over."

She walked back to him. "You stay up here. I'm going downstairs to lock the doors and turn out the lights. I'll find you."

Perspiration soaked his shirt and rolled down the side of his face. He walked to his room, thankful that it had a private bath, stripped and stepped into the shower. In spite of the chasm they'd had to bridge and the reservations it provoked, he didn't want to live without her. He still wanted her as he wanted air to breathe, and he loved her as he'd never loved any other woman. The moment he gave in to his feelings and made up his mind to ask her to marry him, he'd burned with passion and his love for her had almost overwhelmed him. He laughed at himself. Why should deciding to ask the woman he loved to marry him make him sweat? He dried off, found a pair of shorts that would pass for pajamas, got into bed and waited.

Tyra locked the front and back doors, opened a bottle of Chablis, got two stem glasses and tripped up the stairs. She put the bottle and glasses on the floor by Byron's bedroom door, and went to her own room. After showering and pampering herself, she put on a red teddy, covered it with a white caftan and walked barefooted to Byron. One light tap, and the door opened. He reached for her but, with a grin spread over her face, she pushed the bottle and glasses to him. She didn't know where he put them, but it seemed that not a second had passed before he had her tight in his arms.

"Are you sure that everything is all right between us?" he asked her.

She put her palms on his bare chest, keeping him away from her. "I'm positive, but are you?"

"Yes. Yes," seemed to rush out on his breath. "I know you love me and that you believe in me. If I didn't know it, I wouldn't be here with my child in your house."

She wished she knew how to seduce him. "Shall we drink to it?" she asked him.

"Baby, drink is the farthest thought from my mind. This thing is beautiful, but I want to take it off you."

She traced her fingers over his taunt abdomen and across his prominent pectorals. "Who's stopping you?"

He wanted her badly. Looking him in the eye to see the

effect, she cupped his genitals, squeezed and gloried in his shout as he picked her up, and pressed her to his full arousal. She put his left hand into the bodice of her caftan, and he released her breast, pulled the nipple into his mouth and sucked it. She locked her legs around his hips and rocked against his arousal, anticipating her pleasure in it.

"Sweetheart, be still unless you want this to be over before it starts." Easing her to her feet, he unzipped the caftan and dropped it to the floor. She fell across the bed and after staring at the treasure spread before him, he dropped to his knees, pulled her body to the edge of the bed, hooked her knees over his shoulder, and bent his head to feast on the honey that was for him alone. She raised her hips to him and he plunged his tongue into her. She thought she'd go mad from the fire that he sent streaking to her belly, her womb and every one of her limbs.

When she could stand it no longer, he kissed his way up her body, entered her slowly and took her on a lightning-fast ride to oblivion. An hour later, sitting up in bed sipping wine, she said, "I'd give anything if I could put this glass down, snuggle up in your arms and go to sleep. These little crumbs are getting to me."

"Tell me about it. No one wants that more than I do."

But even though she knew that no one would know if she spent the night in his room, she was playing for high stakes, and if he wanted her to spend the night in his arms badly enough, he knew the solution. She drained her glass, pulled on the caftan and got up. "What time do you want breakfast?"

"Andy will be hungry by eight," he said, "so whenever you like." She kissed him, went to her room, got into bed, slept soundly and dreamed beautiful and erotic dreams.

Byron had never been so nonplussed. Andy ignored him all morning, trailed behind Tyra, claiming that he was helping her, and managed to develop a relationship with Maggie. After much difficulty, he held the boy's attention for about ten minutes and then the doorbell rang. Andy dashed to it.

"Well now, who are you, young man?" Byron heard a male voice ask.

"I'm Andrew Whitley, and I'm having Thanksgiving Day dinner with Miss Tyra and Miss Maggie." Not a word about his father who, until he found a mother substitute, had been his whole world.

"My goodness, Andy, you must grow like wildfire. You're supposed to be four," he heard Darlene say.

"That's what my Aunt Jonie says. And I am four. How do you know my name?"

"I'm Darlene, Tyra's sister, and she talks about you all the time."

"She does? Gee."

Byron headed toward the conversation and greeted Darlene and Edward, whom he'd met at the trial. "Hmm," he said. "This is nice. I hadn't realized that you two are an item."

"When you met me, we weren't," Edward said, shaking Byron's hand, "but I figured out that something was going on between you and Tyra. Great to see you again."

"You, too, man. Something was *indeed* going on." The group walked toward the living room, with Andy holding Tyra's hand and chattering as if he'd known everyone all of his life. When the doorbell rang again, Andy pulled Tyra along with him to the door and squealed in delight when he saw his grandfather, who came in along with Clark and his date.

After the introductions were made, Byron joined the group in the family room. He loved the hominess of the fire in the big marble-faced fireplace and the colorful glow that seemed so appropriate to that gathering. When he would have enjoyed relaxing there with his son on his knee, he looked around for him and didn't see Andy.

After searching upstairs, he went into the kitchen and asked Maggie, "Have you seen Andy?"

"He's in the game room downstairs with Clark. Before that, he was in here giving me his Aunt Jonie's recipe for noels. That's a smart little boy. I'd make some for him, but I don't have time right now. Maybe tomorrow."

When he saw Clark giving Andy lessons in ping pong, he went back to the adults. Maybe Andy needed a wider circle of adults in his life. Tyra joined the group, stunning in a burnt orange jersey sheath that stopped at the knee and gave him a heart-stopping view of her flawless legs. In his mind's eye he saw her as she'd been the night before with those legs wrapped around his hips as she thrashed beneath him before exploding in ecstasy, her face shifting from a thunderous cloud to a sky with a thousand shooting stars.

Tyra's gazed locked on him, and demon libido began to stir in him. She moved toward him, in slow motion it seemed, exciting him almost to the point of torture. Suddenly, he could hear a pin drop. The chatter had ceased. He glanced toward his father, whose face bore an expression of fear, and told himself to shove it aside and remember that he and Tyra were not alone.

She dropped down on the arm of the overstuffed leather chair in which he sat, leaned over and kissed his forehead. "Honey, that was close."

His long breath expelled pent-up energy. "Woman, you're dynamite."

They sat down at a table laden with a twenty-pound turkey, cornbread stuffing, wild rice, turnip greens, spiced peaches, cracklin' bread, corn pudding and cranberry relish. Maggie said grace, and each guest offered a toast. Pumpkin pie à la mode completed the meal, and they gathered in the family room around the blazing fireplace for coffee and tall tales.

Byron focused on the people around him who, if he were

blessed, would soon constitute his family and smiled at the thought. He didn't know when he'd last had such a feel of rightness, a feeling that at last the wind had caught his sails.

After lunch the next day, Tyra asked Byron if they could take Andy fishing. "He's been exceptionally good, Byron, and he begged me to ask you if we could catch some fish."

Her pleading tone amused him. Andy had already learned how to get to her. "I suggest we go to the Monacacy River, since it's reasonably close."

"Can you wait till Andy's noels come out of the oven?" Maggie asked. "He wants to taste them."

His brow arched, Byron observed Tyra with mild amusement. "Looks to me as if Andy appropriated your home and your family. I'd better get him back to Baltimore before his head swells to twice its size." To Maggie, he said, "Let us know when the cookies are ready."

"I'm taking them out now," she said. "I'll put a few in a bag for him."

Byron packed the fishing gear in the trunk of his car and drove them the four miles to the river. He baited the hooks for Andy and Tyra and said to Andy, "Sit right here on this plank, and do not stand up for any reason. If you get a fish, I'll help you pull him in. Do you understand?"

"Yes, sir."

He walked back to her. "You're just as sexy in these jeans as you were in that dress you wore yesterday."

"Byron, please, Andy isn't six feet away."

"He's looking for fish," Byron said, gripped her to him and plunged his tongue into her eager mouth. Her nipples hardened, and she sucked him deeper into her. Lord, if she could only get at him the way she wanted to and do whatever she pleased with him. Frustrated and bristling with heat, she backed away from him.

"I wish you'd pick a better place to start a fire, mister."

"Aw, come on, sweetheart. If this is what rocks our boat, let's rock it. All day, I've been dying to get you to my—"

Splash! She looked toward the river, didn't see Andy, raced to the bank and dived in. Luckily, she surfaced beside him, held his head above the water and headed to the shore burdened by Andy and the weight of her winter clothing. Byron pulled them in, removed their coats, got the blankets that he always kept in the trunk and, though the blankets needed cleaning, he wrapped them around Andy and Tyra.

"I'm sorry, Daddy. The fish pulled me in. He musta been real big. Do you think we could go back and get him?"

"Not today, son. There are fish aplenty in that river, but I have to get you and Tyra out of your wet clothes before you both become sick."

"If she gets sick, Daddy, she can come stay at our house and Aunt Jonie can take care of her and me."

"Andy, this is not fun. You could have drowned."

"No, I wouldn't, Daddy. You know I can swim."

She imagined that her teeth chattered partly from the chill and partly from the fact that though she'd had swimming lessons, she'd never before dived or actually swum on her own. "I'm glad t-to h-have evi-d-dence that I can, too," she said, tightening the blanket to her body.

Immediately after reaching Tyra's house Byron put Andy in a tub of hot water, dried him and put him to bed. "Andy's in bed," he said to Tyra. "You should warm up in a tub of hot water."

"I got a hot shower. I'm fine."

He put an arm around her, walked with her into his room and closed the door. "Are you sure that's the only time you ever swam? You looked to me like an expert."

"It's true. And as soon as you began to pull us up, I realized it and nearly panicked."

With both arms tight around her, he closed his eyes and said

a word of prayer. She'd thought of his child before she thought
of herself. "If you're willing to risk your life for Andy, you
should be willing to help me raise him. Will you marry me,
Tyra? I love you, I'll always be there for you and I'll be a good
father to our children."

Her heartbeat began thudding at the pace of a spooked
thoroughbred. "How many? I'm not good for more than three."

"I'll love and care for as many as you give me. Will you
be my wife? In my heart, I have belonged to you since our
first night on that cruise ship."

"I gave you my heart the first time I saw your face. Yes. I
want to marry you."

Byron looked toward the door and, uncertain that he'd closed
it, reached over and locked it. Minutes later he leaned over her
as she lay on his bed with her arms outstretched. "You're more
than I dreamed I would find, Tyra. You're my life."

"I never thought I could love a man so much that just
looking at him makes me giddy." Her hands stroked his hips.
"I don't need your finesse or your expertise right now, love.
Make love to me the way you did the night before last, till I'm
so besotted, so drunk on you that I don't know who I am."

He bent to the nipple that he loved so much, sucked it into
his mouth, eased his hand down to check for her readiness,
and went into her. She pushed him to the limit, and he lost
himself in her as soon as she sucked him into her hot, swirling,
quicksand orgasm.

When he could find sufficient strength, he said, "I want us
to begin looking for a house tomorrow. I don't expect you to
live in a home that another woman chose. Okay?" She kissed
his cheek and shifted beneath him. "And I want us to get
married within the next three months."

"Make it two. What's Andy going to say to this?"

"Sweetheart, Andy's getting his wish."

Hidden secrets…shared passion.

Essence Bestselling Author

GWYNNE FORSTER

Tragedy and depression
drove Justine Montgomery
to give her baby up for
adoption. Determined to
make her way into the
child's life, she conceals
her identity and takes a
job as the baby's nanny.
Single adoptive father
Duncan Banks senses
there's something not
quite right about his
daughter's otherwise
perfect nanny. But when
a powerful attraction
develops between them,
Justine and Duncan must
risk all to attain a seemingly
impossible dream.

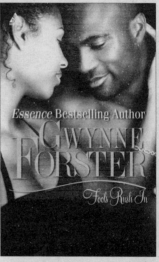

FOOLS RUSH IN

*Coming the first week of August 2009
wherever books are sold.*

**www.kimanipress.com
www.myspace.com/kimanipress**

KPGFI 650809

When it comes
to love...there's
no contest.

Games
of the
Heart

Favorite author
PAMELA YAYE

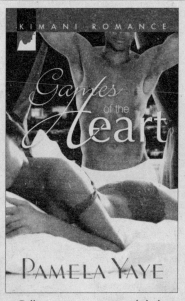

Since celeb manager Sage Collins came to town, she's been
determined to land her first big client—a teenager who could
be the next Michael Jordan. The immovable object in her way?
Marshall Grant, the boy's father and manager. Though Marshall
and Sage are constantly at odds, it isn't long before this country boy
and big-city girl succumb to their desires and let love call the shots!

"With just the right dose of humor and drama, Pamela Yaye's
story compels from beginning to end."
—*Romantic Times BOOKreviews* on *Her Kind of Man*

*Coming the first week of August 2009
wherever books are sold.*

KPPY1250809

KIMANI™
ROMANCE

www.kimanipress.com
www.myspace.com/kimanipress

*Love's calling…
and it may be
destiny on the
other end.*

ESSENCE
BESTSELLING
AUTHOR
LINDA
HUDSON-SMITH

DESTINY
Calls

Ethan Robinson, the sexiest professor on campus, has
fallen hard for the pretty twentysomething student Dakota
Faraday. But when his Ph.D. research to a phone-sex line
divides his attention between the mysterious Dakota and
the sexy Persia, he finds he's got two vibrant women vying
for his heart. Or does he?

*Coming the first week of August 2009
wherever books are sold.*

**www.kimanipress.com
www.myspace.com/kimanipress**

KPLHS1260809

She's gambling on her future… but he's playing his cards close to his chest.

FULL HOUSE *Seduction*

Book #4 in The Donovans

Favorite author A.C. Arthur

Getting her brother-in-law's casino off the ground is Noelle Vincent's big opportunity. But the attraction sizzling between her and developer Brock Remington makes her wary. With her history of disastrous relationships, can Noelle defy the odds to win a lifetime of love?

The Donovans: betting the house and headed full tilt into love!

Coming the first week of August 2009 wherever books are sold.

www.kimanipress.com
www.myspace.com/kimanipress

KPACA1270809

REQUEST YOUR FREE BOOKS!

2 FREE NOVELS
PLUS 2 FREE GIFTS!

KIMANI™
ROMANCE

Love's ultimate destination!

YES! Please send me 2 FREE Kimani™ Romance novels and my 2 FREE gifts (gifts are worth about $10). After receiving them, if I don't wish to receive any more books, I can return the shipping statement marked "cancel." If I don't cancel, I will receive 4 brand-new novels every month and be billed just $4.69 per book in the U.S. or $5.24 per book in Canada. That's a savings of over 20% off the cover price. It's quite a bargain! Shipping and handling is just 50¢ per book.* I understand that accepting the 2 free books and gifts places me under no obligation to buy anything. I can always return a shipment and cancel at any time. Even if I never buy another book from Kimani Press, the two free books and gifts are mine to keep forever.

168 XDN EYQG   368 XDN EYQS

Name	(PLEASE PRINT)	

Address		Apt. #

City	State/Prov.	Zip/Postal Code

Signature (if under 18, a parent or guardian must sign)

Mail to **The Reader Service:**
IN U.S.A.: P.O. Box 1867, Buffalo, NY 14240-1867
IN CANADA: P.O. Box 609, Fort Erie, Ontario L2A 5X3

Not valid to current subscribers of Kimani Romance books.

Want to try two free books from another line?
Call 1-800-873-8635 or visit www.morefreebooks.com.

* Terms and prices subject to change without notice. Prices do not include applicable taxes. Sales tax applicable in N.Y. Canadian residents will be charged applicable provincial taxes and GST. Offer not valid in Quebec. This offer is limited to one order per household. All orders subject to approval. Credit or debit balances in a customer's account(s) may be offset by any other outstanding balance owed by or to the customer. Please allow 4 to 6 weeks for delivery. Offer available while quantities last.

Your Privacy: Kimani Press is committed to protecting your privacy. Our Privacy Policy is available online at www.eHarlequin.com or upon request from the Reader Service. From time to time we make our lists of customers available to reputable third parties who may have a product or service of interest to you. If you would prefer we not share your name and address, please check here. ☐

KROM09

HELP CELEBRATE
ARABESQUE'S
15TH ANNIVERSARY!

2009 marks Arabesque's 15th anniversary!

Help us celebrate by telling us about your most special memories and moments with Arabesque books. Entries will be judged by the Arabesque Anniversary Committee based on which are the most touching and well written. Fifteen lucky winners will receive as a prize a full-grain leather duffel bag with the Arabesque anniversary logo.

How to Enter: To enter, hand-print (or type) on an 8 ½" x 11" plain piece of paper your full name, mailing address, telephone number and a description of your most special memories and moments with Arabesque books (in two hundred [200] words or less) and send it to "Arabesque 15th Anniversary Contest 20901"—in the U.S.: Kimani Press, 233 Broadway, Suite 1001, New York, NY 10279, or in Canada: 225 Duncan Mill Road, Don Mills, ON M3B 3K9. No other method of entry will be accepted. The contest begins on July 1, 2009, and ends on December 31, 2009. Entries must be postmarked by December 31, 2009, and received by January 8, 2010. A copy of these Official Rules is available online at www.myspace.com/kimanipress, or to obtain a copy of these Official Rules (prior to November 30, 2009), send a self-addressed, stamped envelope (postage not required from residents of VT) to "Arabesque 15th Anniversary Contest 20901 Rules," 225 Duncan Mill Road, Don Mills, ON M3B 3K9. Limit one (1) entry per person. If more than one (1) entry is received from the same person, only the first eligible entry submitted will be considered. By entering the contest, entrants agree to be bound by these Official Rules and the decisions of Harlequin Enterprises Limited (the "Sponsor"), which are final and binding.

NO PURCHASE NECESSARY. Open to legal residents of U.S. and Canada (except Quebec) who have reached the age of majority at time of entry. Void where prohibited by law. Approximate retail value of each prize: $131.00 (USD).

VISIT **WWW.MYSPACE.COM/KIMANIPRESS**
FOR THE COMPLETE OFFICIAL RULES

KPI5ARACONTEST